THE HOLLOW

KIERSTEN MODGLIN

KIERSTEN
MODGLIN
Two Lies Aside

Cover Design by Kiersten Modglin
Copy Editing by Three Owls Editing
Proofreading by My Brother's Editor
Formatting & Graphic Design by Kiersten Modglin
Hunter's Hollow Map © Dewi Hargreaves
Author Photograph © Lisa Christianson

First Print and Electronic Edition: 2024

kierstenmodglinauthor.com

To the ones moving forward, but not on.

PRIVATE

16

Playground

Maintenance

9

15

10

8

7

11

6

13

Playground

Swimming

12

14

5

4

3

2

Mckennas' Cabin

PRIVATE

1

Hunters' Cabin

Boat Ramp

Office

Storage

Enjoy your stay!

HUNTER'S HOLLOW
CAMPGROUND MAP

HUNTER'S HOLLOW GUEST LOG
WEEK OF _JUNE 1ST_

CABIN NUMBER	NAME	NUMBER OF GUESTS
1	ROY + LYNN JACKSON	4 (2 ADULTS, 2 CHILDREN)
2	OLIVIA + TED JAMES	3 (2 ADULTS, 1 TEEN)
3	WES + THEODORA DONOVAN	2
4	DAVID + ALEXIS STRAHAN	4 (2 ADULTS, 2 TEENS)
5	DR. REYES	1
6	J~~ACK~~ ELEANOR CUBAN	1
7	RYAN + KELLY SMITH	3 (2 ADULTS, 1 CHILD)
8	CHRISTINE MOORE	2 (1 ADULT, 1 TEEN)
9	CODY + DAN ERIKSON	2
10	WOOLARD (MULTI-FAMILY)	(11 ADULTS, 5 CHILDREN)
11	JANINE + NOLAN WILDERMUTH	2
12	MARGO HUNT	4 (2 ADULTS, 1 TEEN, 1 CHILD)
13	S. BOOTH (BOOK CLUB/GIRL'S TRIP)	7 (ADULTS)
14	JAREN + NATASHA CLEMMONS (ANNIVERSARY TRIP)	2
15	DEAN + JACK (RESERVED FOR SUMMER)	2
16	CARMEN (RESERVED FOR SUMMER)	1

CHAPTER ONE

I should just turn around. There's a reason I haven't come back to Hunter's Hollow in the past eleven years. A reason why I've insisted Mom come visit me for holidays instead of the other way around.

There's still time to back out of this plan and go home.

I could do it.

Really, I could.

But I don't. I drive along the winding dirt road that leads to The Hollow with a lump in my throat that I can't seem to swallow down. The road is empty and surrounded by acres and acres of pine trees. Dust flies in every direction around my little Toyota, despite how slowly I'm going. Which, for the record, is so slow I'm not sure I haven't stopped.

I remember driving this road the day I got my driver's license, when everything still felt okay. Safe. Happy, even.

Things were so different back then. It felt like everything was going to change for the better, like my life was beginning. And, I guess, in a way it was, just not in the way I hoped.

That day was the beginning of the end for me, the beginning of it all falling apart.

I catch sight of the office up ahead, next to a large, wooden sign.

Hunter's Hollow
Boat rentals, recreation for all ages, cabin rentals,
and more.
Established 1952

The office building is small and rustic, a cabin itself, and the smallest of the nearly twenty others that exist on the land. Once, generations ago, it was the cabin where the Hunter family lived before they expanded it to the campground it is today. I pull to a stop in front of the building, inhaling deeply and releasing it with a puff. Stepping out of the car, I shut the door and cross the grassy yard on my way toward the small porch.

I jog up three stairs and reach the door. This place is laden with memories, good and bad. For the good, I remember lazy summers on the porch swing to my right, dozing off with a book in my hands; warm evenings with popsicle juice dripping down my hand as I raced the boys to finish mine; and nights catching lightning bugs in the yard. Of the bad, I remember crying.

2

Sobbing over leaving when we'd just come to visit, over my dad when we came to stay for good, and, eventually, over *him*. I remember the day I left for the final time, driving away from this town and vowing to never look back.

And, of course, there are the awful memories. The kind that, when they sneak past the wall I've built in my mind and catch me by surprise, make my entire body feel as if it's been encapsulated in ice. The memories that still haunt me.

With another inhale of breath, I pull open the door, get blasted by the air conditioning inside, and step into the office.

The space smells of cedar and dust, a combination that brings instant tears of nostalgia to my eyes. I missed this place, and until now, I wasn't aware of just how much.

"I'll be right with you!" I hear my mom's chipper voice from somewhere in the back.

"You'd better," I call, stepping forward toward the hall that leads to Mom's and Jill's offices. The old floor creaks underfoot, and I spot the scuffs on the floor from when Jack and I rode our rollerskates down the hall every day until we were threatened with having them taken away.

I hear, rather than see, her response. An audible gasp, the sudden roll of a chair. Then, with seven quick steps, she's there. Her jaw drops from the end of the hall, and you'd think she had no idea I was coming from the way her entire body seems to go slack and her eyes glisten with tears.

"Carmen?"

I've nearly reached her, but it's not quick enough. She holds out her arms, launching herself forward and giving me one of her signature hugs—squeezing me too tightly and for too long as we rock back and forth from side to side. When she pulls back, her hands run over the sides of my face as if she hasn't seen me in years, when it's only been months—or hours if you include our daily video chats.

"*Te he estrañado mucho, mi vida*," she mumbles, pulling her hands back finally to dry her tears.

"I've missed you too, Mama." I kiss her cheek, realizing there are wrinkles there I haven't noticed on the video calls.

She runs a hand over her graying ponytail—still mostly black, but changing quickly. "You made it okay? No trouble?"

I nod, holding my arms out to my sides as if to say, *Ta-Da!* "Yep. All in one piece."

"It's been too long, *mija*. I can't believe you're here. I never thought I'd see the day."

Before I can respond, I hear the front door slam shut, and then Jill's voice carries through the small office. "Elena, there's a car outside. Any idea who it—"

She cuts off just as I turn around and see her at the opposite end of the hall. Unlike my mom, it truly has been a few years since I saw the woman I once considered

4

a second mother. Her hazel eyes light up at the sight of me, and when she smiles, it's with her full face.

She presses a hand to her hip, rubbing her lips together. "Well, it's about time you came back home. I was starting to take your staying away personally."

"Jill..." I cross the hallway, wrapping her up in my arms. She smells just the way I remember—of the mint body lotion she wears daily, sunscreen, and cotton fabric softener. It's a scent I associate with summers and freedom, safety, and comfort. Despite everything that happened, guilt weighs on me for staying away from Jill for so long. I know it's not just *me* who thinks of *her* as family. The feeling is mutual. She is my second mother, and I will always be her stand-in daughter, the daughter she never had. "I'm sorry. I missed you."

"I missed you too, kiddo." She rubs my back and releases me, her hugs always much shorter but equally as warm as my mother's. She gives me a once-over. "Look at you, all grown up." Her eyes find my mom a few steps from us over my shoulder. "When did that happen?"

"Beats me." Mom shrugs, patting my back as she moves past. "They were all supposed to stay little for a lot longer. That's what the brochures told us anyway."

"Well, I'll be." I turn my head just in time to see Sam walking through the door. "If it isn't Little Miss Big City, come back to see us. 'Bout damn time." He grins at me brightly, the corners of his eyes wrinkling. I see both of his boys in him: Jack's warm, chocolate hair and Dean's dark eyes. His skin is tanned from the sun, and he

5

adjusts the ball cap on his head as he beams in my direction.

Sam should've been my stand-in father. In every way that mattered, I suppose he was. He's married to Jill, and the two of them were there for me through everything growing up, but still, there's an awkwardness that exists between us. Perhaps because he looks so much like his sons, like the boy I loved not so long ago, or perhaps—and more likely—because he's not my dad, and I never wanted to feel like I was trying to replace him. I think, in some ways, Sam sensed that and wanted to be respectful. Which is why, even now, he waits for me to step forward to give him a hug before he holds an arm out.

"Good to see you, Sam."

He presses a soft kiss to the top of my head. "You too, kiddo. Your mom hasn't shut up about you coming."

Before the words have completely left his mouth, a ball of something soft whacks him on the shoulder, narrowly missing me. He chuckles, bending down to pick up a pair of the socks we keep on hand to sell to guests who might need an extra pair during a cold night.

Mom scoffs. "Shut up, Sam."

He chuckles, tossing the socks up and catching them in his palm like a ball. "She's gotten mean in her old age, too." He winks at me just before being pelted with two more pairs of socks, this time from both Mom and Jill.

Laughing, he gathers the three pairs of socks and delivers them back to the counter carefully. He ruffles Mom's hair and kisses Jill's cheek. "Oh, you know I'm teasing, ladies." Getting down to business, he raps his knuckles on the countertop. "Now, why was I here? Oh, right. Cabin eight's all settled in, but there weren't extra blankets in the closet. I need to grab some and run 'em back over there."

My mom steps aside so Sam can move past us and down the hall. She swats at his back playfully as he does. Minutes later, he jogs out the door, blankets in hand, and returns to his golf cart.

"Well"—Jill sighs—"we've got to get you all settled in. We've put you in cabin sixteen, so you'll have some privacy and—"

"Wait. I'm not staying with you?" I look at Mom. "Why? I don't need a whole cabin to myself. I'm just here for two months. I can sleep in my old room."

Mom and Jill exchange a look I can't quite read, one heavy with meaning. They've always been able to do this —carry on conversations entirely in silence.

"What's going on?" I press, drawing their attention back to me.

"Well, of course you *can* stay with me, Car. I just... well, I thought you might like some alone time while you're here. I've already turned your room into a craft space so I can paint the pieces for my little village, but there's always the couch. I just thought you'd be more comfortable in a bed."

Something inside me deflates like a balloon that's been popped. She packed away my room? My things? My bed? Of course she did. It's been eleven years. She had every right to make the house more comfortable for her, but that doesn't make it sting any less.

"Oh. Right. Well, okay. Sure. That makes sense."

She tilts her head to the side, visibly upset. "Honey, we'll get it worked out. You can have my bed, and I'll sleep on the couch. Or we can share the bed. Or I can order an air mattress and set it up in your old room. I'm sorry. I just thought—"

"No, don't be silly." I wave her off, interrupting the numerous solutions. "Honestly, it's fine. I don't mind staying in another cabin. It'll give me more space to work, so it's probably better. As long as there's an opening? I don't want to be taking away two months' worth of rent from you guys. And I can totally stay in one of the smaller cabins, anyway. It's just me."

Jill shakes her head at my concern, moving toward the counter. "Oh, no. You're not taking anything away. Not at all. We've had the cabin set aside for you from the second your mom found out you were coming home." She opens a drawer and shoves the socks back inside, then opens another and retrieves a key, holding it out to me. "It's all yours." When I hold my hand out, she places it in my palm slowly, her hand embracing mine. "For as long as you need. Consider it your 'welcome home' present."

"Thank you." When she releases my hand, I tuck the key into my back pocket just as I hear a truck pull up outside, signaling that more guests have arrived. "I guess I'll go take my bags down and unpack. I'll see you after work?"

Mom nods, squeezing me into a hug again, and plants a kiss on my cheek. "Yes, go get settled in, and I'll see you for dinner once we close up for the day." She checks her watch. "Just a few more hours."

Jill glances out the window. "Do you need help with your bags, Carmen? The boys should be around here somewhere..."

My heart plummets, my chest constricting. "*No.*" I blurt the word, practically scream it, then try—and fail—to recover while both women stare at me with wide eyes. "I mean, no. I'm okay. I've got it."

"Okay." Mom chuckles, cutting a glance at her best friend with a look that is both confused and knowing all at once. "Suit yourself. You remember where it is?"

"Where what is?" The voice comes from behind me, sending a shiver down my spine. I spin around at the sound of it, my eyes landing on a boy—*a man*—I haven't seen in years. He looks equally taken aback to see me, his dark eyes locked on mine in frozen stupor.

He's tall, dark, and handsome in every sense of the word. All long, thick limbs, with a dusting of dark stubble across his chin. He looks so much like his dad, like his brother, it's painful for me.

"Carmen..." My name leaves his lips on a breath. "Wow." He blinks, shaking his head, and seems to snap back into reality. "I..." He takes two steps forward, reaching for me and pulling me into a one-armed hug. "You're...here. Wow."

I hug him back. "Hey, Dean." He smells clean, like

9

soap and an earthy cologne that comes loaded with memories. Cashmere and sandalwood—warm and safe, the epitome of Dean.

"What are you doing here?"

My brows draw down. "You didn't know I was coming?"

He shakes his head, looking up at his mom. "You knew?"

She glances at my mom, wincing, then looks back at me. "Well...yes, we did. Honestly though, Carmen, we weren't sure you were actually going to make it here. We didn't want to...we didn't want to get anyone's hopes up."

She says it kindly, but I hear the words she isn't saying. *My return might not be this welcome by everyone. If they'd told them I was coming, there was a chance Jack would've disappeared.*

"Well, surprise." I give an exaggerated shrug.

Dean's hand still hasn't left my back as he looks down at me. "It's a nice surprise." His gaze is gentle, holding my eyes with so much left unsaid passing between us. Years of awkward **Merry Christmas!** and **Happy birthday!** texts have done little to quell the strangeness that sits between us now. And if our encounter feels odd, I can't imagine how it'll feel to see—

"*Jack!* Speak of the devil. There you are!" Jill's voice rings through the office as I hear the creak of the door.

I turn to see the face of the man I once thought I'd never see again. At one point, *hoped* I'd never see again.

He's shirtless—gorgeous—and drenched in sweat. His once chocolate-brown hair is lighter now, more cinnamon from the sun. He drops the bag of tools in his hand, staring at me as if he's seen a ghost. His skin pales, eyes wide as they dance between mine, then to his mom, my mom, and finally Dean, before they come to rest on mine again.

"Carmen." My name is a full sentence on his perfect lips.

"Hi, Jack," I say, my voice crackling with uncertainty.

Dean's hand leaves my back as Jack and I stare at each other for what feels like a lifetime. There is, in fact, a lifetime of things to say—things I wish I could say, things I will never say—between us.

"Why are you here?" His voice is gentle, quiet and unsure, as if he thinks he might be dreaming. Or hallucinating from heat exhaustion from the looks of it.

"I'm...I'm staying here for the summer. I took some time off of work to visit Mom."

Slowly, he removes the tan, leather utility gloves from one hand, then the other. "You're...you're staying here?"

"We put her in cabin sixteen," Jill says, ever so pleasantly.

His eyes dart up to meet his mother's, and he bends to pick up the bag. "I've gotta get back to work." With that, he's gone, and even in a room full of people, I'm completely alone.

CHAPTER TWO

BEFORE — AGE 13

After today, everything will be different.

More different than it already is.

A year ago, everything was normal. Mom was happy. I was happy. Dad was alive. Then came the accident, and there hasn't been a moment that felt anywhere close to normal since.

I load the last of the boxes from my room into the back of the car. It's the room I grew up in, the room I've had sleepovers in, the room that still has *The Little Mermaid* stickers stuck to the back wall of the closet and my height marks on the door frame. It's the room where all of my life has happened, and as of tomorrow at 9:00 a.m., it will belong to someone else.

Clearing it out over the last month, taking down the posters I carefully picked out, unplugging the lava lamp Dad got me, and packing everything into boxes to be taken to our new home has felt like losing him all over again.

I don't understand why we have to leave. I know Dad left money for Mom, and the house has been paid off. This place was our home, and he would've never wanted us to leave it. He loved it as much as he loved us. In its walls, we were a family. Wherever we go now, it won't feel like home.

I spin around to see Mom headed down the long side-walk that leads to the front door. She's smiling, but it's sad. I don't understand it, really. She's the one who made the decision, the one who said we had to sell the house and move to the middle of nowhere—Cody, North Carolina. More specifically, to the campground her best friend owns, the place where she and her *happy, alive* husband live and work. *Hunter's Hollow, our new home.* She could take it all back. She could fix this easily. With a single phone call, probably. So what right does she have to be sad? I know for a fact that nothing is official until the papers are signed by the buyers at nine tomorrow morning.

I've asked. Twice.

"Is that the last of it?" she mutters, not really looking at me.

"Mm-hmm." I shove my hands into my back pockets and move away from the car.

She turns back toward the house, her shoulders rising and falling with a heavy breath. I can't look at it, though. If I do, I'll cry again, and I desperately don't want to cry.

My entire body aches from spending last night curled up in bed, sobbing silently into my pillow. I thought somehow, by some miracle, she'd change her mind. That she'd rush into my room and tell me she couldn't go through with it. But she didn't.

Instead, I woke up this morning to a stack of boxes on my bedroom floor and the instructions to pack up the last of my things. It was official. Done. And now I can't bring myself to feel anything but anger.

Her hand slides into mine, surprising me, and I look down at it. When I meet her eyes, she smiles at me with a silent apology.

"We're going to be alright, *mija*."

It's a lie, and she knows it. Once this is done, once it's irreversible and someone else calls our home theirs, we will never be alright again.

She squeezes my hand gently, then drops it and turns away with tears in her eyes that she tries and fails to hide. I look at the house just once, a final time, as I hear the car door open and shut.

Goodbye, Dad, I whisper internally to no one. He's not in the house. Even if I believed in ghosts, I know he's not. If I believed in ghosts, if I thought his ghost was still in the world, he'd be roaming along the interstate where he died, twenty minutes across town. Not here. But still, this is where I feel him. The memories of his laughter, our games and fun, the warmth of his love is still here.

And now, thanks to Mom, we're leaving it behind.

It takes six hours to drive from our old hometown of Atlanta to the rat-infested swampland of Hunter's Hollow. For most of it, I pretend to be asleep. My head rests on the seat, face turned away, eyes slammed shut. If Mom knows I'm awake, I know she'll try to talk to me. To explain—for the millionth time—why abandoning our old life and moving to Hunter's Hollow with her best friend and her family is the best thing for us, but I don't want to hear it.

I don't want to live in a swamp. I'm not Shrek.

She rides mostly in silence. Mom has always loved music. As a kid, I have very few memories that weren't set to a soundtrack of her favorite music. Family game night? She had a record going. Christmas morning? Christmas songs playing. I'd wake up to the sounds of her music wafting through the house like a scent on the wind.

Since Dad died, though, she hardly listens to anything.

Our lives have become nothing but deafening silence.

Once, I came out of my room to find her holding one of their favorite records and crying. I snuck back to my room and never mentioned it again.

When we get close to Hunter's Hollow, I feel her hand on my arm. "Honey..." She shakes me gently. "Carmen. Wake up, *mija*. We're here."

I glance over at her slowly, sitting straighter in my seat as I pretend to rub my eyes. I stare out the windshield at the dirt road we're traveling on and the building that's coming into view.

The road is lined with trees, and in between them, I'll occasionally get a peek at the lake that surrounds this plot of land. It's like an island here. A peninsula, technically. Either way, it feels cut off from the world.

I already miss my friends. My city. My life.

This isn't going to be some storybook ending where we move to a small town, connect with nature, and become closer as a family or some crap like that. It's going to be a nightmare, and the first chance I get, I'm going to bolt.

She'll have no one to blame but herself.

"Jill is going to be so excited to see you," she says, smiling at me. Apparently, all of her sadness from leaving the house behind has evaporated. Or maybe it was all just an act in the first place.

"Why?" I ask, scowling. My anger isn't directed toward Jill. In truth, I hardly remember Jill. I remember Jack and Dean from the few times we visited when I was younger, but my mother's best friend and her family are hardly a permanent fixture in my mind. In fact, now that I think more about it, since she's the reason we're here, I guess I *am* mad at her, too. If she hadn't offered Mom the cabin that used to belong to the boys' grandparents, if she hadn't suggested we come live in this dump of a campground and Mom could help her and Sam run the place, we'd still be at home.

"She loves you, Carmen." Mom's using her no-

nonsense voice. Once, I was scared of it. Now, it barely affects me. "She's family."

"She's not," I say firmly. "She's your friend, that's it. *Abuela* and *abuelito* are family."

She sighs, eyeing me as her hands wring the steering wheel. "And they're in a nursing home. We can't go and stay with them. The Hunters are the closest thing we have to family. I know you're upset about moving, but it was really kind of Jill to let us come and stay here. To give me a job."

"You already had a job," I point out angrily. "A good one at the hospital. And we had a place to stay."

"I've told you, Carmen, my job required me to work all hours of the day and night. There was no schedule. No consistency. When your dad—" She cuts herself off. "When there were two of us, someone could be home for you. But now it's all on me. I don't want you home alone all the time. I see how those kinds of kids turn out—drugs, alcohol. This job means I can be home with you every evening. Every morning before school. There's flexibility when you're sick or need something—"

"I'm not a baby. I'm practically an adult, Mom. Stop treating me like a child. I don't need a babysitter. I don't need you to always be there. And you know I'm not going to do drugs. Jesus." I scowl.

"You're thirteen years old. A child, Carmen. But no, you're right, you don't need a babysitter. You need a mother. More than that, I need to be there for you. Losing your father has been hard on us both, which is why we have to be there for each other. And the city is expensive. Even with what I was making, losing a whole income was hard, *is* hard—"

"You have Dad's life insurance—"

"And that has helped," she says, her voice somehow firm and gentle at the same time. "Some. But not enough. Not enough for it to be permanent. We've been over this. I paid off the house and the car, but that didn't leave us with a lot. All of the rest of the bills, the things you need, I was barely going to be scraping by. We would've had to cut into the insurance money any time something unexpected came up, any time the bills ran a little high. Eventually, it would've been gone, and then what?"

"We'd figure it out." Finally, I see an in. I see that she might be changing her mind. "We'd figure it out, Mom. We always do. When—if—the time comes. But it would be okay. I can get a job soon. I can help you."

She slows the car to a stop before we reach the office, turning to face me. "That isn't your job. I don't want that for you. I want you to be a kid. To have fun. Freedom. I want you to enjoy your life, and this will give us that. Carmen, you're going to love growing up at Hunter's Hollow. Don't you remember how much you loved it there when you were little? There are always kids around, a playground, the lake for swimming and boating, and you've always gotten along with Dean and Jack. We'll have family there. Support." She pauses, tilting her head to the side. "I know you didn't want to leave the house behind. I didn't either. But eventually, this place will come to feel like home, too." She reaches across the center console and takes my hand. I pull it away. "It's not about forgetting your dad or moving on from him. It's about moving forward. This is what he would've wanted for us."

I slam my hand down on my leg, radiating with fury. How can she say that? "Really, Mom? I don't need a place to grow up. In case you haven't noticed, I've already grown up. In Atlanta. Dad loved our home. You can't honestly believe he would want us to move away. This is all because it's what *you* wanted. That's it. Don't you dare put this on Dad."

She huffs, clearly trying to maintain her composure. "Your father would want us to be safe. Supported. He would want us to be with family, and yes, Jill *is* family. She's the closest thing we have to it, anyway. She loves you—and me—and she's doing this very nice thing for us. So you can be mad at me all you want, but this *is* happening. It's already happened. We're moving to Hunter's Hollow, and you're going to be nice to the Hunters. This is our home now. Like it or not."

With that, she put the car in drive.

For the record, I didn't like it. Not one bit.

CHAPTER THREE

PRESENT DAY

At our mothers' suggestion, Dean follows me to my cabin to help unload the few bags I've brought with me. Cabin number sixteen, the one where I'll be staying, is set back at the far end of the property behind a tall fence. The drive is gated, giving both cabins fifteen and sixteen privacy and access to their own private pond, playground, and firepit. Mostly, the properties are used for wedding parties or big groups traveling together, so I can't help feeling that it's strange Jill and Mom would give one of them to me. Aside from cabin ten, which is the largest cabin on the property, these two are The Hollow's most substantial money makers.

I drive up to the gate, slowing down in front of the keypad to input the passcode—1-9-5-2. Same one it's always been.

The rusting black gate swings open, allowing Dean and me to pass through. It's as if an ice pick has wedged itself deep into my stomach as I try to avoid looking toward the woods, try to avoid thinking about them at all, though how I'll manage that during my stay is beyond me.

Maybe this was a terrible idea.

Maybe I'm not ready for this.

I spot the two cabins sitting just behind the pond, sunlight sparkling on the surface. The cabins are roughly the same size, with cedar siding and cozy front porches. We arrive at cabin sixteen first, and I pull up to the dirt path next to the house.

I put the car in park and sit there, staring up at the place I'll be calling home for the next two months. What feels both like a lifetime ago and just last week, I moved here for the first time and thought it was going to be the worst thing that ever happened to me.

As it turned out, I was wrong. At least for a little while.

A rap on my window has me jerking my head toward the sound. Dean stands there, one knuckle on the glass and that crooked grin on his lips. I open the door, and he steps back, allowing me space to step out.

"The place hasn't changed a bit," I say, breathing in the scent of the woods all around me—pine, pond, and freshly mown lawn. It's so familiar I can practically conjure it without meaning to.

"Well, that was always the appeal, wasn't it?" He makes his way back toward the trunk of my car. "A place that stands still while the rest of the world can't move fast enough."

I pop the trunk and help him unload my two suitcases and duffel bag. "Are you still teaching?"

He nods, appearing almost shocked I remembered. I guess that's fair, since we haven't spoken in any detail at all over the years. "Yeah, but while I'm off for the summer, Mom asked if I'd come and stay to help get things fixed up, so I am."

"You're staying here?" My jaw drops, but I quickly recover. "Don't you live in town?"

"I moved to Wake Forest two years ago, so it's easier to just stay here for the next few months. What about you? What brings you back home?"

Home. The word feels strange and foreign. In truth, my life was split in half when I was thirteen. There was the home before and the home after, and I never know which to claim. I've never actually felt like I have a home, I guess.

We make our way halfway up the wooden steps to the front porch before I answer. "I'm between projects right now, and Mom's been asking me to come back for a while, so I thought this was as good a time as any. I'm just here for a few weeks."

"Well, it'll be nice having you around again. For however long." He pulls open the door and allows me to step inside the cabin. The smell, even inside here, is familiar. Dust and heat and cedar, like an attic on a hot day.

"What are you doing these days anyway? Last your mom told me, you were illustrating books?"

"Yeah, sort of. Mostly fantasy maps and children's books. I work for an email marketing software company, too. So...a little of everything, I guess."

He sets the suitcase down next to where I've stopped and places the duffel on top of it. "Oh, right. Speaking of maps, the map you designed for the campground turned out great."

"Thanks." I've never been very comfortable with compliments, but coming from Dean, it feels honest and important. *True.*

"I always knew you'd end up doing something with art."

"What, because I hid it so well?" I chuckle. "How many times did you make fun of my drawings as a kid?"

He smiles. "Well, I was a little shit back then."

"As opposed to now?" I tease.

"I'll have you know I'm a perfectly respectable, upstanding member of society now." He shoves his hands into his pockets.

"I'll believe that when I see it." I nudge my bags out of the way and walk across the room to the kitchen. "I can't believe our parents put me here. It's way too big for just one person."

He watches me from the living room. "I think they were trying to keep us all away from the guests."

I pause. "What?"

"Joking. Sort of."

"Us all?" I glance out the window to my right, toward cabin fifteen. "You're staying..."

"Oh. Next door, yeah." He rubs his lips together. "Me and Jack. Jack usually lives in cabin six off by himself, but one of the summer guests is an older lady who needed a place to stay for the season and asked for the cheapest cabin we have. She's visiting her kids, and they didn't have room for her, or they're doing a renovation, or something like that. Anyway, since they were already trying to figure out whether I'd have a place to stay this summer or have to drive back and forth, and then—I'm assuming—they found out you were coming too, it made the most sense to put us all back here together."

"Made the most sense, hmm? Sounds like a recipe for disaster," I mutter under my breath.

He steps closer to me. "Don't worry about Jack. It was just a shock to him. He'll come around."

I meet his eyes then, my chest tight with words I can't say, questions I can't ask. "Are you sure about that?"

He opens his mouth, then closes it again, rethinking. "Jack's Jack. He'll take some time, but he'll be okay. The last thing he expected was for you to show up here again after everything, but...that doesn't mean it's the last thing he wanted."

"You really think so?" I hate the vulnerability in my voice, hate that he's the only one who can offer me the assurance I need. I pull a glass from a cabinet and fill it with water from the sink. It tastes like pond—a muddy aftertaste that's so different from the chlorine-scented tap water back home, but it's a taste I don't hate. One I was once very accustomed to.

His smile is enough of an answer. Then he asks, "Are you seeing anyone, Carmen?"

The question catches me off guard. I set my glass down. "What? You mean like dating?"

"Yes."

"No. I'm not."

One corner of his mouth upturns into a wry grin. "Then, yes, I think Jack will be very happy you're back."

His words surprise me, and I can't tell if he's serious. "It's never going to happen between the two of us again. There's too much baggage. Too much...everything."

Suddenly, the room feels stuffy and small, when only moments ago, it felt positively cavernous. He takes a step back with a deep breath. "Hey, summers are for possibilities, right? Someone smart told me that once." I grin at him, and he takes another step back. "Anyway, I should get back to work and let you unpack and everything, but I'll be around if you need me."

"Thanks again, Dean," I say, crossing the room and pulling him into a hug.

"Anytime." His hands grip my back like he may never let go.

CHAPTER FOUR

BEFORE — AGE 13

We stop at the office, and Mom steps out of the car, leaving me there while she goes in and does whatever she needs to. I close my eyes and pretend this is all a dream.

A nightmare.

But it's not, and I know this because, a few minutes later, Mom reemerges with Jill next to her and the two of them rush to my side of the car and practically yank me out.

"Come here, kiddo." Jill pulls me into a quick hug, kissing my cheek. She leans back, studying me as if I'm a science exhibit. "Oh, Elena, she's a doll." Her eyes flick over to my mom for a second but return to me quickly. "When did you grow up? Oh my gosh. Last time I saw you, you were just this little girl, and now you're practically grown." She squeezes me into another hug. "We're so happy you're here, Carmen. You and your mom. You're going to love growing up at

Hunter's Hollow, truly. It's like summer camp all year long."

Her pep talk sounds suspiciously like what Mom already said to me, and I can't help thinking they must've already had this conversation many times, deciding on the best way to sell this lame idea to me.

I press my lips inward, nodding. I have no idea what to say. I don't want to be rude to Jill, honestly, but I just don't want to talk about it anymore.

Seeming to take the hint, she places a hand on my shoulder and turns back toward Mom. "Why don't we get you guys all settled into your cabin, and Sam and the boys will come help unload everything."

The cabin Jill is giving us sits directly next to hers, and the two are on a peninsula entirely their own across the road from the rest of the campsite. In the distance, I can vaguely see a few of the cabins, but for the most part, it feels like we've been separated from the rest of the world. As we pull up, Jill leans forward from the back seat and beeps the horn three times.

Mom slows the car to a stop, and within seconds, I see three men coming around the corner. Well, *men* is a stretch. A man and two boys.

Sam is everything I remembered. Unremarkable as far as dads go, but with kind eyes and a soft smile. The older son, Dean, just turned sixteen and has this sort of knowing gaze about him. I don't like him very much. It's like he always thinks he is better than everyone else. Better than me, specifically. Jack, the younger son, is my age at thirteen. He has dark-brown hair that curls up around his ears like his dad and brother, with a square face and dark eyes that catch and hold my attention even from where I am.

When I was younger, Mom used to bring me here for a week every summer, and I'd play with Jack and occasionally Dean, but as I've gotten older, we've come less and less. Right now, they feel like strangers with familiar faces.

People I might know from somewhere, but I can't put my finger on where or how.

Mom and Jill step out of the car, and Mom gives Sam a hug, then moves down the line to Jack and Dean. When they're done, they seem to realize I still haven't gotten out of the car because Mom glances back and gives me a forceful wave toward her.

Come here. I could swear I hear her words despite the fact that her lips don't move.

I step from the car and slam the door shut with more force than necessary, my heart racing as I stand in front of the group. It's as terrifying as standing on a stage at this moment, with all eyes on me.

Jill nudges Jack's back softly.

"Hey, Carmen," Jack says, a blush spreading across his cheeks. "Welcome."

"We're glad you're here, kiddo," Sam adds.

I nod.

"Alright, boys. Can we help Elena and Carmen get their things inside?" Jill claps her hands together, turning to us. "Put us to work, you two. Jack, maybe you could show Carmen her room?" Her brows dart up with a sort of intense stare.

"Sure." He presses his lips together with a small smile.

"Okay, great. Here we go, then." Mom hurries toward the trunk, and the other adults follow suit, eagerly chatting about the drive and how happy they are to have us here, how much fun it's going to be.

Mom is thanking Jill over and over, telling her how good it is to see her again, and Jill is thanking her right back, telling her how much they've needed the help and how grateful they are that someone will get use out of the cabin that's been sitting empty.

"Jesus, Carmie, you ever heard of the sun? Those legs are so pale, they're blinding." Dean puts up a hand to shield his eyes as he heads in my direction.

I swat at him, scowling. "Get a life, Dean."

"Says the little girl." He walks past me on his way to the car and grabs one of the boxes from the trunk, following his parents and my mom toward the stairs that lead to our cabin.

"I'm not a little girl," I shout after him, but he just shakes his head without looking back.

"Could've fooled me," he calls seconds before disappearing into the house.

"Ignore him," Jack says, his voice soft as he makes his way toward me. "He's a jerk. It's been worse since he got his license last month. But if you ignore him, he'll get bored."

"Bully 101. Thanks." I turn back toward the car, walking slowly beside him. Suddenly, I worry I've been too rude. If there's anyone I don't want to be rude to, it's Jack, so I add, "I...uh, I guess we're going to be neighbors now."

"I guess so, yeah. Mom and Dad have been preparing us for a while." He nods.

"Preparing you?"

He runs a hand over his neck. "I just mean...they've been telling us to make you feel welcome. And we've been cleaning my grandparents' old house so it would be ready for you."

"Oh. Right. Well, thanks, I guess."

"You must be sad to leave home."

I look up at him then, shocked by his words, though they're so simple and obvious. It's as if he's the only one who can see me, the only one who cares to look.

"Yeah. I didn't have a choice." It's probably the dumbest response in history, but he doesn't look at me like it is.

"Well, I'm sorry. About your dad, I mean. And about the move. But...it's not so bad here."

"Thanks. That's what Mom keeps saying. It's not about the place, honestly. I've always had fun here with you guys. It's just...I hate leaving my friends."

"I get it." He grabs a box, waiting for me to do the same before he heads toward the house. "I wouldn't want to leave my friends right before high school either."

"At least I know someone," I say, looking over at him.

He seems shocked by my words, but he smiles and bumps my arm with his. Without saying a single audible word, he seems to say exactly what I need him to. I'm no longer alone, and that feels like the greatest gift I could be given.

CHAPTER FIVE

PRESENT DAY

The woods surrounding Hunter's Hollow are growing dim by the time I get my things unpacked. I walk across the porch and down the stairs, then toward the tree line with extreme focus.

They've haunted me ever since that night and now, so close to them again, it's as if I'm drawn to them by some magical force. Like I can't stay away. Or maybe I just need to face them, face what happened, once and for all.

Maybe it's the only way to move on.

If I remind myself the woods are just the woods, that what happened is over, that the danger is gone...

When I close my eyes, I still see...

No.

I can't think about what happened that night. If I do, I'll run away from this place and never look back. I force the thoughts away before they even fully form.

I have to face this place—this summer—without allowing myself to go back there mentally. I have to remind myself there is nothing to be afraid of anymore.

Long before that night, there were plenty of good memories made on this land, in these woods. Those are what I will focus on.

Right now, more than anything, I just need a moment to feel like I'm alone. In that cabin, a place that purposefully looks ambiguous so anyone and everyone can feel at home in it, I'm just another visitor. Surrounded by things that belong to other people. With neighbors who carry with them so much weight and baggage it's painful.

The forest provides a privacy I won't find anywhere else during my stay. As soon as I step into the solace of the trees, I'm surprised to find it's as if the vise gripping my lungs releases in an instant.

I inhale deeply, continuing to move forward.

Maybe I'm braver than I thought. Maybe I can do this.

Sticks crack underfoot, but except for that, I'm surrounded by silence. I'm not even sure which way I'm going; I'm just walking. Traveling. Needing to move in the same way a runner needs to get miles under their feet.

CRACK. I hear a sound and travel toward it without thinking.

I walk for ages before I hear the sound again and come out of the trance I seem to be in. When I look up and realize where I am, my heart drops and lungs seize.

No.

No.

No.

No.

No.

I didn't mean to come here. I shouldn't be here.

I never meant to...

But I should've known. I knew this direction was where...

A vision flashes in my head, my chest seizing with panic. I can't breathe.

A body.

Blood. Purpling, mutilated skin.

I'm going to be sick.

I turn, preparing to run away or vomit—whichever comes first—when I hear the sound that originally drew me this way. I'd nearly forgotten I heard it in the first place.

CRACK.

I jump.

"Carmen?"

My heart stops.

I spin around to find Jack standing between the little cabin and a tree, axe in hand. His dark brows draw down. His bare chest rises with a deep breath, sweat glistening on his skin. "What are you doing out here?"

"I was...going for a walk."

He bends down and grabs a shirt from the ground,

pulling it over his head. It's a small mercy, but I'm still finding it hard both to look *at* and to look *away* from him.

"I didn't know you were out here."

He places the axe down, resting it against the side of the house. "I just needed to clear my head."

"I'm sorry I'm here," I blurt out.

"Here? As in...literally right here? Or at Hunter's Hollow?"

"Both, I guess. Is it weird for you? Mom never mentioned that you still lived here. If I'd known, I would've..." I'm not sure how to finish that sentence.

"It's not weird for me," he says, seeming to understand I won't be completing my thought. "It's fine. I mean, was I expecting to see you? No. But it's not the worst thing." One corner of his mouth upturns. "And I know it means a lot to your mom. So it's fine. Welcome home."

It's weird to see him now. The man who, at one point, was a boy I knew so well. His hair is shorter than it once was, his face faintly lined with proof of the years we've spent apart. He has stubble now, a hint of a beard he must keep shaved. His body is stronger than it was then—all hard lines and angles, and muscles I've never seen up close under that all-too-familiar skin. But still, I see the boy. When his dark eyes meet mine, I see the boy who once saw me like no one else could. The eyes that understood me in a way I never understood myself.

"She's been trying to get me to come back for years..." The cabin beside him is exactly how I remember it.

Devil's Cabin.

I actively try not to think about how it got the nickname.

It's smaller than what would be necessary for anyone to stay there for any length of time, which was why the Hunters never made it into a cabin for guests to rent.

Well, at least that was the first reason why. Before the...

I shake the thought away.

It's wooden and rickety, showing signs of its age more than ever. One of the windows has been boarded up with plywood, and there's a padlock on the door to keep it from blowing open in the wind.

Noticing me staring at the lock specifically, he says, "We've had some weirdos and lookie-loos trying to break in after what happened. Dad locked it up after that."

"Speaking of"—I turn my attention back to him—"why are you out here? *Here*, specifically. I thought, after that night, after what happened, I thought everyone would stay away. My mom told me she'd kill me if she ever found out I was out here."

He sighs. "For exactly that reason. Because, ever since Dad put the lock on it, this is the one place on the property no one ever goes," he says, his voice low. "Until now, I guess."

"I wasn't planning to come out here," I tell him. "I wasn't paying attention to what direction I was walking. Being back home has my head all over the place."

"No harm done. I'm, um"—he scratches the back of his neck—"for what it's worth, I'm glad you're here. Here"—he points toward the ground—"and here." His hands gesture around the woods.

"Thanks." I glance over my shoulder. It's getting dark, and I know I should head back soon, but I don't want to leave him. I should. I have no reason to put myself through this torture, but I can't walk away. We need to talk about everything. I know that. I have so much to say to him, but not now. Not yet. "Mom mentioned a family dinner tonight, like old times. Are you planning to go?"

He nods. "Now that you're home? Wouldn't miss it."

"Cool." I start to walk away, but his voice stops me.

"You don't have to go."

"It's getting dark." My eyes fall to the cabin again. "And my mom really will kill me if she finds out I was out here. I should get back."

He picks up the axe again. "Okay, well then, for Elena's peace of mind, let me walk you."

"Only for my mom?" When I glance over at him, his brow quirks up, which is answer enough. Something warm passes between us, and I feel the questions bubbling up inside me, but I can't bring myself to ask them. Just like I couldn't back then. Jack is my weakness. A part of me will always love him and wonder what could've been. So much has changed, yet that never will. "Yeah, okay. Sure."

"Okay." He rubs his lips together. "Have you, uh, how have you been, I mean? What's life like for Carmen McKenna these days?"

"Life is good. I'm working as a book illustrator now, which is fun."

"You always hoped you'd be an artist."

I smile. *He remembered*. "Yeah, I did."

"And you live..."

"I moved back to Atlanta a few years ago. I assumed Mom told you."

"We don't really talk about you," he says simply. Then, maybe to cut down the sting of his words, he adds, "We don't really talk much at all, honestly. Mom keeps me busy with projects around here, and then I go home."

"Home." I repeat the word. "Dean, uh, he mentioned we're neighbors for the summer."

He grins and bumps my shoulder with his playfully. "Just like old times." *Old times*. A heaviness fills the air at his words as memories pass over me. "Are you...are you seeing anyone?"

"Nope," I say, maybe too quickly. "You?"

"No," he says. "Not really, no."

"Okay." I'm not sure what to make of that. We still need to talk about so much, but it can wait for now. I just want to be here. To feel at peace among the people who once built a home for me, even if I didn't realize it until I was gone.

"I'm really glad you're here," he says again.

A tickle forms in the back of my throat, threatening impending tears. "Me too."

CHAPTER SIX

BEFORE — AGE 13

"Last one in's a rotten egg!" Jack shouts, running up behind me. I spin around, spying him with his blue swimming trunks and a white shirt, towel whipping behind him before he drops it, continues to zip past me, and heads for the water.

I roll my eyes playfully, dropping my own towel and darting in after him. We hit the lake water quickly, mud squishing between my toes as I make my way out toward him.

"Loser," he teases, sticking his tongue out and splashing me with water as I draw closer to him. I try not to think about the fact that I'm in a two-piece bathing suit in front of him. The water has only just reached my chest, and I bend down, forcing it to cover me more.

"Cheater," I reply. "You didn't tell me it was a race until you were ahead of me."

"I was still behind you, technically." He walks farther

out in the water, until it's up to his shoulders, and spins around to wink at me.

"Yeah. For all of two seconds," I point out, following him.

Now that the rest of our things have been dropped off by the movers and unpacked, Mom and I are settled into the new house, and Mom is learning the ropes of working here at Hunter's Hollow, which means I've been left to figure everything else out on my own.

Thankfully, Jack has been around to help with that. He's not so bad, really. Not just because he's cute, but because he's kind, too. He's funny. He actually listens to me and has been here to help me navigate the strangeness of being in a new place. In the two weeks since we've been here, it's possible I've told him more about myself than some of the friends I had back in Atlanta.

Of course, Dean is around sometimes, too, but only when he's not with whatever girl he's dating that day. I'm not exaggerating, either. There have been at least four different girls that I can think of since our arrival.

As it stands, Jack was right that I'd eventually learn to like it here. I do. And in a much shorter amount of time than I thought it would take me to come around. I still miss home, and I still wouldn't admit this to anyone except him, but I'm learning to love the lake and the busyness of being here, the fact that something is always going on and interesting people are always showing up. There are quite a few kids around our age that have stayed at Hunter's Hollow since our arrival, and even more that have come just to hang out. It seems to be the place for people our age to spend their days, both friends of Jack and Dean, and complete strangers.

There's never a dull moment, which I appreciate when my head is still in a place that's very dangerous. When sadness seems to be lurking around every quiet moment, every lull in conversation.

"Did you watch *The Covenant* last night like I told you to?" he asks, waving his arms through the water.

"Yeah, it was pretty good." I fell asleep midway through it, but I won't tell him that.

"I watched *John Tucker*." His eyes light up with laughter. "It was funnier than I expected."

"I told you."

Without realizing it, he's suddenly closer to me than he was before. "Um"—he wipes his hand across his mouth, water droplets shining on his skin—"I was thinking we could watch a movie tonight...if you want. Together, I mean."

My heart leaps in my chest. Does he mean it like a date? Or just friends hanging out? There's no way I can ask for clarification. "Oh, um—"

"No pressure or anything. I just thought—"

At the same time, I say, "No, I mean—"

We both laugh and stop speaking, but before we can finish our thoughts, a new voice interrupts us from over my shoulder. "Well, look at the two little love birds."

Dean pulls our attention to where he stands on the

shoreline with two boys I haven't seen before. They're laughing at his lame attempt at a joke.

"Shut up," Jack says, but I can't help noticing he's backed away from me slightly in the water. "Where've you been? Mom was looking for you earlier."

"Devil's Cabin." Dean turns and grins at the boys behind him.

"Devil's Cabin?" I ask, looking at Jack. I know all of the cabins here by now, but they're all just numbered. I haven't heard of any that are nicknamed anything so terrible.

Jack's jaw tightens. "You were supposed to help clean the boats."

"I had...other things to take care of."

The boys laugh in that sort of perverted way boys do, like they know a dirty secret.

"What are you talking about?" I demand, refusing to be the only one not in on whatever this secret is. "Which one's Devil's Cabin?"

"It's not one of the cabins in the campground," Jack tells me, still not looking my way.

"It's farther out in the woods, Carmie. Adults only." Dean peers at me with a smug look on his stupid face.

"Like you're an adult." I fold my arms across my chest. "Why is it called Devil's Cabin?"

Dean steps farther into the water, moving toward us with a sly expression.

"Because of all the devilish things we do out there," one of the boys says.

43

"Although I don't know why they call it *devilish*," Dean admits, but it feels like he's about to tell the punchline of a joke. "Practically a religious experience if you ask me, the way I have the girls screaming for God."

The boys bend at the waist, cutting up with laughter. One high-fives Dean. "Nice one."

My cheeks flame with embarrassment, a lump caught in my throat. He's only sixteen. Is he really already having sex? And bragging about it? My mom would kill me.

"Anyway, don't mind us." Dean runs a hand over the dusting of hair on his bare chest and stomach as he and the other two boys continue to make their way farther out into the water. "We just needed a swim." He eyes me. "Your cheeks are a little red, Carmie. Do you need sunscreen, or is that just from adult conversations? Don't worry. Maybe someday Jack will take you out to Devil's Cabin and show you what it's all about."

"You're disgusting," I snap.

"Dean, stop," Jack says at the same time.

It's as if Dean loves to see how angry he can make me. As I feel the rage bubbling in my belly, he only seems happier.

"What's wrong? The two of you like each other, don't you?" Dean teases, and now they're circling us like sharks in the water, the three boys moving around us and getting closer. Sweat trickles down my back. "Are you boyfriend and girlfriend?"

His friends snicker as they continue to circle us. Dean toys with a piece of my hair as he moves past me.

"We're friends," Jack says before I can say a word.

He scowls. "Well, maybe when you're older."

"Maybe I already have a boyfriend," I say plainly.

Dean's eyes dart to Jack's. "Oh. Sorry, bro. There go your chances."

"Go away, Dean," Jack says through gritted teeth.

"What's his name?" Dean glares at me.

"I don't have to tell you anything," I say, my face flaming with heat.

Dean looks back at his friends. "What do we think, guys? She's clearly lying, right?"

Before either can answer, he launches forward and grabs me, tossing me over his shoulder.

"Liar! Liar! Liar!" the boys chant in unison.

"Put me down!" I cry, slamming my fists into his back.

He spins around, and I notice both of his friends' eyes are glued to my butt.

"Nice view!" one of the boys calls, fist over his mouth. The other laughs, covering his own mouth but making no attempt to look away.

He whistles loudly.

Dean notices what they're doing and drops me back into the water, shoving them both backward seconds later. "Dude, seriously? She's a kid, you assholes."

"*I am not a kid*," I argue, pausing to enunciate each word as I adjust my bathing suit.

Dean turns back to me, his eyes searing into mine. He's too close, and I can smell the scent of his sunscreen and cologne—something warm and familiar. Earthy. "You're a kid, Carmie."

"Her name is Carmen," Jack says, moving to stand next to me.

Dean's lips quirk up cruelly, and I see something dangerous behind his eyes. "You ever been kissed, Carmie?"

"Carmen," I reiterate, avoiding the question as my cheeks heat. He makes me so angry I feel sick.

"I didn't think so." He winks. "You're a kid."

"I didn't answer."

"Didn't have to. Don't worry, little Jack hasn't either." He bats his eyelashes at me. "Maybe you'll be each other's firsts. Unless that fake boyfriend is going to come along and surprise us all."

"Awww." There's an echo of laughter and teasing from the boys, as if he's just made the best joke of the year, and Jack turns away from him.

"Shut up, Dean. Come on, Carmen. Let's go."

"No need to rush off," Dean calls, but we're already going. He waves at us with just his fingers, grinning proudly. My entire body radiates with heat as I step out of the water. As I follow Jack out of the water, I can still feel their eyes on me.

"Ignore them," he tells me, grabbing his towel and wrapping it around his neck. "Dean's just bored."

When I look back, Dean blows me a kiss with a wink, then dives into the water.

CHAPTER SEVEN

PRESENT DAY

I'm freshly showered and dressed when it's time for dinner at the Hunters' cabin. I press the button to open the gate and make my way across the campground quickly. It's bustling with people, like always. The smell of campfire smoke and meat roasting on grills fills my nose as a group of teen girls walk past me in their bikinis, towels draped over their shoulders as they giggle about something I can't hear.

Teenage girls will always make me nervous. Even now, as a fully grown adult, when they laugh, I'm right back in middle school knowing they're talking about me.

"Carmen, wait up!" I hear a voice behind me and spin around to see Jack jogging to catch up.

"Oh, hey."

He's freshly showered, too, his wet hair clinging to his head. It instantly takes me back to the many days we spent in the water together. He runs a hand through it as if he can hear my thoughts, and I shove them away just as quickly.

"Heading to dinner?"

I nod. "Yep. Walk with me?"

"Happy to." His eyes dart over at me, then back to the ground. "You look pretty."

It's as if I'm thirteen again, my stomach flipping over a silly compliment. The weight of it swells in my chest, radiating with heat. He shouldn't still make me feel this way. "Oh. Thanks."

"You're awfully dressed up, I mean," he adds, looking away. "For dinner at Mom and Dad's."

I run a hand over the shirt I'm wearing. "It's just a shirt and jeans. It's not as if I'm wearing a gown."

He laughs. "I guess I'm just not used to seeing you dressed." The words leave his mouth, and his cheeks are instantly bright crimson as he fumbles to correct himself. "I mean, not in a bathing suit or, you know, like...not real clothes. Pajamas, shorts." He puts a hand over his face, and I laugh. "No makeup. I didn't mean—"

"It's fine, Jack. I know what you mean."

He smiles, but it looks pained. His cheeks are still incredibly red. "So what are your plans for the summer? Are you taking time off work?"

"I'll be working here when I can, but I'm between projects, so I can take my time with it."

"What are you working on, then?"

My eyes drop. I haven't told anyone yet, but I feel like I can tell him. Jack was always the one who listened.

48

"Actually, I'm working on a book of my own. I've already got the story for the most part, but now I'm working on illustrations."

"Wow, really?"

"Yeah. I mean, I'm trying. It'll probably never amount to anything, but it's a fun way to kill time anyway."

"I'm sure it's great."

"Thanks. We'll see." I look over at him. "What about you? Dean mentioned you stuck around here to help your parents."

"Yeah. Well, I'm useless with maintenance and repairs, so Dad still takes care of all that, but I can handle the boat rentals and cleaning and lawn care and landscaping, and our moms take care of the office stuff. Plus, I never really had any plans anyway, and someone will have to run the place once Mom and Dad retire. Dean doesn't want it, so I guess it'll be me."

"You never had any plans? Last I heard, you wanted to be a film director."

He laughs, brows shooting up toward his hairline. "Well, okay, I never had any *realistic* plans, then."

"You don't know that until you try."

"Maybe." With a shrug, he adds, "I'm happy here, though. This land has been in our family for generations. Someone has to take care of it."

"It's not like your parents are planning to retire any time soon, are they? There's nothing to say you can't do what you want until that time comes."

"Yeah, maybe." He runs his teeth over his bottom lip as we cross the dirt road and head over to the peninsula where our parents' homes sit. It feels like returning to my past here, as the cabins come into view. More than ever before, I'm reminded of the first day we moved to The Hollow. That day, so full of uncertainty and confusion, anger and stress, is at once nothing like today and so much like today.

We make our way toward the cabins, past Mom's, and Jack lets me walk up the stairs first on our way into his parents'. He pulls open the door for me, and we step into the kitchen, where our moms are working side by side at the counter.

At once, both of their heads turn toward me, eyes wide. Their mouths crack into smiles, and Jill's gaze falls between Jack and me. My mom instantly drops the knife she'd been using to chop the veggies and crosses the room to pull me into a hug.

"I still can't believe you're home." She kisses my cheek, then turns back to Jill. "It's like nothing's changed around here."

"Plenty has changed." Dean appears from the living room, grinning broadly. "Including the fact that Carmen and Jack are actually on time for once."

"Shut up," Jack and I say at the same time.

"Plenty's exactly the same, too," Jill says with a chuckle, turning around with a platter of burgers in her hands. "Alright, who's hungry?"

She carries the platter to the table across the room

and sets it down while Mom drops the cucumbers into the bowl of salad before carrying it to the table as well.

Soon, we're all seated. Jack is to my left with Mom to my right, and Dean is directly across from me. Like usual, Jill and Sam sit at opposite ends of the table.

Dean reaches for a burger, but Sam waves his hand at him, gesturing toward me. "Easy, hoss. Guest of honor first," he teases.

Dean eyes me as I lean forward and grab a burger as slowly as possible, inching forward with my hand outstretched, a smirk playing on my lips.

"*She's* the guest of honor?" He grimaces. "Since when?"

Once I've taken my pick, everyone else dives in, grabbing their share of burgers, potato salad, regular salad, and macaroni and cheese.

"This all looks delicious, Jill," I tell her, ignoring Dean.

"Well, we had to celebrate our girl coming home." She grins and pats Mom's arm. "Tell us all about what you've been up to in the big city."

I give them the same spiel I've given to both Dean and Jack—a little about my art and much more about life in general.

"How's Greg?" Mom asks, and every eye in the room falls to me.

Dean puts his burger down, folding his hands in front of him with a shit-eating grin on his face. "Greg?"

"Who's Greg?" Sam asks, a hint of warning to his tone. "Boyfriend? Do I need to talk to him?"

I shake my head. "Greg is...fine, I think. We haven't spoken in a few months."

"Oh." Mom's face falls, and I see the disappointment in her eyes. "I was hoping he'd come with you. I still haven't gotten to meet him."

"Uh-oh. Is Carmie making up boyfriends again?" Dean teases, returning to his food.

"I've never made up a boyfriend."

"I beg to differ." He chuckles. "Right after you moved here, you told me you had a boyfriend back in the city."

My heart drops as I recall the memory. I groan. "Why are you so obsessed with me, Dean? Who even remembers that?"

"You wish I was obsessed with you." He playfully kicks my leg under the table.

"Trust me, I do not."

"Alright, alright." Sam cuts off the impending argument. "Some things never change." He turns his attention to Jack, who's being oddly quiet. When I look over, he's checking his phone. "Speaking of girlfriends, how'd we get lucky enough to get solo-Jack tonight?"

"Sam," Jill chides.

The table falls silent as everyone looks her way, though I'm looking at Jack. *Solo-Jack? He told me he was single earlier...didn't he?*

"They broke up," Jill whispers. *Who?* I want to ask. *Jack had a girlfriend?*

"Thanks, Mom," Jack says, looking up from his phone finally.

"You did?" Sam asks. "I didn't know that. When?"

Jack leans back in his chair and runs a hand over his forehead. "It's not a big deal. Can we move on from this?"

"She cheated on him," Dean says.

"She did?" Sam's eyes widen.

"You didn't tell me that," Jill adds.

"Jesus Christ," Jack growls. "Can we talk about something else?"

"We can go back to Carmie's love life, if you want. I'm dying to learn more about *Greg*," Dean teases.

I purse my lips, inhaling deeply. "My name is *Carmen*, and if we're going to talk about anyone's love life, why don't we talk about yours? What poor girl are you dating this week?"

"Oh, come on, Carmie. You know me better than that. I don't date poor girls, only rich ones." He winks and takes a large bite of his burger. His antics don't bother me like they used to, but still, I roll my eyes.

"You're impossible."

He chuckles. "And what about you, Elena? Mom said you went on a date the other night."

I dart my attention toward Mom at his words. "A date?"

53

"It's not a big deal," Mom says quickly, placing her glass down on the table. "It was one date."

"So there won't be a second?" Jill asks.

"I haven't heard from him." Mom distracts herself, appearing unbothered as she searches for the perfect bite of salad.

"His loss, then," I tell her. Since Dad's passing, Mom hasn't tried to put herself out there, no matter how much we encourage her to do so. If she's dated someone, even just once, it's a good sign. She's only in her fifties. She still has a lot of life left to live, and she put so much into me as a child, she never had time for herself.

She gives me a placating smile. "Enough about everyone's love lives. I want to hear what your plans are while you're here."

"I'm going to help you guys out, same as Jack and Dean," I tell her.

"No, you're not," she says.

"Not a chance," Jill says at the same time.

"What? Why? The boys are."

"Men," Dean corrects, his mouth full of food.

"Exactly. They are. We have enough help around here, young lady." Jill smiles at me with adoration. "We want you to have fun while you're home. Explore. Enjoy yourself. You aren't here to work."

"They're trying to convince you to move back, is what she's saying," Jack says.

Jill's eyes grow mischievous as she looks at Mom. "We

are not." She's actively fighting a smile. "But...it certainly wouldn't be the *worst* thing."

Mom glances at me, throwing her hands up in surrender. "I've already told her she won't convince you. Carmen loves the city too much."

"I love it here, too." I pick up my fork. "But Atlanta is my home. I'm just here for a few months."

What I want to tell them but can't is that Atlanta doesn't feel much like home anymore either. I guess maybe it's why I'm here if I look deep enough. For so much of my life, I've just wanted there to be somewhere I belong. Since my dad died, part of me has craved that stability we had in my early childhood. Moving to Hunter's Hollow was an interruption to the life I once had, and then, just when I felt like I'd found my place, everything went wrong.

I ran because this place no longer felt good or safe, but running away didn't fix anything no matter how badly I wanted it to or how hard I tried to pretend it had. Coming back here has filled me with so many conflicting emotions, but until I deal with them, until I learn the truth about everything, I just don't know how I can move on.

Maybe that's why Greg and I didn't work out.

My eyes flick toward Jack. Maybe there are other reasons, though.

Looking down, I take a bite of my food. The rest of the meal is filled with casual conversation about repairs needing done around a few of the cabins and stories about some of the more interesting guests I've missed over the years. It feels so normal it's almost surreal. Some things really don't ever change.

When dinner is over, Mom takes me over to her cabin to see what's become of my old bedroom. Like she told me, the space is set up with paint supplies and tables all along the perimeter of the room, and the latest addition to her little ceramic village—a grocery store—is midway through being painted.

"I hope you aren't upset with me," she says, her voice soft and hesitant. "I should've told you I was packing your things away before I did it."

"Mom, of course not. It's fine. I'm happy you've found the space to start painting again. The corner of the living room was never really big enough. You deserve it." I hesitate. "And you know I'm okay with you dating, too, right? Dad would want you to be happy...and so do I."

She nods but doesn't meet my eyes. "Thank you, *mija*." She crosses the room and adjusts a few of the tubes of paint on the table silently. After several seconds, she turns back toward me. "And I want you to be happy, too."

"I am happy," I assure her.

Her dark eyes dart back and forth between mine, trying to read me like she always has. "Are you? You didn't tell me about Greg."

"Nothing dramatic happened, I promise. I just realized he wasn't what I wanted."

"That seems to be happening a lot." She leans back against the table behind her.

"What does that mean?"

"Well, it's not just Greg. It was Anthony. And Jevon. And...who was the other one? Mark?"

"Marco," I correct. "It's not a big deal, Mom, I promise. I'm picky. Isn't that better than settling?"

She puffs out a breath. "Of course it is. I just...I can't help wondering if you're picky because you're scared of getting hurt like...like I did." Her voice cracks, and she looks away again.

"No." I step toward her quickly. "No, Mom. It's not about Dad. I saw how much it hurt when we lost him, yes, but that's only because of how happy he made us. You guys taught me why love matters. If anything, you've made me want to find that." I rub a hand over her arm. "Dad is a hard example to live up to, that's all."

She smiles through her glassy eyes. "That he is."

"I'm okay. I'll know when I find the real thing. I just...I need to figure out who I am first. What I want."

She dries her tears, and a wry grin fills her lips. "The *real thing* may be closer than you expect. You might not have to look so hard."

"Meaning?"

"I don't know what happened between you and Jack back then, but I always liked you two together. You know that."

"Yeah." I huff, shoving my hands into my back pockets with a step back. "I know. I liked us, too."

"I'm just saying...the two of you are here. You're both single. Maybe it's the second chance you've always needed."

I look away. "Well, don't get your hopes up. Jack and I could never make it work."

"Back then, sure. But you're different people now."

"Maybe." I don't feel so different. In certain ways, yes. But I think part of me never grew out of the heart-broken young woman who left this place. Maybe part of me never grew up from the girl who found love here even before the heartbreak.

When I really think about it, sometimes it feels like I'm trapped—stuck in the past and the pain, confusion, and unanswered questions that have followed me for years.

I'm lost in my thoughts—of back then, of all the heartache and the grief, but also the love and happiness —when she draws in a long inhale. "Is there anything you want to talk to me about? Are you really okay?"

"Yes. Of course. Mom, I'm fine."

She presses her lips together, clearly not convinced. "Don't get me wrong, I'm glad you're back. But eleven years, and I haven't been able to get you to step foot in Hunter's Hollow for even a holiday, and now you're here for two months? And it was your idea? I feel like there's something you aren't telling me."

"I just missed you." I shrug, though I know I'm not very convincing.

She folds her arms across her chest. "Carmen..."

"Look...I promise I'm fine. I just...I guess Greg and I broke up, and I was between projects and work, and I felt...lonely." My voice cracks. "Atlanta has always felt like my home, but suddenly, I started missing this one. I can't explain it."

She places a light hand on my arm. "Your home is where your family is, *mija*. I've told you that. Atlanta will always hold a piece of you, but..." Tears line her eyes, and she pauses to collect herself. "It doesn't mean you're giving up on your father—or...or betraying him in some way—if you let this place start to feel like home just as much. If you let this place, this family, have a piece of you, too."

I fight back tears of my own, faking a yawn. "You're right. I'm just stubborn, I guess."

She nods, dusting tears from her cheeks. "It's late. You should probably get going, honey. Before it gets too dark."

Glancing out the window, I see she's right. The evening sky outside is getting darker, and it's a relatively long walk back to the cabin. "Yeah, okay." With a kiss on her cheek, I head for the door.

"I'm so glad to have you home, Carmen. We all are."

For some reason, her words crack in my chest. *Home.* I'm not sure I know what that is.

I open her door and step out. The world around me

is a mix of pinks, purples, and oranges. The sun fading into the horizon over the lake is just as pretty as a painting.

"Ready?"

I jump at the sound of his voice, and when I look over, it's the last brother I expected to be waiting for me. "Dean?"

"Last I checked." He appears from behind Mom's cabin, looking down as if searching for something on his shirt. "Seems I've lost my name tag, though." He walks toward me with that cocky attitude that's practically part of his DNA.

"What are you doing?"

"Waiting for you, clearly. It's dark. Didn't think you should be walking home alone."

I make my way down the stairs with a scowl, then poke him in the chest when I reach the bottom step. "Okay, *one*, I'm perfectly capable of walking myself home, thank you very much. And *two*, it's not dark, Grandpa."

"Well, it's getting dark." He waves a hand in the air. "And with how slow you walk, it'll be dark before you get there."

"Not everyone has mile-long legs."

"Obviously." His eyes fall to my legs skeptically. "I'm not even sure those qualify as legs, Carmie. Shrimpy little things."

"Oh, I know. They're too short and too pale for you." I turn, walking toward the road. "Newsflash, Dean, not everyone can be the models you date. I happen to like my legs, thank you *very* much." My words come out more vengeful than I feel, and the look on his face tells me he felt every bit of that.

He stops in his tracks, taking hold of my arm with one hand to stop me, too. "You know I'm just teasing, right?" His eyes are more serious than I've seen them—maybe ever. "Your legs aren't..." He looks away, running his tongue over his bottom lip like he's especially angry at it. "They're fine."

I bark out a laugh. "Well, thanks, I guess. It's fine, Dean. You didn't hurt my feelings. I was teasing you back. It's what we do." I wave a hand between us. "Sort of our thing, remember?"

"Kind of hard to remember. It's been a long time. Besides, for the record, I haven't dated anyone in a while, models included."

My jaw drops, and I look over at him. "Wait, wait, wait. Dean Hunter, single? Is this the apocalypse? I don't have my go-bag prepared."

He rolls his eyes and shoves me with his shoulder. "Shut up."

I laugh. "I guess you've probably run through every girl in this town, and they all know to avoid you. Warned their friends. Maybe there's a Don't Date Dean Club." I pause, thinking, then let out a hum. "Hmm. Very fitting initials."

"You're such an infant," he growls, his eyes on me again. "I haven't dated every girl, and you know it."

Something heavy sits in his voice, something he's not saying.

"Well, no. I guess there are some married ones you've missed, but surely there aren't many left. Definitely all of your class and most of mine, and the ones in between. Plus, with the Triple D Club hard at work..." I pause to feign running the math in my head, then click my tongue. "Dude, you're going to have to come visit me in the city sometime. Or else become celibate."

His mouth twists with an unreadable expression.

Moments later, my face flames as I realize what I've said. What I've implied. "To see other women, I mean. You'll have to come see me in the city to see *other* women. You know, because there are more in the city. Women, I mean. More women. Not...I didn't mean me. Obviously."

"Relax." He puts a hand on my shoulder, and suddenly, I can't breathe. His touch is doing the exact opposite to me as what he's requested. *Why can't I catch my breath?* "I know what you meant, Carmie."

After removing his hand, he continues walking, but I stay rooted in place. "Why do you call me that?"

He doesn't look back, but stops and waits for me to catch up. "Why do you hate it so much?"

"Because it's not my name."

"It's called a nickname. A sign of affection. Is that an unfamiliar concept for you?"

"What if I called you Deanie?"

He chuckles. "Would it make you think of my weenie?"

"You're such a child." I shove him away and hurry forward.

"That's why I call you Carmie." His voice comes from behind me, his tone suddenly sobering, and I realize he hasn't resumed walking yet.

I spin back around. "Because you're a child?"

"Because *you* were." I can't understand the look on his face, the way he's standing all still and uncomfortable. I've never seen Dean look uncomfortable. "Because you were a child."

"I was three years younger than you—hardly a child."

"You were a child, Carmen." He barely looks at me as he walks past, and I swear I feel a shot of electricity run through me as he says, "And I needed to remember that."

"What is that supposed to mean?"

When I catch up with him, whatever just happened has passed and the casual demeanor has returned. "You know what I mean. Anyway, Tye and Daniel needed to be reminded, too."

I physically recoil at the mention of his old friends. Somehow, they were even worse than he was. Or maybe I just managed to care about him more than them. "Whatever happened to them, anyway?"

"They're still around. Tye's the principal at our old school, actually. Daniel's on the force with his dad. He'll probably be sheriff when Robbie retires."

"Well, you guys just run the town, don't you?"

"I'm a high school history teacher," he says, his voice low and self-deprecating. *How very unlike him.* "Hardly running the town."

"Just the basketball team."

He nods. "Fair enough. They'll, uh, probably be around at some point."

"The basketball team?"

He inhales, pursing his lips before chuckling with forced annoyance. "My friends, smart-ass."

"*Here*, here?" I can't help the shrill tone of my voice, and he doesn't miss it.

"Is that a problem?" One brow quirks up.

"No, obviously not. I just didn't realize you were still close."

"They're not like they used to be," he assures me. "They both calmed down a lot after everything that happened."

I swallow. "That night changed us all—the whole town—didn't it?"

He shoves his hands into his pockets. "I think so. How could it not?"

"Speaking of, I, um, I went for a walk earlier and ended up at the cabin. Did they...did the police ever arrest anyone? Mom never talks about it, and it feels weird to ask. Like bringing it up is bad luck or something. Everyone is just trying to forget and move on." Guilt swells in my throat, a lump I can never seem to swallow.

He's quiet for a long pause, then shakes his head.

"No. They never figured out what happened. I know they questioned everyone, but last I heard, they said it was just...probably someone passing through. I don't think the case was officially closed or anything, but it may as well have been. You're right...no one ever talks about it."

My skin lines with chills. "Someone passing through." I pinch my lips together, inhaling deeply. "You believe that?"

"I don't know. I mean, the campground draws all kinds of people here, and they have guests, too. There's really no way to keep track of who was here when it happened. And the woods back up to several different properties. It seems unlikely, but I don't want to think it could be anything else. The alternative is so much worse." Several seconds pass before he changes the subject. "But no one's asking my opinion, and there was no evidence to the contrary, so I guess I try not to think about it either."

As much as I hate to admit it, he's right. It's likely we'll never know what happened the night that changed all of our lives, and that fact has haunted me for the last eleven years.

"So, what happened with George?"

I eye him.

"Wasn't that his name? Something boring like George or Gabe or Gus?"

"Greg."

"Greg. Right. What happened with him?"

"I don't know. Nothing interesting. He was nice, but...it didn't work out. We'd gone two weeks without talking when he reached out, and...I guess I just realized I hadn't missed him, and that probably wasn't normal."

He winces. "Was it because of his boring name?"

"Greg is a fine name. What do you have against the name Greg?"

"Nothing against the name. Something against the man."

I grip his arm, shoving him playfully. "He was fine. You guys would probably get along."

"Doubt it."

"He's a teacher, too, actually. English."

He wags a finger at me. "There's your problem. English is *way* more boring than history."

"So says you."

He laughs, turning his head to look at me. "You disagree?"

"I was always better at English."

"That's because you didn't have me as a teacher."

As he says the words, I think of my history teacher, Mr. Jones. Awkwardly tall, with a bald patch, a protruding stomach, and clothing that never seemed to fit. Add to that the monotonous voice and teeth that always seemed to have a bit of lunch left in them, and he was right. I study Dean, who is conventionally attractive, objectively speaking. Dark hair and eyes, tall enough to make you feel small without towering over you, with a sharp jaw and neatly trimmed facial hair across his cheeks and chin. Yes, I suspect he's right. If my history teacher had looked more like Dean, there's certainly a chance I would've paid more attention.

"I'm a great teacher," he adds, making me realize I've been staring at him for far too long.

"I have no doubts."

"You were looking at me like you had several doubts."

I snort, letting him believe that rather than telling him the truth. "I'm sure you're a great teacher, Dean. Honest. You forget that it's you who taught me how to drive."

His brows draw down. "What? My dad taught you."

"Yes," I agree, "but I remember the night you took me out when I was upset after a lesson. I hadn't done well, and your dad was stressed out, which meant *I* was stressed out, so you offered to take me. Do you remember?"

We've reached the gate to our cabins now, and we stop to enter the code. Dean looks over at me like maybe he doesn't remember. Maybe it's silly that I remember it so well.

"Of course I remember that night, Carmen," he says after a moment, staring at me. "I'm just surprised you do." Something warm passes between us, and I can't understand the way he's looking at me. Then, before either of us makes a fool of ourselves, the gate swings open with a loud, slow groan.

We both turn away, the heat of the moment heavy on

my skin like a sunburn. "You were a good teacher then, so I'm sure you're even better now."

He swallows, looking up at the cabin. "I should let you get some sleep."

For some reason, the idea of him leaving me alone makes me sad. "You sure? I have some drinks in the fridge if you want one. It...wouldn't be the worst thing to catch up. Dredge up the past. Make it really awkward."

His gaze falls between me and the cabin, but eventually, he shakes his head. "Yeah, I probably shouldn't. It's late. Maybe another night."

The bitterness stings, but I don't know why. I shouldn't care what Dean wants to do. He's probably going to call one of his many girlfriends.

"Okay. Yeah. Sure. I'll, uh, I'll see you in the morning."

He nods, taking a step back. "Sure. See you."

As he disappears across the yard toward his cabin, I make my way to mine. Inside, I crack open a bottle of wine and pour a glass before changing into a pair of shorts and a T-shirt for sleep.

When I return to the living room, I grab my iPad out of my backpack and flip open the cover.

I shouldn't care that Dean didn't want to come inside. It was probably for the best that he didn't. I guess, in a way, I just miss our friendship. Growing up, Dean and Jack were the closest things I had to friends, even when things were complicated between us. They made me feel less alone out here.

Now, even with my mom not so far away for the first time in years, even knowing I could call five different people and they'd be here in seconds, I feel more alone than ever.

I sink down onto the couch with my glass of wine and my iPad, and I open it to my latest sketch, turning the television on to some mindless reality show.

Grabbing my Apple Pencil, I begin shading in the picture I've been working on. I've chosen a porcupine as my main character, and with each new page, I'm finding him easier and easier to draw. His quills are familiar now, his little button nose coming to me with ease.

I'm lost in my drawing when I hear a knock at the door and look up. I check the window behind me, but I see nothing out of the ordinary.

Did I remember to lock the door?

Out here, it shouldn't be necessary, but my city instincts are still front and center, and I'm certain I did. The world outside is dark, and I'm not expecting anyone.

I stand up, place my iPad down, and cross the room slowly, my heart ratcheting upward in my chest. With a hand on the doorknob, I hesitate. Suck in a deep breath.

Then, I swing open the door.

Dean's back is to me, like he was just about to walk away, but he turns around again. "I didn't want to wake you."

"I wasn't asleep."

"Is it too late to agree to a drink?" Why does he look as if he already regrets this?

"No. Of course not." I step back and allow him inside.

He walks past me and into the cabin, hands shoved into his pockets.

"Is everything okay?" I ask, shutting the door.

"Yeah, I just...I thought it might be weird if I came over."

"Why would it be weird?" I ask, but we both know the answer to that question.

"Jack wouldn't like it," he says finally. "I thought you might...rather have him here."

"Jack and I are friends, if that. Besides, he's welcome to come, too. If he'd been around, I would've invited him. You and I are just two friends having a drink. It's not a big deal, and I guarantee you Jack doesn't care what I do anyway." I lead him into the kitchen and open the fridge. "I've got beer or merlot."

"Beer's good." He reaches for the bottle as I hand it to him, and he twists the top off with ease.

"Where is Jack, anyway?" I ask, trying to seem nonchalant.

"He wasn't home," he tells me, taking a swig of his beer. "His car's gone, so I'm guessing he went out."

"Oh." Just like that, the desire for company dissipates. I'm no longer in the mood to entertain, but for Dean, I'll manage.

"He disappears sometimes. I think he's annoyed with having a roommate." He rests an arm against the bar-height countertop of the kitchen peninsula. "Can't say it's my favorite thing either."

"It's just a few weeks," I point out.

"Says the girl living alone."

"I was always alone," I say, more sad and pitiful than I'd meant it to sound. "Only child, remember?"

He tips his beer forward as I cross the room and grab my glass of wine, making room for him on the couch. "You were never alone, Carmie. You know that."

"No, my mom was here, of course. And Jack was around, I guess. And then there was you, but you were mostly a jerk."

He smiles, taking it as the joke it is. "Your favorite jerk, though."

I roll my eyes. "I want to hear about your life, Dean. How're things?"

And just like that, we fall into step. Back to how we were before things got very, very complicated.

CHAPTER EIGHT

BEFORE — AGE 14

Mom bursts out of the kitchen of cabin ten as the last of my friends makes their way through the front door. Sam is on jacket duty, greeting everyone as they enter and taking their coats and purses to put them in one of the bedrooms, while Mom and Jill set out the food and drinks they've prepared for my birthday party.

I tried to tell Mom I didn't need some elaborate party, especially since I still don't have that many friends at school, but being the new girl apparently has perks because practically everyone I invited has shown up.

Mom and I are on good terms now, I guess. I don't hate it here like I thought I would. I still miss home, but Hunter's Hollow isn't the most awful place to live, and the town—Cody—is also fine.

I guess it helps that Jack is so well-liked at the school, and I've clung to his side, which means everyone is kind to me too, but in general, there are worse places to be.

In the living room, there are ten girls and eleven guys, Jack and Dean included. I asked Mom if we could exclude Dean, but I don't think she realized I was serious. Either way, it is what it is.

At sixteen, he's too cool to hang out with *fourteen-year-old babies* anyway—his words—but it was the only way the parents would agree to leave us alone for the party.

Of course, they've told us they'll still be popping in randomly, the doors have to remain unlocked, and they've checked the house and everyone's things for alcohol or anything else that might get us into trouble. If I know Mom, it means that if we break a rule, this will not only be my first birthday party in The Hollow, but my last.

"Happy birthday, Carmen," Alissa Burton says, hugging me quickly as she walks past the gift table and sets down a large bag.

"Thanks," I call after her, but she's not really looking at me. As usual, she's followed by a gaggle of her most loyal cohorts, and they're already lost in conversation, scoping out the place.

Alissa is the most popular girl in school, so getting her here is like royalty accepting an invitation. The happiness in my chest wilts when I notice the way Jack's watching her as she walks into the living room, his eyes hopeful and strangely intrigued.

It's how most people look at Alissa, myself included, but I thought—hoped—Jack was different. The girls surrounding her, Sarah and Nicole, whisper something in her ear, and she giggles, looking back at me. My hand goes to my hair instinctively, wishing mine looked anything like their perfectly shiny locks, or that my makeup was as freshly applied and pristine as theirs.

"Hey, Jack." Alissa waves with just her fingers, toying with a piece of her hair. "Hey, Dean."

"Hey," Jack says from where he's sitting, staring at her like a dog waiting to be called.

Dean barely looks up from his phone. "'Sup?"

Drawing my attention away from my worst nightmare coming to life in the living room, Mom makes her way toward me as Jill finishes arranging the food on the table. She claps her hands together in front of her stomach with a long breath. "Okay. That's everyone, right?"

"Yep, that's it."

She kisses my temple, hugging me. "Okay. Then I guess I should go." Her eyes search mine, waiting. "Happy birthday, sweetheart. Are you sure you don't want us to stay? You know your mom will still kick everyone's butt at karaoke. We could sing some Selena, like old times."

I cover my face. "No, Mom. Please don't."

She grins. "Oh, fine. You're all grown up and too cool for me now. I get it." She plants another kiss on my head, my cheeks heating as Jill crosses the room with an inhale.

"I think everything's all set up. Do you need anything, Carmen?"

"Nope. That's everything. Thank you both." I smile at them, hoping they'll take the hint and get out.

"Remember, we'll be back to check on you occasionally, so...be good." Mom's eyes are full of meaning.

I groan. "Mom, stop. It's fine. We're just going to hang out."

She turns but then stops again, practically toying with me at this point. "Okay. Well, if you need anything, you call, do you hear me?"

If she doesn't leave, she's going to ruin everything. "Yep."

Jill wraps an arm around her shoulder. "Okay. Come on, Elena. Our little girl's all grown up, and she wants us annoying old people to leave her alone." She winks at me as Sam comes out of the bedroom.

He rubs his hands together. "You ladies ready?"

"You bet. Take us home for ice cream?" Jill slips an arm through Sam's, still holding my mom with the other.

"You read my mind." He chuckles. "Dean, you're in charge. Best behavior, you hear me?" He snaps his fingers. "Dean!"

"Got it," Dean groans, his arm tossed over his forehead, eyes locked on his phone screen. "Just so we're clear, I expect to be paid for babysitting."

"You remember when you woke up in a warm house with food in your stomach? Consider that payment." Sam's joke elicits a sigh from Dean, and the adults finally leave the room, then the house, and we're alone.

I cross the living room, where the party seems to have

started without me. Everyone appears to be having fun, which is a plus, I guess, but I'm not sure where I fit in at my own party.

I don't even know half of these people.

I'm starting to think letting Jack send out the invites was a bad idea. When I recognize a friendly face from several of my classes, Shelby Brewer, on the floor, relief floods me. At least there's someone here I'd consider a friend aside from Jack and Dean.

Jack is standing in the center of the group, across from Alissa and bookended by two of his friends—Brett and Colton—that I know from school, though only vaguely.

"There's the birthday girl," Shelby calls when I move to squeeze in next to her. I've always liked Shelby. She's a bit obnoxious, but always friendly. She scoots over, making room for me next to her. "Fourteen and fabulous. How are you feeling? Older and wiser?"

I smile. "Thanks, Shelby. I feel...the same, I guess."

"Well, let's fix that, shall we? What are we doing first? Dancing? I brought some CDs."

"I vote we play spin the bottle," Alissa says, her voice carrying across the room until everyone falls silent. I hadn't even realized she was listening to us.

Before anyone can respond, the front door opens, and for a split second, I just know our parents were waiting outside the door for someone to say something as scandalous as that.

Within seconds, Tye and Daniel—Dean's closest friends—appear. I definitely didn't invite them.

Dean stands, doing that weird high-five-handshake-hug thing boys do with each of them. "'Sup, boys?"

"What are they doing here?" Jack asks, stalking toward them. "We didn't invite them."

"I did," Dean says, turning away from him with a quick dismissal.

"It's *my* birthday. My party," I say, joining Jack behind Dean. "Who said you could invite anyone? Our parents wouldn't be okay with this."

"Relax, pipsqueak," Dean says. "You won't get in trouble. The guys are here for me. Mom and Dad don't care. Now run off and play pin the tail on the donkey or something, would you?"

"It's my birthday," I repeat.

"Awww. Happy birthday," Tye says, bending down like he's talking to a small child. He's blond and beautiful, and god does he know it. Everything about him drips with arrogance. Together, these three boys run the school. "I left your present in my car, Carmie. Want to go out there and get it with me? That way you can thank me properly." He pokes his tongue into his cheek, and Daniel snorts, but Dean shoves him. Hard.

"Enough. Leave her alone," he warns.

I ignore him, focusing only on Dean. "You weren't allowed to bring anyone. If Mom finds out there are extra people, she'll make everyone leave, and then I'll be the one in trouble."

"Who's going to tell them?" He eyes me, then Jack, as he walks up to stand next to me. "You two?"

I shake my head and look at Jack, who's also denying it.

"Okay then," Dean says. "Run along to your little party and leave the grown-ups to their business."

"I know you aren't talking about yourselves," I say defiantly.

"She's got a mouth on her, Dean," Daniel says, stepping closer to me. "I always forget about that."

"Be a shame if someone kissed the sass right out of her," Tye agrees. "You gotten your first kiss yet?" Clearly, he remembers that humiliating day at the lake as well as I do. His voice is too loud in the small space, and soon enough the entire room has fallen silent, listening to us.

"None of your business," I tell him.

"I said leave her alone," Dean growls at the same time, shoving his friends back.

"Come on, Carmen." Jack steps between us, pushing me away toward the group of our friends. When we return, I see Alissa has moved forward with her plan to set up spin the bottle. Everyone is sitting in a circle, a single bottle of water in the center.

"Birthday girl first," she says, gesturing toward me.

"Oh, that's okay." My entire face is burning red from my interaction with Dean's creepy friends, and my chest races with fear that we're going to be caught and my birthday's going to be ruined. "We could do something else. We have Xbox and music. Food. We could watch a movie or something. Or there are some board games around here somewhere."

"Come on, Carmen," Shelby says, holding out her hand to me so I'll sit next to her on the floor. "You'll be fine."

"You don't have to do this if you don't want to," Jack says.

"Do *you* want to?" I ask him, a lump forming in my throat.

His eyes flick down toward the circle, toward Alissa, perhaps. "I won't if you don't want me to."

"Oh my god, you guys," Alissa says, standing and pulling us over to join the circle. "Just play. Come on, I thought this was a party."

I sink down with no real choice. To my relief, Jack sits down beside me.

Everyone is still watching me, waiting for the birthday girl to go first, apparently. I've never played spin the bottle before, but I've seen it in enough movies that I get the idea.

I lean forward, hoping my hand doesn't shake as I take hold of the water bottle and give it a good spin. It spins, zipping around the circle, and slows down. When it stops, I look up while holding my breath. The bottle is pointing toward Shelby, who grins at me playfully and, without hesitation, shouts, "I get a kiss from the birthday girl!"

She leans forward, plants a kiss on my cheek, and hoots loudly, both hands in the air. Then it's her turn.

She spins the bottle and lands on Jack's friend, Colton. It continues around the circle, and each time the bottle nearly lands on me, my entire body holds a breath. To my mortification, I notice Dean and his friends are now watching the game intently, no doubt ready to make fun of Jack or me when the bottle lands on us.

When it's Jack's turn, he looks at me once, then leans forward and spins it gently. It goes around just twice, and my muscles clench when I see it coming back toward me and slowing down.

The bottle finally stops, and my entire body tenses and floods with warmth all at once. It's pointing right at me.

When I look up, Jack's eyes are locked on mine. He licks his lips and looks down at the bottle, like he's checking to be sure of what he's seeing. I don't know what to say. What to do. He doesn't seem to either.

"Kiss her, Jack." Dean's voice fills the silent room.

Jack glares at his brother, and I follow his sight line to where Dean is standing, the most serious look I've ever seen on his face. His jaw is so tight it looks as if his teeth might crack.

"No." I hear Jack's answer before I turn my attention back to him. I can't help feeling like I've been rejected. My face burns. He shakes his head.

"You have to kiss her," Alissa says. "It's how the game works."

Everyone in the circle agrees enthusiastically.

"Go on."

"Kiss her."

"Come on."

"Do it! Do it!"

"It's fine, Jack. It's just a game," I say, my voice low. *Why doesn't he want to kiss me? Have I been totally misreading everything happening between us? Is the idea of kissing me really so awful?*

"I'm not going to kiss you. Not here. Not like this." He's practically whispering, talking only to me. "You deserve better than this for your..." He pauses, saving me the embarrassment of letting everyone here know this would be my first kiss. "For it to happen like this."

"Kiss her," Dean says again, and when I look over at him, his eyes are locked on me. He swallows. "Before someone else does."

"I'll volunteer," Brett says playfully, a hand in the air.

"Easy, tiger." Tye pushes up his sleeves. "I'll handle this if he doesn't want to."

A murmur of agreement runs through a few other guys. I don't feel flattered, though. I just feel dumb. Like the little charity case no one actually wants. Like a project.

"It's fine." I tuck a piece of my hair behind my ear, moving to stand. "It's a stupid game anyway. Let's play something else, okay?"

"Yeah," Jack agrees. "Okay."

Heavy footsteps cross the room, and before I know what's happening, Dean is standing next to me. He takes hold of my arm, then my chin. His eyes search mine with an unspoken question. My brain malfunctions. I can't answer. I can't breathe.

A beat passes, and then his mouth is on mine. It's different than I expected—the kiss. Better, I guess. It's Dean, but somehow, I can overlook that. His mouth is warm on mine, both hands on my cheeks suddenly, thumbs guiding my jaw as it opens slightly. His tongue swipes over mine just once and then, seconds before my chest explodes, it's over.

He pulls back, eyes wide, jaw slack, and stares at me. The crowd hoots and hollers, but I barely hear it. I'm stunned into pure silence. A cocky grin grows on his lips, and he turns as movement to my right catches both of our attention.

Just like that, I'm slammed back to reality as Jack storms out of the room.

No. I chase after him, shame riddling my body as if I've done something wrong, though I know I haven't. Then again, I'm not sure why I enjoyed the kiss so much. It was *Dean*, so in theory, it should've been disgusting. It's probably just the fact that he's so well-practiced.

Now I wish I had mouthwash.

"Jack, wait!" I shout after him.

He stops, finally, in the hallway and turns back to me. His hands are gathered into fists, face beet red. "What, Carmen?"

"Don't be mad at me," I bite back, his tone infuriating me.

The anger evaporates from his face, lines disappearing from between his brows. "I'm not mad. I'm just..." He turns away. "He shouldn't have done that. I can't believe he did that."

"It was just a game," I tell him, reaching for his arm.

He flinches, pulling his arm from my grasp. "It wasn't a game. It was your first kiss, Carmen. You don't get it back. Don't you see that? For the rest of your life, your first kiss will be from..." He gestures toward the hall behind me, his face growing stoic then cold as he locks eyes on something—more likely, some*one*—there.

"Take it as a lesson, baby bro." Dean's voice fills the hall.

"Get out of here!" Jack shouts.

"No can do. I'm babysitting, remember?" Dean moves to stand next to me, and heat crawls up my neck. I glare at him. His gaze flicks to my lips again, clearly remembering what just happened between us.

"Dean, please. Give us a minute." Suddenly, I can't bear to look at him.

"Go!" Jack bellows.

"Take it as a lesson," Dean repeats, unmoving.

"What the hell are you talking about?" Jack shouts, his voice breaking. He looks on the verge of tears. Either that, or he's going to punch Dean soon. I've never heard him cuss before.

"If you don't go after what you want, someone else will."

"She wasn't yours to *go after*," Jack cries, waving at me as if I'm a doll on a shelf, some inanimate object rather than a living, breathing person with thoughts and opinions of her own.

"She isn't yours either," Dean says, stepping forward. He towers a full head over his brother. "Unless you do something about it. And soon. You should be thankful it was me who did it and not someone who actually wants her." With that, he casts a cutting glance my way before he disappears, leaving us in the silence of the hallway.

My chest is heavy with the awkward, strange weight of all that's happened—my first kiss taken by someone who clearly finds me repulsive; the boy I like apparently humiliated by the idea of kissing me and angry that anyone else would either. I feel discarded and pathetic.

Unwanted in every way.

Just an hour ago, this was supposed to be one of the best days of my life. A day I hoped I'd always remember. Now I wish so desperately I could forget everything about it.

I wish I could disappear.

A loud wave of laughter from the other room tells me that I might as well *have* disappeared as the party continues on, not bothering—even for a second—to notice I'm gone.

CHAPTER NINE

PRESENT DAY

I spend the early hours of the next day working on my illustrations, nearly perfecting the drawing I've been creating for the last week. It's not totally there, but it's good enough that I'll be okay moving on to the next one for a while and coming back to it once I've had a break.

With that taken care of, I check the pantry and make a mental note to do some grocery shopping soon. I brought a few essentials with me—mostly alcohol and chips—but not nearly enough. I grab a pack of dried mango and munch on it while I get dressed and ready for the day, then head out.

When I get outside, I see Jill walking down the steps of the guys' cabin next door.

"Morning!" I call, waving a hand over my head.

Her gaze searches the air until she finds me, and a smile cracks across her face. "Oh! I didn't see you there! Good morning. You look pretty today." She jogs down the steps faster, meeting me at the bottom and wrapping her arm around my shoulder. "Sleep well?"

"Yeah, awesome."

"Good. We just upgraded those mattresses last season. They're supposed to be top of the line."

"It was magical," I assure her. "What are you out and about doing?"

"Oh, I was just coming by to talk to Jack about one of our accounts. I haven't seen him around yet this morning, and he didn't answer my call. So I thought I'd stop by and see if I could find him, but he wasn't there. What about you? Where are you running off to?"

"I'm not sure yet. I was just going for a walk to get some fresh air."

"No shortage of that here." She inhales deeply as if to prove her point. She pulls her arm back, releasing me as we walk down the dirt road. We stop at the maintenance shed just outside the gate, and Jill opens the door. "Just one second," she calls from inside the dimly lit shed, grabbing two light bulbs from a box and tucking them under her arm. "I have to ask Jack if he ordered more of these. We're running low." She closes the door on her way out, turning her attention back to me. "Anyway, we're all so happy to have you home, kiddo. I know your mom is the reason you're here, but it's a treat for all of us. We've missed you around here."

"I've missed being here," I tell her honestly. "It's good to be home." I say the word more for her benefit than anything, but I quickly realize how badly I don't want it to be a lie anymore.

"And everyone's making you feel welcome?"

I look over at her, noticing a hint of stress in her voice.

"The boys, I mean?" she prompts. "I still don't know all the details about what happened between you and Jack back then, but...I'm hoping it's in the past. Even if the future doesn't look like what we all thought it might, I'm hoping you guys can be friends again."

"Jack and I are fine," I promise her. "Honestly. We were just silly kids back then. We've both moved on from it."

Her mouth opens slightly as if she wants to say something, but eventually she closes it and nods again. "Okay, good. And you'd tell me if that wasn't the case, right? Or if there was anything I could do to make you feel more welcome?"

"Of course I would."

She runs a hand over my arm. "Good girl. Because we want you home as much as we can get ya. Your mom looks like a new woman today. I heard her singing in the office this morning." Her eyes beam with delight. "Even Sam's in a better mood. And the boys, too, but they show it in their own ways."

I look around, not sure what to say as a family strolls past us. Both parents are carrying happy children on their shoulders, the four of them giggling and waving at us.

"This place is really something," I tell her. "You've done an amazing job with it. All of you, but especially you."

"Well, thanks. It's a team effort. I'm just trying to keep it as magical a place as Sam's parents had it before we took over. There was always something special about The Hollow. I hung out here as a kid, just like you guys did. It's where I met Sam. Did we tell you that?"

I shake my head.

"It's true. And all I want is to maintain it for the kids and grandkids, hopefully, someday. But also for the town. For the kids who need a place to go and the adults who've stuck with us. This town has been really good to us. Especially after..." She trails off, running a finger across her lip. "I thought we were going to lose every-thing back then, thought no one would want to stay somewhere where something like *that* happened. And yet, people just kept showing up for us." She waves at an older couple as they walk past us, hand in hand. "Good morning, Mr. Donovan. How'd that fire work for you last night?"

"Amazing." He beams at her. "Just what we needed. Thank ya, miss."

"I'm glad to hear it. You'll let us know if there's anything else we can do to make your stay better, won't you?"

"You've done more than enough," the woman next to him says, taking his arm.

Jill gives them a sort of salute with that charming

quality only she seems to have mastered and walks on past, with me just beside her.

Once we're far enough away that we can talk again without being overheard, Jill goes on to say, "You know, I thought after what happened with that girl...I thought we'd have to shut down."

"But it wasn't your fault," I say quickly, feeling protective of her. If Hunter's Hollow had to shut down over her death, there would be someone to blame, but it wouldn't be the Hunters. Of that, I'm sure.

"I know." She pats my arm. "I know. And I wish the police had been able to prove it, but still, people don't always like to vacation where someone has died. Especially not in a place like this. So, for everyone to come back here anyway..." She touches her chest. "It's always meant a lot. Made me want to make this place even more special."

"Have you..." I pause, trying to find the right words. "Have you thought about tearing down the cabin?"

She turns her head toward me quickly.

"I sort of stumbled upon it the other day. I guess I always assumed you'd tear it down after the investigation ended."

She looks down. "Your mom tells me I should, but...I haven't been able to bring myself to do it. I don't know why. I guess in some strange way, I worry that it makes us look guilty or...maybe just heartless. Like it would be trying to erase what happened. I wish I could explain it better than that. I know I should tear it down—we gave up on restoring it years ago—but the boys' great-great-grandparents lived there at one point, before they moved into the cabin that's the office now. That little one-room building was their entire world. Sam's great-grandfather built it from the ground up. Does one terrible event—and of course it *was* terrible, I don't mean to be disrespectful about what happened—but does that give me the right to tear down generations of history?"

Her face is sort of crumpled in on itself, and she's staring through me rather than at me. Like she's asking herself the question, not me. "I don't know the answer to that. I wish I did." Finally, her eyes find focus on me again. "Anyway, what a depressing conversation. Let's talk about something happier, hmm? How's your drawing going? Your mom tells me you're illustrating children's books now. The guests are just loving the map you made for us."

We walk the rest of the way back to the office discussing work and life and everything except the past, which is exactly how I prefer it.

When Jill and I make it back to the office, Mom pops up from behind the counter. "What'd he say?"

"He wasn't at home. I'll find him around here some-where and ask. I'll bet anything he managed to switch the cards again and used the wrong one." She scratches the space between her eyes. "Men, I swear."

Mom chuckles, but I catch a hint of sadness behind her eyes. "I want to hear about this date you went on, Mom."

She eyes me. "I told you it was nothing."

"Well, who was he?"

Jill beams at me, sidling up against Mom and waiting for her to spill.

"Robbie Dunlap," Mom says finally. "But it was nothing. Just a date."

"The sheriff?" I cringe. "Seriously? Daniel's terrible. That can't say much about his parenting."

Jill shrugs. "He's a sweet boy deep down." After a second thought, she adds, "Way, way deep down. But Robbie is nice."

"Where did he take you?" I try to get on board with this, even though I definitely do not want to be Daniel Dunlap's stepsister.

"I—"

The door opens to the office, announced by a small chime, and two men walk inside, followed by a couple with a young girl.

"Saved by the bell," Mom mutters. "Hey! How can we help you?"

While the men purchase sunscreen and the couple asks Jill about buying floaties and bug spray, it becomes obvious I'm in the way. With a silent wave to them, I see myself out.

I leave the office and, without really thinking about it, find myself heading toward the peninsula where the two family cabins are. Somehow, in this place that feels very much like it belongs to the world, just a few steps away, the peninsula feels like my own private oasis. With everyone at work, I hope I'll have it to myself.

I pass the cabins and make my way down toward the water. The lake water's muddy scent fills my nose as I get closer, the sound of the water lapping at the shore growing louder. I can't count the number of days I spent right here growing up, can't explain the way the water always seemed to be what I needed even when I didn't know myself. This place healed me in some ways, wounded me in others.

I inhale deeply.

In some strange way, I feel my dad here. Though I know it's impossible, this is the place I feel like I can talk to him the easiest. Maybe because it's so quiet. Maybe because it's the only place I could ever be alone with my thoughts, though not usually for long.

In a bustling world filled with new people and adventures every day, this was the one place I was always guaranteed a bit of solace.

I kick out of my shoes and feel the grass and mud of the shore squishing between my toes. I close my eyes and inhale deeply, feeling a scream building in my chest.

"*Watch out for that snake!*"

"*What?*" I startle, eyes snapping open, and scream. I jump in the air, searching for the snake. "Where?"

When I don't see anything, my eyes fall on the person who warned me. Jack looks positively pleased with himself, a wide grin stretching into his red cheeks. He's squinting in the bright sun, one eye shut completely. He chuckles, placing a hand on his chest.

I squeal, slapping a hand in the air. "Jack Hunter, you're the worst."

"That always works on you. You'd think you'd learn eventually."

"No, because the one time I don't freak out, that'll be the one time there *is* actually a snake. It'll be like the boy who cried wolf." I stomp across the ground toward him, and he stands there waiting, a cocky grin on his face that I want to slap right off. "What are you doing out here, anyway?" I demand when I reach him.

"Dad asked me to run and get a key to the maintenance shed padlock from the house, but I saw you out here looking entirely too safe. Thought you could use a scare."

I scowl. "You're the actual worst."

"You've said." He scratches his eyebrow.

"Your mom was looking for you, by the way. Did you see her?"

"I've been cleaning boats all morning. What'd she need?"

"Something about an account. I don't know."

He shakes his head. "She's probably locked out again. The bank upgraded their system, and she can't seem to figure out the new login. I'll go check on her once I get Dad the key." Even saying this, he doesn't seem in a hurry to go anywhere.

"Where'd you go last night, by the way?"

His eyebrow quirks up as he shoves his hand into his pocket.

"Dean mentioned you weren't home."

"Dean." He puffs out his name, looking away with a certain attitude that annoys me.

"Yeah. He walked me home when you disappeared."

He nods slowly. "I didn't disappear. I ran into town for a drink with some friends."

"What friends?" I don't know why I ask. I have no right to know anything about him anymore, but I want to. I want to know who he's become since I left.

"Colton Ray. He was in our class, and we've stayed in touch. Do you remember him?"

That's only one friend, not plural, but I don't bother pointing it out. "Yeah, of course."

"He's going through a divorce," he says simply.

"Oh." Well, now I feel like crap. "That's awful."

He shrugs one shoulder without responding.

"Well, anyway, we missed you. It would've been nice to hang out last night."

"Maybe," he says. "Or it might've been a bad idea."

I swallow. "What do you mean? There are some things we need to talk about, and I was hoping we could do that soon."

"I don't know if I'm ready for that, Carmen. I don't know if I trust myself around you." As if to prove it, he takes a step back. "I should really leave you alone."

It's hard not to feel insulted by his words. "What are

you talking about? You're the one who came over here, remember?"

He nods. "Yeah, I remember. I said I *should* leave you alone. Doesn't mean I want to."

"Why can't we hang out? We're friends, aren't we?"

He scoffs and looks away. "Friends. Yeah. Sure. We're friends. What do you need to talk to me about?"

"I don't want to do it like this. Not fighting."

"We're not fighting." His voice is pointed and empty.

"What is your problem, Jack?"

He takes a sudden step forward, stopping just inches from me. I can feel the heat of his body from where I'm standing. When he inhales deeply, his chest practically touches mine. He takes his time, his eyes scanning every inch of my face, like I'm a test he desperately needs to pass. "I've never wanted to be your friend. Not then and not now." He raises his hand, touching my chin and lifting it toward his. "You know that."

My heart skips a beat when his eyes land on my lips, and I finally understand what's going to happen. I'm thirty years old. I have no business getting butterflies like some silly teenager, but there they are.

My eyes flutter when he leans in, and I prepare for the feeling of his lips on mine. I should stop this. I should talk to him, ask him the things I need to know. Finally get answers.

This is a terrible idea.

"Jack!" We jump apart at the sight of Dean standing just a few feet away. I swallow down whatever feelings are currently soaring through me as Dean looks between us. "Don't you answer your damn phone?" he shouts.

Jack pulls his phone from his pocket, staring at the screen. "It died. I forgot to charge it last night. What's wrong?"

"A kid's missing," Dean says. "A girl. All hands on deck."

"A what?" I ask, sure I heard him wrong. The seriousness on Dean's face says it all. I haven't heard wrong at all. It's happening again.

Just like that, the world implodes once more.

CHAPTER TEN

BEFORE — AGE 14

The campground always slows down during the wintertime. Though we have a few families staying with us, compared to how it usually is, this place is a ghost town. Which is why this evening Jack and I snuck onto the playground for cabins fifteen and sixteen. It's private, hidden behind a gate, and meant only for these two cabins which are usually booked, so I've only seen it a few times. It feels like a whole secret world just waiting for us to explore.

Tonight, the cabins sit empty, all the lights off, which means the only light I can see is coming from the moon and the matching lamps on the outside of either side of the gate.

"Are you ready for Christmas?" he asks from behind me, pushing me forward on the swing.

"Yeah, I guess so." In truth, I'm trying not to think about the fact that this will be the first Christmas morning of my life where I won't wake up in the house I've always been in.

"It's probably weird, hmm? Being here this year."

I nod, not surprised in the least he's read my mind yet again. "Weird, yeah. Not bad, necessarily."

"When we were little, Mom and Dad would always go all out for Christmas."

I look over my shoulder at him. "Yeah?"

"Yeah, like Mom would make what she called 'reindeer food' which was just, like, carrots and oats, I think, and have us sprinkle it in the yard. And Dad would always spend Christmas Eve keeping track of Santa's whereabouts on some website to let us know how close he was."

I chuckle, suddenly overcome with Christmas memories of my own. "We always had a Christmas cookie decorating contest. Dad was the judge, and he'd always say he had to do a taste test to determine the winner, but then he'd say he forgot what they looked like after he ate them, so we all won and should help him finish them off." It's the smallest memories that make me miss him, even now. The tiny flickers of who we used to be. Of how bright and full the world once was.

Because it isn't now.

It's not full, not bright. Even when things are happy, something is always missing, and there's no doubt it's him.

That's the burden we, the living, are forced to bear. The cost of loving someone so much their loss leaves a them-shaped hole inside our lives. That every moment should have the slight aftertaste of them, the quiet whisper of 'he should be here, and he isn't, and that will never not hurt.'

"Your dad was funny," Jack says, his hands catching the chains of my swing as I come back. "That's what I remember about him. He was funny, and he was kind. And..." He leans over my shoulder and tucks a piece of hair behind my ear. "And he reminded me of you."

Tears sting my eyes, and I look away. I know I look like my mother more than my father. We both have dark hair and dark eyes. I have her bone structure and small smile, but it's my greatest hope that people who knew my father see him in me. Like usual, Jack seems to know exactly what I needed to hear.

Still, I'm grateful when he changes the subject.

"Did you watch *Enough* yet?"

"Yeah. I've got the DVD to give back to you. J.Lo was amazing as always, but it was so hard to watch."

"I told you. It's fantastic, though. Those are the kinds of movies I want to make. The ones that make you look at things differently."

"You'll be great at it." I really mean it. The way Jack sees the world is so different from anyone I've ever met.

He pulls me back on the swing before pushing me forward again.

"Have you thought about what you're going to do for your birthday next month?" I ask.

"Uh, no. Not really. Why?"

Something flips in my stomach as I edge toward the conversation I'm dying to have. "I just wondered. Hopefully we won't be playing spin the bottle again." A nervous laugh bubbles out of me.

"Yeah, I guess so. Seems kind of childish."

"I mean, at this point, you'll know when you're ready to have your first kiss. And, like you said, it's weird to have it in a game."

The silence is deafening as I wait for him to answer.

When I turn back to him, I notice the flurry of snow that has begun to fall. It's like something from a movie, the white sprinkles falling to the ground. Snow is rare in North Carolina—just as rare in Atlanta—but it's not my first time seeing it. I hold out a hand, letting snowflakes land in my palm.

It won't stick. The ground is too warm. The snow melts as soon as it hits the grass, but with each falling flake, I find myself holding out hope it'll last just a bit longer.

"I can't believe it's snowing already, and it's not even winter officially." Jack walks around from behind me and sits in the swing to my right.

"I love snow," I muse. "Maybe this will mean we'll get a snowy winter."

"It's always quiet around here when it snows."

"Speaking of snow and winter"—I fold my hand, crushing the melting snowflakes in my palm and sucking in a deep, determined breath—"are you planning to go to the winter formal at school?"

His face goes serious, and he looks down at his feet. "I'm not sure yet. Maybe. It's kind of silly, isn't it?"

"I don't know. It could be fun, I guess." I swallow. *Come on, Carmen. You can do this.*

"Megan asked me."

My chest deflates. "What?"

"Megan Griffin. You know, from algebra?"

"Yeah. She asked you?" I force a smile that feels so fake it makes me sick.

"Yeah." He rubs his lips together. "We've been hanging out at school. In class, mostly. But after some, too."

"I've never seen you together." I try to think back.

"We've sort of been...kissing, too."

An ice shard stabs through my stomach. "Oh."

"And she asked me to go to the dance today."

"Oh." It's the only word I can muster.

"It's really not a big deal. We aren't dating or anything. Just...hanging out, like I said."

"Do you like her?" Obviously he must if he's kissing her.

"She's cool."

My chest aches, and my voice is so strained it doesn't sound like mine. "Okay. Well, good. What did you tell her?"

"I told her...probably."

"Well...do you want to go with her?"

No. The only answer to this question is no. He has to say—

"Maybe. Yeah."

My entire body feels as if it's been crushed by a truck.

"I mean, she's fun," he adds. "Has...has anyone asked you yet? Do you know who you'll go with?"

I don't realize I'm going to lie until the words slip out. "Yeah, I think so. I mean, it's not set in stone. You should go with her. With Megan. That'll be fun. You're right. She's cool. Super cool." I'm making this all so much worse, but I can't stop the indignant word vomit that is currently spewing out of my mouth.

"Yeah?" His brows rise.

"Yeah, sure. And you've been kissing her. Which is... you know. Great. She's great, right? So great."

"Yeah, I guess so." He's using the toe of his shoe to draw in the dirt under his feet as he says it.

I shiver, rubbing my hands over the sleeves of my coat. "I think I'm going to go home, Jack. It's getting cold."

"I'll walk you." He stands, zipping his jacket.

"No, it's okay." I try to think quickly, just needing him to go away. "I'm going to call my *abuela* on the way. I haven't talked to her since we got settled in." I pull out my cell phone, my voice tight, chest aching. "I'll catch up with you later."

"Are you sure?"

"Mm-hmm. You should go. I'll be fine. S-see you in the morning." My voice cracks, and I turn away from him, just hoping he'll leave. Hoping he'll get the hint and walk away, leave me alone.

Which is why, when I hear his footsteps retreating, I'm surprised to feel disappointment, not relief, filling my gut. I guess a part of me was hoping he'd stay. That he'd see through my lies and realize how badly he's hurt me.

Jack and I never promised each other our first kisses, and he didn't even get mine, so I have no right to be angry or hurt, but I am. I feel like something precious has been stolen from me, something I can't get back. The entire trajectory of my life feels thrown off its axis, like the picture I had for my future has now shifted into something unrecognizable. Something where Jack likes Megan, not me.

Is this how Jack felt when Dean kissed me? Worse, is that why he's kissing Megan? To get even with me?

I listen as the gate opens and shuts, and then, with a final look over my shoulder to be sure I'm alone, I shove my phone into my pocket and cover my eyes, sobbing silently into my hands.

Why did I think this would go any other way?

He made it clear at my birthday party he didn't want to kiss me. I don't know why I keep expecting something different from him.

And who the heck does Megan think she is? Why should she get to go to the dance with him? What gave her the right to kiss him? I had no idea she even liked him. Then again, who wouldn't like him? He's so perfect and sweet and cute and funny and...

I sniffle, drying my eyes. I have no idea what I'm

going to do. I could ask Colton to go to the dance with me, I guess. He seems nice enough. But I don't *want* to go to the dance with him. I only want to go with Jack.

I could try to convince him to go with me. Tell him he should say no to Megan. There's still time. He hasn't given her an answer.

But that feels...pathetic.

When I asked if he wanted to go with her, he should've said no. He didn't, and that's that.

As much as I hate it, I have no choice but to move on.

A crack somewhere in the distance draws my attention to the treeline like a magnet. Someone is there...just ahead. Someone is walking out of the woods.

I dry my cheeks, sniffling as I back up toward the gate.

No one is supposed to be out here. It's private. No one is staying in the cabins, and no one knows the code to get inside the gate except those of us who live here.

It can't be Mom or Jill—the figure is too large. Jack just left. Which only leaves Sam or...

Just as the thought crosses my mind, I hear his voice. "Carmie?"

"What do you want, Dean?"

"What are you doing out here?" he demands, moving toward me faster. "You shouldn't be here by yourself. It's not safe."

"I was with Jack." I dry my eyes with my hands again, shivering.

"Where's Jack now?" He has nearly reached me when he asks, "Are you crying?"

"No," I lie, albeit unconvincingly.

He groans, like this is the last thing he wants to be dealing with right now. "What happened?"

"Nothing happened. I'm fine." I turn away from him, heading toward the gate, but he pulls me back to face him.

"I said what happened, Carmen?"

Something about the way he says my real name sends chills throughout me. Like when my parents use my first and middle name—*Carmen Elizabeth*—to scold me. But this is different. Warmer, somehow, even as his tone is cold as ice.

"It doesn't matter." My voice breaks again as I try to pull away from him. He jerks me forward into his chest as if someone is forcing him to do it and holds me there. A hand goes to the back of my head, soothing me in a very Dean way. He's rigid, like a statue, but his touch is gentle. Kind.

Slowly, his other arm goes around me, and he's holding me. Both hands rub my skin—one on my neck, the other on my back—and I feel myself break all at once. My body goes slack in his arms, and he holds me without trying, without exerting any energy at all, it seems. He just holds me without saying a word, without asking any questions.

We stand still in the dark silence for several minutes, me soaking his shirt with my tears, him stroking my hair with his thumb. When I finally pull away, I rub my eyes again, asking through my tears, "Why are you being nice to me? Did you hit your head?"

"Haven't you ever heard not to look a gift horse in the mouth?" he snarls. "Why are you crying?"

I run my arm under my nose. "It's nothing."

"It's clearly *not* nothing. Tell me, or I'm going to assume the worst."

"What's the worst?" I glare at him with a hint of suspicion. He equally drives me mad and makes me want to hear everything he has to say. The more I get to know him, the more interesting Dean seems to be. Maybe he could help me somehow, but it's unlikely. The only thing he's interested in is making me look silly or childish.

"Your mom's finally sending you to that military school," he says with a shrug.

I smack my palm against his shirt, then throw my attention toward the treeline where he came from. "Where were you, anyway? Why were you in the woods?"

"You answer my question, and I'll answer yours."

I pinch my lips together, swirling the possibility through my mind. What's the worst that could happen? He makes fun of me? He tells Jack I was upset? Dean's a jerk, but he's no snitch. I can't believe he'd rat me out.

"It's just this stupid school dance. The winter formal."

The worry and confusion evaporates from Dean's face like alcohol in a chemistry class beaker. "Ahh. You have a terrible fear of dances, then? A phobia of sorts?" The corner of his lip upturns.

"Could you be serious for one second?"

"Sure, but just one." He holds up a finger. "Why are you crying over the dance?"

I put my face in my hands. "It's stupid."

His hands come to rest on my arms, and when he speaks, his voice is as soft and slow as a caress. "*Why* are you crying over the dance?"

"I thought Jack might want to go with me." I'm unable to meet his eyes as I spit out the words.

He's quiet for a pause. "And he didn't?"

I look up at him finally, afraid I'll find judgment or teasing, but instead I only find a boy who's trying desperately to understand. "He's going with someone else. Someone he's apparently been kissing."

"Megan," Dean says the name firmly. He's not asking. Apparently everyone knows this has been going on except me. His jaw drops, and he looks up over my head, staring at nothing as his eyes dart back and forth in thought. When he lowers his gaze back to me, his hands fall away from my arms, and I instantly miss their warmth. "So, you should go with someone else, too."

"But who?" I groan. "I could ask Colton, I guess, but I don't really know him that well and—"

"Me." His voice—that word leaving his lips, what he's proposing—sends a jolt of shock through me. He can't be serious. I'm sure I heard him wrong.

"What? I can't do that." I spit out the words like they're hot coffee.

"Why not?"

"Because you're"—I wave my hand in his direction—"*you.*"

His brows bounce up. "I'll try not to take offense to that."

"I'm sorry, I just mean...you can't exactly be excited about taking me to a dance. Were you even planning on going?"

"Plans change," he says with a shrug.

"And you actually *want* to do this?"

"I never said that. I said I will."

"I don't want to be your charity case."

His hands come around my arms again. "Let me be clear about this. I don't do anything selflessly, and you should know that by now. I want to go with you, Carmen. I want..." He pauses, inhales, then continues. "I want you to let me take you to the dance. Please." His forehead wrinkles with a distinct pout that sends a wave of power coursing through me.

"Seriously?"

"Don't make me beg." His laughter makes me forget I was crying only moments ago. "You'll be safe with me. We'll have fun. It'll be great."

"And you won't tease me all night?"

"Not once. I swear."

I sigh, pretending to think on it, though we both know I'm not. Dean is a better prospect than any guy in my grade. "I owe you one, Dean." I throw my arms around him quickly, pulling him into a hug. He seems shocked by my actions, standing stiff as a rod for several seconds, but just when I'm about to release him and let the awkwardness set in, his arms encircle my waist and the side of his face comes to rest on the top of my head.

Something warm and weird passes through my stomach, and I drop my arms away, stepping back. "Now, a deal's a deal, so fess up. Why were you in the woods?"

"I was..." He swipes a hand over his nose, looking away. "I was down at Devil's Cabin."

"Devil's Cabin?" The name washes away any warmth I previously felt. The snow is picking up, and several snowflakes are caught in Dean's hair and eyelashes. "Were you with someone?"

"Yeah." His Adam's apple bobs. "Don't worry about her."

"Do I know her?" A flare of jealousy scorches through me, though I have no idea why.

He quirks his lips. "I gave you one question, Carmie, and you've already asked and gotten an answer for two." A shiver runs through him and, apparently contagious, passes to me. "Now, come on. Let's get you home before those pretty, little legs turn to popsicles."

CHAPTER ELEVEN

PRESENT DAY

Jack and I follow Dean toward the golf cart waiting in the driveway.

"What happened?" I ask, still trying to catch my breath.

"I don't know. It's some teenager." Dean turns the cart around, pointing us toward the driveway and off the peninsula. "Her mom said she didn't come home last night. She was hanging out down by the water when her mom went back to cabin eight, where they're staying. She told the girl to be home by midnight, but when she woke up this morning, she was gone."

"And she's just now reporting her missing?" Jack asks skeptically. "It's noon."

"I guess she stopped by the office this morning to ask if Mom had seen her, but at that time, she just thought she was off with some friends she'd made here or something. But since then, she's tracked down all the girls she's seen her with, and she can't find her. They just called Robbie to come down and help us search."

My chest is tight, and I can't seem to catch my breath. This feels eerily similar to what happened back then, and though I want to believe it's a coincidence, something inside of me says it might not be. Like a branch growing inside me, twisting and curling, thorns scraping and reminding me they're still here, I feel the terror growing. It never went away, not really. It was just lying dormant for a while.

"How old is the girl?" I ask.

"Eighteen." Dean's eyes meet mine. "Which is another reason this is complicated."

"Shelby was eighteen, too..." I say, understanding the implication. Another connection, aside from the place and the circumstances. "Could it be related? Could the same person be back?"

"What?" He scowls at me, then shakes his head, and I realize I'm going down the wrong rabbit hole. "No. No. It's just...she's eighteen, so she's legally an adult. The police can try to find her for a welfare check, but there's not a lot that can be done in terms of searching for her unless they believe there's foul play involved. Otherwise, she's free to come and go as she pleases."

"So they don't think there's foul play involved?" Jack asks.

"I guess we'll find out. Her mom doesn't seem to, but she's worried, obviously." He speeds up as we reach the center of the campground, near the public playground and swimming area. There, a group of people have gathered. Jill, Sam, and Mom are here. Mom is standing close to the sheriff, and they both keep looking at each other as if to check in. This is probably the first time they've seen each other since their date. There's a woman with swollen, frantic eyes and dark hair that looks unbrushed. She looks our way when she sees us coming, scans each of our faces, and decides all at once that we aren't whoever she's looking for. I see the moment she realizes it—the disappointment that washes over her expression—and know this must be the woman looking for her daughter. Aside from her, there's the older couple I saw earlier with Jill, a younger couple with two small girls, Sheriff Robbie Dunlap, and a face I haven't seen in years: Daniel Dunlap, his son.

Dean shuts off the golf cart and we all jog across the grass toward the group.

"Anything?" Jill asks.

"Did you find her?" the woman asks at the same time.

Dean shakes his head and, when the woman looks at me, so do I.

"Mrs. Moore—"

"Ms.," the woman corrects Sheriff Dunlap firmly, and I get the feeling she's already told him that once or twice.

"Right. *Ms.* Did April tell you that she might go anywhere else? Did she mention any friends she might see while she was here?"

"No." The woman shakes her head, her hands clasped in front of her. "I know my daughter. She wouldn't have just run off. April is a good girl. She's...she wouldn't have left without telling me where she was going and when she'd be back. And she doesn't know anyone here anyway, just...well, she met some kids around her age since we arrived. Taylor in cabin two and...um, Selena and Tom in cabin four. But they're all still here, and none of them have seen her since last night. I checked this morning."

Sheriff Dunlap passes a look toward his son. "We'll need to talk to each of them. And their parents."

Daniel nods and jots down a note in the notepad in his hands.

"We already checked with them, too," Sam says. "The kids were all together by the water last night, but they said the girl, er, *April,* left around eleven and none of them have seen her since."

Anywhere else, what he said wouldn't matter, but here, Sam's and Jill's words carry weight. Not just because they're friends of Sheriff Dunlap's, but because they mean something to this town. Hunter's Hollow is one of the things that keeps this place going. They bring in tourists, they've raised two amazing men, and people in town can count on them.

So the sheriff nods at Sam, clearly takes his words to mean something. "Thanks, Sam. We'll need to look at records for everyone staying here if you don't mind, just so we can talk to them all. Make sure no one saw anything strange."

"Of course. Whatever we can do to help in any way."

"I'll run and print a copy of the records now," Mom says, backing away to leave for the office.

"Thanks, Elena." He touches her arm before she goes, and she smiles at him before he turns back to the woman—Ms. Moore. "Have you tried contacting any of April's friends back home? Classmates? A boyfriend? Girlfriend?"

"She...she's not dating anyone. She and her boyfriend just broke up because they're going to separate colleges." She pinches the bridge of her nose. "I could call some of her friends."

"Do that." He nods. "And contact the ex-boyfriend, too. Anyone you can think of who may have heard from her recently. Anything you can find out will be extremely helpful. You said she has her cell phone with her, but it's turned off. What about her purse?"

"It's still here. Her wallet, too. It doesn't look like anything is missing."

"Okay, I'll want to see that. And she didn't have a car, right?"

"Not here, no. We rode here together in mine."

"And yours is still here? We'll need to take a look at it, too, if so."

She nods and hands over her keys. "It's the red Hyundai parked outside our cabin."

"Right. Okay. Well, Daniel will get to interviewing

the guests as soon as Elena returns with the paperwork, and I'm going to check out the car and the woods." He juts a thumb over his shoulder. "We'll get to the bottom of this, Ms. Moore. You all just sit tight."

"Is there anything we can do?" the older woman from this morning asks, holding her husband's arm tightly and offering a soft, apologetic smile to Ms. Moore.

"What was your name?" Sheriff Dunlap asks.

"Dora," she answers. "Theodora, but Dora, Donovan. And this is my husband, Wes. We're staying in cabin three. We're happy to help with the search."

"For now, I don't think it'll be necessary, but I appreciate the offer. Did you see the girl at all?"

"We saw her..." She looks at her husband. "Well, we saw her two days ago, right? When you all arrived." Her eyes find Ms. Moore again. "We saw you checking in and then saw her swimming yesterday on our evening walk, but nothing out of the ordinary. She was with another girl."

"Do you know which one?"

"She had...blonde hair, I believe."

"Taylor," Ms. Moore says quickly. "Selena is a brunette, so it has to be Taylor."

"Well, thank you, Dora. We will keep everyone posted and may take you up on the offer to help with the search moving forward, but for now I just want to get a quick lay of the land. See what we can figure out."

With that, the two men break up and spread out.

Daniel waits for my mom to return with the guest list and contact info, while the sheriff begins his search.

Slowly, the rest of the guests disperse, including Ms. Moore, who walks away, already on her phone placing a call.

When a car pulls down the road slowly, dust flying behind it, I hold my breath. *Could it be the girl? April? Could she have come home?*

When the car stops, a woman, not a girl, steps out of the driver's seat. She's our age, with blonde hair and a face I'd recognize anywhere. My stomach clenches when I see her.

Jack steps forward, and she makes her way to him, arms outstretched.

"You weren't answering your phone."

"It's dead. What are you doing here?" His entire body is tense, shoulders drawn up by his ears.

"Can we talk?" she asks, wrapping her arms around him. He doesn't fight her off, but he doesn't lean into her either. "Please?"

What the hell is Alissa Burton doing here? And why is she with Jack?

I don't have to wait long for an answer, because when she pulls back from her hug, her lips curve into a smile and she says, "I missed you." Then, before he can answer, before anyone can say anything, my entire body turns to ice as she presses her lips to his.

CHAPTER TWELVE

BEFORE — AGE 14

The night of the dance, I meet the boys in the driveway. I'm wearing a plum-colored, floor-length gown with layered mesh material, a band of silk around my waist, and straps that cross in the back. It took us ages to pick it out. Mom put a few extra stitches in to move the neckline up higher, and we found the perfect golden, sequined, strappy heels.

Despite the chill in the air and the nerves in my belly, the fact that my hair has already begun to frizz and fall out of my updo in certain places, and that I couldn't get the wings of my eyeliner to match perfectly, I'm buzzing with pride and confidence.

Mom walks me out of the cabin to where the boys are waiting outside. They're dressed almost identically, both in black suits with their hair neatly combed. Though upon closer inspection, Dean's is a bit messier, with a piece of dark hair falling in his face.

They're talking to their mom and hardly notice me as I descend the stairs, so not exactly the fairy-tale moment I pictured, but when I get nearly to the bottom, Dean's eyes lock on mine, and he turns to face me, his expression suddenly serious.

I smile at him and look at Jack, who's glaring at me with a stony expression.

"Not bad, Carmie." Dean steps forward, pulling my attention back to him.

"Gee, thanks." I roll my eyes. "You guys look great, too. Both of you."

Jack studies me, his eyes cold.

"Um, you okay?" I ask.

"You're going with him?" he asks, gesturing toward his brother as if it's the ultimate betrayal.

"Yeah, so?"

"You didn't tell me."

"You didn't ask. I told you I was going with someone."

"Not my brother!" he says, his voice exasperated.

"*Jack*," Jill warns.

"He's my friend!" I shout right back.

"You hate Dean!" he cries.

"That's not true." I give Dean a guilty look. It's mostly true, to be fair. But lately, it feels *less* true.

"Okay, guys," Mom says, stepping between us. "There's no sense arguing over this. Jack, Carmen is a big girl, and she gets to decide who she goes to dances with."

She crosses over toward Dean, adjusting his tie. "And Dean is a nice boy. He's going to treat her well." Her eyes lock with Dean's, her words both an instruction and a warning.

"Yes, ma'am," Dean says, unblinking.

She steps back, pats his chest with a nod, and turns to me with a smile. "Alright, *mija*. You kids should get going."

"Come on." Dean pulls the keys from his pocket.

"I'm not riding with you," Jack says firmly. "I'll get Mom to take me."

"Of course I'll take you, honey," Jill says, looking between the three of us with a pained expression. "If you're sure that's what you want."

"Suit yourself." Dean shrugs one shoulder and looks down at me. "You ready?"

Not at all, but I nod anyway with a final, apologetic look back at Jack.

In the car, Dean adjusts the heat so the vents are pointing at me. I nudge them down just a bit so they aren't blowing my hair all over the place and making my eyes water.

"You good?" He looks over at me just before we pull away from the cabins. I watch as Jack slides into the car with his mom without looking our way. He's angry at me, I guess, and I understand why. But what was I supposed to do? Go with one of his friends instead? Would that have been better?

"I don't understand what his problem is." I fold my

arms across my chest, then unfold them just as quickly as I realize the dress is uncomfortable to do that in.

"Jack's?" The question seems like it's asked more to buy time than anything.

I nod.

He blows a puff of air from his lips. "I'm not sure he knows what his problem is either."

"If he was so worried about who I planned to go with, he could've asked me, but he didn't."

"Mm-hmm," he agrees, adjusting the radio.

"What was I supposed to do? Go alone? Not go at all? At least it's just you and not someone else, right?"

He cuts a glance at me out of the corner of his eye. "I'll try not to take offense to that."

I groan. "It's like you said at my birthday party. The night that you..." I trail off, unable to say the word. We haven't talked about that night a single time since it happened.

"Kissed you," he finishes for me.

"Right. You said it was better that it was you than someone who actually wanted me. It's the same thing tonight, isn't it?"

He swallows, but he doesn't answer right away. "Look, Jack has no idea what he wants or doesn't want. He never has. He just knows that he doesn't want anyone else to have what he might sort of, kind of want someday."

I wait for him to go on, but when he doesn't, I prod, "What are you saying?"

"I'm saying—look, I love him. He's my brother, but he's not exactly the boldest guy on the planet, you know? If you want him, you're going to have to make the first move. Just like Megan had to ask him to the dance. Jack's just never going to put himself out there like that."

"I never said I wanted him."

A small smile overtakes his lips. "You never said you didn't either."

"Jack's my friend. He's been nice to me since I moved to Hunter's Hollow. He was nice to me before, too. Every once in a while, I get the feeling he wants to be more than friends, and...I don't think that would be the worst thing. But I don't want to ruin our friendship by pushing for more than he's into. Maybe he doesn't like me at all, maybe I would just make it weird."

"Maybe." His response is soft. Clipped.

"Really? That's all you're going to give me?" I turn my head to look at him.

He chuckles. "What? Isn't that all you need? That's life. But"—his face goes serious, his fingers practically choking the steering wheel—"if you're into someone, if you really want to be with them, doesn't that kind of make it worth the risk?"

I cannot believe those words just left his mouth. I stare at him in utter shock—the only sign of life is the fact that my chest is still rising and falling with slow breaths.

"What?" he asks when I haven't responded in a while.

"Nothing." I shake my head, brows drawn down as I stare at him. "It's just...is *Dean Hunter* a secret romantic?"

His eyes roll back so far in his head they practically disappear. "Oh my god. Really? That's what you're going to do? I give you this excellent advice—which *was* excellent, if I do say so myself—and instead of thanking me, you tease me?" His eyes are whimsical and playful. It's always easy with Dean. The lines are clear. With everything else in my life feeling so fuzzy, I can't help appreciating that.

"That's what we do, isn't it? Tease each other?"

His lips press together as he puffs a breath from his nose. "Yeah, that's what we do."

"And...thank you," I add, after a few silent minutes pass. So long, in fact, that I think he's forgotten what I'm thanking him for. "For the *excellent* advice. And for taking me tonight."

"Better me than anyone else," he says.

"Agreed." Something strange and unwelcome flips in my stomach, and I shove it down, leaning forward to turn up the radio.

It's twenty more minutes to the school, and when we arrive, the lot is overflowing with cars, trucks, and even a few limos. This isn't even prom, and already people have gone all out. Girls are dressed in gowns much fancier than mine, their hair perfectly styled. Groups pose together for pictures.

Dean finds a spot to park in the grass, and we step

out of the car. The air feels colder than it was when we left The Hollow. I wrap my arms around myself as we make our way across the parking lot, trying and failing to hide my shivers. I look around, trying not to make it too obvious that I'm looking for Jack.

When my head is turned away from him, I feel something come down over my shoulders and realize instantly it's his suit jacket.

"Oh." I look up and meet his eyes, dark and warm and always just...there. "Thank you." I pull the jacket farther around myself. "You didn't have to do that."

"You were cold."

"In hindsight, maybe I should've taken my mom up on the wrap she offered me." At the time, I'd claimed the faux fur cloth was outdated and pointless since the dance was happening inside, but now, I have to admit she was right about me needing it. Then again—I snuggle into Dean's oversized jacket—this isn't so bad.

I slip my arms into the sleeves, folding them across my chest.

He adjusts his tie. "Yeah, well you just make sure you mention this moment when she asks if I was a perfect gentleman tonight. I'm still racking up points with her."

Chuckling, I nod. "Can do."

Inside, I hand Dean his jacket, and he slips it back on. I miss the warmth of it almost instantly. Six of our teachers are seated at a little table in the lobby, and it's Mrs. Kirkland who calls me over with a wave of her fingers.

"Carmen, Dean, this way, please!" We approach the table, and she crosses our names off the list in front of her. "Any bags I need to check?"

We shake our heads, and I hold out my arms to show I'm not hiding anything. I even left my phone at home tonight, something I never do, but there was just nowhere to put it in this dress, and I didn't want to have to carry around a bag all evening.

"Pockets?" She pins Dean with a suspicious glance.

He turns out his pockets. "Just a wallet and phone." Laying them on the table, he flashes an innocent grin at her.

She nods and waves them back to him, and he shoves them into his pockets. "Okay, you kids have fun. Don't get into any trouble." She eyes Dean especially hard, who seems completely unfazed as he throws his arm around me.

"It's like you don't know me at all, Mrs. K." He winks. He actually winks at her—*a teacher!*

My cheeks flame with secondhand embarrassment, but she just purses her lips and shakes her head, turning her attention to the next couple in line.

The school gymnasium is lined with snowflakes and clear balloons on strings with twinkling lights. There's a white carpet—meant to look like snow, I guess—leading a trail toward a snowy, flocked garland arch toward the back of the room, where couples and groups of friends are lined up to have their picture taken by the school secretary, Mrs. Walsh.

Dean clears his throat, placing a hand on my back so delicately it's barely there. "Do you...want a drink?"

Hardly anyone is dancing yet. Most people are mingling around the edge of the dance floor, at the punch and snack tables, or sitting at the round tables that line the room along the edges.

"Sure."

He leads me toward the snack table where Tye, Daniel, and another boy named Treylan are standing.

"'Sup, Hunter?" Tye stands, nodding at me quickly. "Dude, seriously? You brought the infant?"

I scowl at him, then turn my attention to the plastic cup Dean hands me, taking a cautious sip. "Thanks."

"'*Sup, Sharpe? You brought the idiot?*" Dean teases, mocking his voice as he eyes Daniel. I snort with laughter.

"Real funny." Daniel flips us both off without missing a beat, and the guys all chuckle.

I'm not really listening as they begin to talk about something that happened during a football game. Instead, almost involuntarily, my eyes search the crowd for the one face I have yet to see.

When I finally find him, it's the moment he's walking in the door. Almost as if we're connected, I seem to sense him. My head spins toward the door just in time to catch Megan looping her arm through his. She tucks her head against his shoulder, staring up at him with a smile that curdles the contents of my stomach.

"Carmen, hey!" Shelby launches into me from

behind, wrapping her arms around my shoulders. I spin around, taking in the sight of her golden ball gown. She looks like a real-life princess, just missing her tiara. Her red curls are pinned up, lips painted crimson.

"Shelby! Look at you! Wow!"

She does a twirl, confidence radiating from her pink cheeks. "I know, don't I look hot?" She lets out a barking laugh. "And what about you? Look at this dress." She plays with a piece of the fabric, fanning herself. "Whoo, sexy lady!"

"Ha. Thanks."

Her gaze moves past me, eyeing Dean and no doubt noticing the plum-colored pocket square that matches my dress and sticks out of his suit jacket, then comes back to me. "Who'd you come with?"

It's like she suspects, but doesn't want to ask. Doesn't want to believe it. Shelby came alone. We had this conversation this morning in physics. I just happened to leave out the fact that I was coming with Dean.

Fighting against a guilty grin, I cast a look back at my date, still mostly lost in conversation with his friends, though when I look back, his eyes find mine and one corner of his mouth upturns.

"Um, Dean, actually." When I turn back to face Shelby, the shock of the answer is evident on her face.

Her eyes go wide, mouth drops open. "*What?* Girl! When did this happen?"

"Nothing's happening," I say quickly, keeping my voice low. "Nothing. We're here as friends."

"Honey, *I'm* your friend, and if I ever look at you the way he's looking at you—"

"Do you want to dance?" Dean cuts her off, loudly and rudely. I can't help wondering if he overheard her, or if it's a coincidence.

"I, um..." He steps up, holding out his hand and not giving me a choice, though the answer obviously would've been yes either way. "Yeah. Okay." I offer Shelby an apologetic look, but not before Tye steps toward her.

She puts a hand on his chest. "Don't even think about it, Sharpe. You're out of your league, my friend. Trey, let's go." She holds out a hand, and a shocked-looking Treylan steps forward. He gives a sheepish look to Tye, who appears absolutely appalled. My guess is he's never been told no in his life, which just makes me love Shelby more.

Dean and I place our cups down, and together, the four of us make our way out onto the empty dance floor. It's only when we reach the middle of the floor that I realize we're interrupting a slow, romantic song.

Which means I'm going to have to do a slow, romantic dance—*with Dean!*

The look I give him must scream that I'm nervous because he quickly wraps his arms around my waist, drags me toward him until our bodies are touching, and smiles. "It's just a dance, Carmie. Don't worry. Perfect gentleman, remember?"

"You weren't such a gentleman when you kissed me." I don't know why I brought it up. *Twice in one night—what am I doing?*

To my surprise, he responds without missing a beat, the corners of his mouth twitching playfully. "Oh, trust me. I was."

Heat swells somewhere deep inside of me. "I, um, I guess I just never took you as much of a dancer."

"I'm not," he admits.

"So, why did you ask me to dance?"

"Nothing wrong with trying something new. Besides, someone had to make the first move."

I swallow, not sure I heard him right.

He lowers his face toward mine and, for half a ridiculous second, I think he's going to kiss me. Instead, he gets very close to my ear and says, "If someone didn't start dancing, there'd be an empty floor all night."

So that's what he meant. My ears burn. "Right."

"And that'd be a shame because we all know how hard the student council worked on these decorations."

My eyes fall to Alissa, surrounded by a gaggle of girl-friends, looking every bit the prom queen she'll be in just a few years.

"Oh, yes. Can't let them down."

Alissa's not your classic mean girl. Not like I experienced in Atlanta. In truth, she's never done anything outright awful to me. But she's the type of person who you know will always turn against you if the time comes to help herself. The type of friend you hold at arm's length and don't tell any secrets to. The one you invite to your birthday party but who doesn't invite you to hers.

"And it clearly has to be someone cool who starts it out. I mean, if I wasn't Dean Hunter, no one would be joining us, would they?"

I look up at him. "Did you really just say that?"

"Am I wrong?"

Looking around, I see several other groups of people starting to make their way onto the floor. "It's still kind of a jerk thing to say."

"Maybe so, but I'd rather be a jerk for knowing who I am than be a pushover for pretending I don't."

"And who *are* you?" I challenge.

"I'm..." For a boy with all the confidence in the world moments ago, he wavers. His dark eyes go distant, searching the room like he expects the answer to be there waiting for him. Then, like the flick of a switch, his confidence returns. "I'm the person who's about to make your day a whole lot better."

"What?"

His grin grows as he nudges me backward. When I turn, he points me toward the photo setup, which, thanks to the now-crowded dance floor, is completely empty. Poor Mrs. Walsh is sitting alone, watching us dance with a sort of cynical whimsy, though how that combination is possible, I'm not sure.

"What are we doing?" I ask as he takes my hand and

leads us to stop just underneath the garland arch. He wraps his hands around my waist as if we were dancing, pulls me in close, and rests his head against mine.

"Smile, Carmie," he whispers, his voice low and deep in my ear.

Fascinating. It's the only word I can think of to describe him. He's completely and utterly fascinating.

I smile on cue, and Mrs. Walsh snaps the photo. Then he turns me around and places his back to mine, using his fingers to make a gun which he draws up next to his mouth. I laugh so hard I snort again when he purses his lips, drawing his brows down into a mock-serious face.

I mimic his actions, and Mrs. Walsh takes another photo, and even she is smiling from behind the camera.

When we're done, Dean turns away from me, squatting slightly. "Now, get on my back."

"What? No. I'll tear my dress."

"You won't." He scoffs. "Come on, chicken. Just try." He waves me up, and, for a reason I still can't explain, it takes no further coaxing. I jump up on his back, my hands wrapped around his neck. Mrs. Walsh snaps two photos mid-laugh, and though I probably look like a witch cackling, I can't bring myself to care. I slip down his back, and he turns around, his own face lit up with laughter. "See, that wasn't so bad, was it?"

I look up at him, ready to answer, but the words die on my tongue. We're too close. His face is just inches from mine. The laughter fades from his eyes, and there's a hint of that nervous boy from the dance floor earlier. He moves forward an inch more. The move is barely perceptible, but his chest is against my own, and I can't tell if the racing heart I'm feeling is mine or his.

Flash.

The bright light of the camera causes me to jump. I'd nearly forgotten Mrs. Walsh was there. I skitter away like a squirrel caught in the middle of the road, and an unbothered Dean crosses the floor toward Mrs. Walsh, pulling out his wallet to hand her a fifty-dollar bill. "We need one of each, please."

She hands him change and jots down a note. "They'll be in the office for you on Monday."

He turns back to me and takes my hand, pulling me back to the dance floor. "Now you'll have something to remember what a perfect gentleman I am."

It's only when I notice Jack sitting across the gymnasium at a table with Megan, I realize I have nearly forgotten about him. What a terrible friend am I? He's mad at me, disappointed in me maybe, and I completely forgot about him.

"Do you want to be with him?" Dean's voice interrupts my thoughts, and I look up to meet his eyes. Clearly, I've been caught watching Jack, probably looking like a pathetic little girl, which is exactly how I feel. But I don't want to be a little girl anymore.

"Yeah," I admit. "I do."

The words feel like a bandage that's finally been ripped off. As if he's heard me, Jack's eyes find me, going serious. He pulls his brows down, probably trying to understand whatever look must be on my face.

Dean's hands leave my waist, and his voice comes out in a whisper. "Go get him, then."

I look up at him. "What? I'm here with you."

"No. You're not." He draws in his lips.

We both know he's not wrong. Even when I'm with someone else, my head and my heart are with Jack.

"If you want him, it's worth the risk. Go tell him."

"He's with someone else."

Dean's eyes follow mine, landing on Jack, who is still looking at me, and again, his words are clearly the truth. "No. He's not."

He nudges me forward again, and this time, it doesn't take much. I step forward, then run, heading for Jack across the crowded room, but it's as if there's no one else in it. I zigzag between people as he waits for me, looking as if he doesn't completely understand or believe what's happening.

When I reach him, I'm out of breath.

"Carmen?" He blinks, shoving his hands into his pockets. "Are you okay?"

"I'm sorry," I say, dragging him away from his friends and date. To my relief, he comes willingly. "I'm sorry I'm here with Dean when..." I look back at Megan, who is staring at us in disbelief, then return my attention to Jack. "When I should've been here with you."

His body physically reacts to my words, folding in on

itself in the smallest way. When he speaks, his voice is soft. "What?"

"I should've been with you, Jack. And when you asked me if you should come with Megan, I should've said no, because you should be here with me."

"What are you saying?" His hands reach for mine, touching my fingers ever so gently, like a whisper between us.

"I'm saying I want to be with you. You're worth the risk, and I know this is the worst possible time because you're on a date, but...you're who I want to be with. And maybe that's tomorrow. Or maybe it's a week from now. Or maybe it's never because you don't feel the same—"

"I do." His words seem to shock him as much as they shock me.

"You do." It's not a question.

"I do," he repeats, his hands taking mine completely then.

"What about Megan?"

"I told you, Megan and I are just hanging out. It's not serious. She likes Jacob anyway, but he's been hanging with Destiny," he says. "We're just here as friends. I wanted to ask you, but I didn't know how."

"I'm..." I suck in a breath, making a decision. "Okay." Without second-guessing, I lean in, pressing my lips to his. The room disappears except for the two of us as his hands come to rest on my waist. He tugs me into him, and I breathe in the fresh, clean scent of his soap. One that reminds me of evenings spent together after days of swimming or car rides to school. One that reminds me of butterflies and my racing heart.

His tongue enters my mouth, and the room disappears completely. The world is gone. There's only us, and I could live and die in this moment.

In fact, maybe I will.

CHAPTER THIRTEEN

PRESENT DAY

The moment I see him kissing Alissa, I'm fourteen years old again, having my heart ripped out of my chest. I want to run and hide, leave Hunter's Hollow, and never come back. But I can't.

I'm not that little girl anymore. I'm an adult. Thirty years old. With a mortgage, a career, two plants at home counting on me—*shoot, I forgot to bring them, so probably no plants by now. How long can succulents go without water?*—and a whole life between then and now.

No one is going to scare me away from this place again. So, instead of running away as fast as my legs will carry me, I turn and head toward the road, making quick work of getting to the gate and typing in the code. Once I have, I try to catch my breath. I have no reason to be angry—except that he lied to me. He said he wasn't dating anyone, yet here he is, kissing Alissa freaking Burton.

I suck in a deep breath and cross into the woods, focusing on what really matters. The missing girl, the potentially hurt or even *dead* girl, just like all those years ago.

I never believed it was just someone passing through, not back then and not now. It never made sense. But then again, nothing about those years makes sense.

It feels like that's the whole world, your whole life, when you're in them. As a teen, there's no sense of reality. No sense of the bigger picture. Looking back now, I can only cringe over the things I thought and did.

Like last time, I don't plan to make my way through the woods and to the cabin, but I do it anyway. All those years ago, I could never bring myself to come back here after we found her body.

Purpling, shredded skin.

Bruises.

Cuts.

Blood.

Her empty, soulless eyes.

It was too painful, too scary. I came up with all sorts of ideas about what might've happened to her. Monsters in the woods, cults, serial killers. Mom kept me out of the woods, like Jill made the boys stay out, but I don't think either of them had to try. No one wanted to go into the woods after she died. It just felt too much like testing fate.

It can't be a coincidence, can it? Two girls. Two young women, really, but they both disappeared here?

I have to see for myself, and I know if I told anyone else my plan, they'd call me crazy or dangerous, or both. I cross the small path in front of me on my way toward the cabin. Leaves and sticks crunch underfoot, and my forehead drips with sweat as I make my way toward the front door.

I still see her body sometimes. In my nightmares, when I close my eyes, when I watch scary movies. It's like she's still with me, still haunting me. I was one of the only ones to see it, in fact. Most people were kept far away from the crime scene, and her funeral was closed-casket, but still, I have this image in my head of the moment I saw her, as my brain processed what I was seeing. Tried to piece together the puzzle that was once a person.

As it tried to understand what must've happened.

Her body was mangled—there's no other way to describe it. Bloody and bruised, torn to shreds. Her entire stomach was hollowed out, one arm ripped completely off. They said animals had gotten to her inside the cabin, making the wounds worse. That was when they were telling us all that it might've been an accident. She'd been drinking and could've passed out. Been attacked by someone or something. Whatever that something was, it got hold of her and tore her to shreds. When her autopsy results came back inconclusive, her cause of death impossible to determine because of all the damage to her body, the mystery was all but forgotten about by everyone, it seemed. And we never got any answers.

When I close my eyes, the image flashes in my head, just like back then. It kills me to think about it, but I can't help it. As I reach for the cabin door, I remember just how it felt to find her. The ice-cold horror was unlike anything I'd ever felt.

I threw up everywhere when we discovered her, like my body was physically rejecting the sight.

I approach the door to the cabin and suck in a breath. No one will be here. Not the girl. No one. She's not here.

But I have to check...just in case.

With a heavy breath and a rush of adrenaline, I reach for the door and stop. The padlock. *Shoot.* I forgot they keep it locked now.

Reconfiguring my plan, I move over to one of the windows on the side, one that isn't covered in plywood, and press my face to the glass. I half expect someone to jump up and scare me like in a movie. My heart thuds in my chest as my eyes take in the empty room.

But there's nothing.

The cabin sits empty and dust-covered, except for a few old cans of cleaner, empty mason jars, and a crate of tools. No bodies. No girl.

Just dust, dirt, leaves, and history.

If I look close, I can see the bloody outline where her body lay until it was found. I try not to look closer.

Instead, I turn away from the window and check over my shoulder.

When I see someone there, I jump, alarm bells going off in my head until I realize who it is. I hadn't heard him coming up. "*Jack.*"

"Sorry." He holds up a hand. I'm not sure what he's apologizing for, and I don't know that he does either.

"I didn't hear you following me."

"Robbie says we have to keep everyone out of the forest until he's done a thorough search."

"Oh." My heart falls. I knew that. Of course I knew that. How guilty must I look now that I went running straight to the place he's going to be searching?

"It's okay," he says. "As far as anyone knows, you just went home to your cabin. But we should get back before they find us out here."

"Right." I can't move, suddenly planted in place. I certainly can't move with him leading me.

"Were you..." He pauses, collecting himself. "Did you think she might be..."

"No. I don't know. I just had to check."

His head drops forward. "Me too, honestly. It was the first thing any of us thought about."

"It can't be a coincidence," I say on a breath. As angry at him as I am, I need to say the words aloud. I need to know I'm not the only one who believes them.

"What else can it be? We don't know anything yet. For all we know, the girl ran off. For all we know, she's asleep in a cabin with someone her mom forgot to check with."

I don't think he believes the words coming out of his mouth, but if he does, it makes me even angrier.

"They never found out what happened to Shelby," I say. "And now this? Now another girl?"

"Shelby was drunk," he says. "Robbie says she probably came in here to get warm, and a coyote got her. It's awful, and yes, it hits close to home—"

"Literally." I wave an angry hand at the cabin.

"But that doesn't mean it's connected."

"Speaking of connected...were you planning to tell me you and Alissa are a thing?"

"We aren't," he says quickly, then runs a hand over his face. "We weren't. I don't know. We were seeing each other for a while, but we broke up. I didn't lie to you when I said I wasn't dating anyone, Carmen."

"And now? What are you doing now?"

He sighs. "I wish I knew."

If I don't start walking, my knees will give out. I nod without another word, another syllable even. I can't muster it. Instead, I walk back to the cabin. Mercifully, Jack doesn't speak either.

CHAPTER FOURTEEN

BEFORE — AGE 15

"Happy birthday, old man," I tease Dean, finding him standing in the kitchen of cabin ten. His birthday party is loud and full of people, some of which I know from school, and several I don't. Given that our school isn't that big, I know most of these people have either already graduated or aren't from here.

He turns to look at me, tipping the beer in his hand toward his lips. The alcohol didn't come out until Jill and Sam left us alone, but something tells me Dean isn't the least bit worried about being caught.

"Old man, hmm?"

"You're eighteen now."

"Last I checked."

"Old." I poke his chest.

"Last I checked, you'll be here in three years. Better watch what you say."

"Three years is a lifetime."

He sighs. "Yeah. Tell me about it." His eyes flick around the room, to the many people filtering in and out to grab food and drinks. He nods at them as they pass, tossing out a few "thank yous" to the people wishing him happy birthday. When he finds me out of the corner of his eye again, he asks, "Where's my brother?"

"He's around here somewhere. I think he went outside with Colton and Tanner."

He nods slowly. "Did he tell you the good news?"

My eyes widen. "Good news?"

He turns toward the sink, resting his hands on the countertop. "I'm leaving Hunter's Hollow. Saying goodbye to North Carolina in general."

A boulder sinks inside of me, a heaviness I can't explain sitting squarely in my stomach. It's as if I'm standing on the shore, and my footing has been ripped out from under me by a massive wave. "What are you talking about?"

"I got accepted to Vanderbilt," he tells me. "Nashville. Their education program is one of the best."

"Nashville..." Dean has mentioned once or twice that he wants to be a teacher, but I guess I never actually thought about the fact that he'd have to go to school to do that. Or that it might require him to leave. I guess I never really thought about the fact that he'd be graduating at all until recently. "You don't want to go to Duke? You could stay here, and..." I can see he's not really listening. His mind has been made up.

"Duke's fine, but I've had my eye on Vanderbilt for a while."

"And your family knows?"

He takes another sip of his beer and nods. "Yep."

"Wow." I sink against the counter next to him, feeling as if the life has been sucked out of me. "Congratulations, I guess. I'm really happy for you, but sad you won't be around anymore."

He grins. "When did that change? The summer you moved here, you would've been glad for me to be gone."

It's funny. He's right, I guess. Two years ago, when I moved to Hunter's Hollow, Dean was basically the bane of my existence. I was annoyed by him constantly, and I genuinely looked forward to days when he'd be away. But it hasn't felt like that for me in a long time.

"It's different between us now."

He nods, though I'm not sure if it's in acknowledgment or agreement. "Well, Jack will be glad to have the place all to himself. It can't be easy living in my shadow." It's a joke, I know, but his voice is soft. Sad, even.

"When do you leave? In the fall?"

"No. Two weeks from now. Right after graduation."

"Before the summer?"

"Yeah, I don't have any reason to stay."

"But summers are full of possibilities. We always have so much fun. How can you leave already?"

"Possibilities." He laughs under his breath. "Maybe for you, but I already have an apartment there, so any possibilities I'll be looking for will be far from here.

Besides, it'll be good to move in and get settled before school starts."

"I thought you were going to take me driving a few more times before I turn sixteen this fall."

The look on his face tells me he wants to say more than he is. "Dad will keep working with you. You're doing fine."

I take a sip of the Sprite in my hand, fighting off the dryness in my throat. "Right. Okay. Two weeks. Wow. Well, I'll miss you."

His eyes flicker with something that looks like surprise. "You'll have your friends. And Jack. And I'll be back for the holidays."

I don't know why I suddenly feel like crying. Dean's graduating in just a few weeks, but I'll see him tomorrow. And the next day. So why does this feel like it's already goodbye? Maybe because it's the beginning of the end.

"It's not the same—"

"Dude, basketball game outside. You in?"

I turn my head to see Tye there, watching us. His cheeks are pink from alcohol, his smile lazy.

"Yep." Dean steps forward, draining the last of the beer from his bottle. Just when I think he's going to leave me alone—a trial run, perhaps—he turns back. "You coming?"

And so, I do.

CHAPTER FIFTEEN

PRESENT DAY

Seeing Tye Sharpe again for the first time in over a decade is like coming back to a travel coffee mug with milk in it that you've forgotten in your car for several days before you remember it's there.

It's the only way I can think of to explain it.

Like I forgot he existed, and now I'm forced to accept that he's still around.

He steps out of the car with the confidence he's always had. His blond hair is still perfectly thick, and he continues to wear that all-too-cocky grin, though it's now surrounded by neatly groomed facial hair.

When he sees me, he stops in his tracks, eyes flashing toward Dean, then Jack, before coming back to me. "No shit? Little Carmie McKenna? Is that really you?"

"Do I know you?" I ask, wrinkling my brow with mock confusion.

He chuckles and walks forward to hug Dean. We're

all sitting on my front porch, waiting for the sheriff to finish his check of the woods. "Daniel told me there's someone missing out here." Tye clicks his tongue.

"*Daniel* isn't supposed to be telling anyone anything," I say, disgusted. "It's an open investigation, and he's a cop."

"Relax, Carmie. I'm not gonna tell anybody." He winks and leans against the railing.

I scoff and turn away.

"What are you doing here anyway, Tye?" Dean asks, tucking his phone into his pocket.

"Well, you told me before I should come visit this summer. And then when Daniel told me about the kid, I thought the place must be missing me. Time to come back." He pats his chest. "Is there anything I can do to help?"

The last thing Tye wants is to help, and we all know it. He wants to be nosy and make himself feel important.

"Not really. Robbie has everyone waiting around while they check the woods and talk to all the guests staying here." Dean stands and moves toward the house. "You want a beer?"

"Yeah, sure."

When he disappears inside, Tye turns his attention to Jack. "How'd things end up last night? You both ducked out before I got a chance to ask. She seemed upset."

She?

My body tenses as I turn to look at Jack and find his guilty eyes peering back at me.

"Fine," he mumbles.

"I thought you were with Colton last night," I say, sitting straighter in my chair.

In the grand scheme of things, none of this matters. A girl is missing, and Jack and I are nothing.

We are friends, though, at least, aren't we? I thought we were friends, and friends don't lie to each other. Except this is what he does, apparently. Why do I keep forgetting that?

Tye's face goes ashen, and he looks between us, clearly realizing he's said something wrong.

"I *was* with Colton," Jack says after a beat. "I mean... at first I was. I went to the bar, and he was there."

I notice he doesn't say he was meeting him, just that they ran into each other. Suddenly his story has changed.

"Alissa asked me to meet her and talk." He sighs. "It wasn't a big deal."

"I didn't mean to start anything," Tye cuts in, his hands held up.

"Why didn't you just tell me when I asked, then?" I keep my eyes pinned on Jack.

"I didn't want you to assume anything."

"Oh. Well, that's convenient. You were with her last night, and then she showed up today. What could I possibly have assumed?"

Slowly, Tye creeps away into the house.

Jack stands out of his chair and walks toward me. "Look, it's complicated with me and Alissa. We dated for a while and broke up, and she thinks we can work it out.

I'm not sure what I want. That's the answer. I told her I needed time to think."

"That's not how it looked this morning."

"I don't care how it looked. It's the truth."

I pinch the bridge of my nose. "Jack, you don't owe me anything. If you're dating her, great. If you're not, cool. But don't lie to me, okay? That's all I ask. I'm just here for two months. You're allowed to have a life, but if you want me around as your friend, you can't lie to me."

Dean comes outside before he can answer. "Everything okay out here?"

"Fine," we both say at once.

"Obviously." He steps forward. "I ordered us some pizzas for dinner. What do you say we all have a few drinks, eat dinner, and swim? I think we deserve a break. And we could clearly all use some stress relief."

"From all our hard work, you mean?" I ask dryly, still angry at Jack.

"Exactly." Dean beams at me.

"I'm not in the mood," Jack says.

I want to agree with him, to say that it hardly feels appropriate to be partying and enjoying ourselves when a girl has gone missing, but I also want to disagree with Jack in any way possible. It's silly of me, I know, but in the end, the pettiness wins.

I stand. "I'm in."

Tye pops out of the kitchen, holding his hand up with fingers pressed together like a chef's kiss and adopting a Spanish accent. "*Excellent.*" I'm not sure if it's meant to insult or impress me, but since he pronounces it wrong, it does neither.

God, I hate him.

———

The sheriff concludes his search of the woods an hour later when the sky grows too dark to see. Jill comes by to tell us the news, along with the updates that he didn't find the girl or any signs she'd been out there, and Daniel has spoken to everyone staying at the campground. Though a few people saw her around The Hollow in general, no one claims to have seen anything strange, and no one has spotted her since she left the swimming area last night, which means they'll be searching for new leads.

The updates come just before our pizza arrives, and with the relief that there's—at least—no bad news, I feel slightly better about trying to relax.

It's past time for the office to be closed, so Jill tells us Sam's going home, but she and Mom are going to stay with the girl's mother while they try to work out what may have happened with her.

The disappearance is weighing hard on all of us, but maybe it's the hardest on Jill, who just wants this place to be the magical escape it's always been despite the fact that something seems to be fighting against this.

It's Sam's family's land, but the burden falls on Jill to keep up the reputation, even if it's never spoken aloud. I feel a sort of kinship with her as she tells us the news and asks us all to be safe and stay out of the woods tonight. The weight she feels is something the three men here will never understand.

Even as Dean, Tye, and Jack try to tell her it's going to be okay, the girl will be found, and everything will work itself out, the fear she's feeling is palpable. I know that whatever happens, she'll be blamed in some way. And, unlike before, the community might not be so forgiving a second time.

When she leaves, we sit down at the kitchen table to eat the pizza Dean ordered.

"So, what's going on with you two?" Dean asks, staring at Jack and me between bites.

"Nothing," I say.

Tye, who's already had a few drinks too many, is happy to fill him in. "Jack lied to her about meeting Alissa at the bar last night."

Jack's gaze is so sharp I don't know how Tye doesn't fall onto the floor gasping for breath. "I didn't lie."

"It doesn't matter," I say. "We're moving on, and we're fine." I take another bite of my pizza. "Let's talk about something else."

"Like what I'm up to lately? How kind of you to ask." Tye winks. "You're looking at the principal, the head honcho, of our old school. Did you know that?"

"Unfortunately," I answer without looking at him.

He visibly deflates. "Oh. You did?"

"I told her the other day," Dean says.

"Couldn't stop thinking about me, hmm?" Tye recovers quickly. "Hey, whatever happened to you two anyway?" He points between Jack and me. "Weren't you, like, high school sweethearts?"

The three of us go deadly silent, but I'm the one who has to answer. "It didn't work out."

"Now she has Georgie," Dean teases.

"Georgie?" Tye's eyes widen. "Spicy. Give me deets."

"Greg," I correct. "And don't say *deets*. Also, I don't have Greg. We broke up."

"Aww, I'm sorry, Carmie."

"*I* broke up with *him*," I say firmly.

"Because you were coming back here for your one true love?" Tye puts his hands on his chest, gasping as he looks at Jack.

I down the rest of my beer, the buzz already setting in. Unable to take any more of this, I stand from the table. "I'm going to change into a swimming suit. I'll meet you guys at the water."

Dean smacks Tye's bicep without any force. "Cut it out."

Tye laughs. "What?"

"Lay off her, man. It's been a rough day."

I make my way out of the house. The darkness that covers the land is unsettling. There's a charge in the air that I can't quite describe—like heat lightning on an otherwise clear night.

The hairs on my arms stand up, every nerve in my body tugging me back to that night, demanding that I remember. The wind howls through the trees, practically pushing me toward the woods.

Everything feels heightened. Dangerous. Like we're right on the precipice, and at any moment, everything could crumble beneath our feet, just like it did before.

I feel the ground shifting underneath me as I walk, a steady rumble that warns something's coming.

As real as a pulse.

Run. Run.

Run. Run.

Run. Run.

I felt it back then, too, but this time I won't listen.

Everything that has happened today, though I know there's not really any chance it's connected to what happened that night, has brought all those old feelings back. The fear, the uncertainty, the anger, the heartbreak —it was all there, waiting for me to acknowledge it and feel it, and now I have no choice.

I don't think these are things you ever get over, really. The five years from thirteen to eighteen are stressful for everyone, but when you throw in a murder investigation, I guess it all gets a bit more complicated.

Once I've changed out of my clothes and into my bathing suit, I make my way outside and find Jack at my door. His chest puffs with a deep breath of air.

"Can we talk?"

"About?" I move past him.

"I'm sorry I lied to you."

I stop, turn toward him, and blink. "Okay. Thank

you." My head is fuzzy with alcohol and stress. His face is sort of hazy, even just a few feet in front of me.

He's still dressed in his regular clothes, his hair messy. "I shouldn't have lied. I know that. I didn't plan to, it just came out, but that's no excuse. Ever since you got here, my head has just been a mess. I thought I knew what I wanted. I thought I knew where my life was going, but now you're here, and..." His eyes dance between mine.

"And what, Jack?"

"And I don't know anything anymore."

I wait for him to say something else, but when he doesn't, I say, "Look, what happened between us is complicated. Messy. I get it. I didn't mean to come in and confuse you or screw anything up for you. If you want to be with Alissa, please don't let me stop you. You deserve to be happy, Jack. You always have."

He nods, but it's sad. Distant. "So we're okay?"

I should ask him about what I know. The truth from years ago, but I can't. Not in my current state and not when we've already been fighting. My emotions are too raw and stormy right now. If I break down the wall, I'm afraid of the tsunami that awaits. "Yes. We're okay. Just don't lie to me again."

He pulls me in for a hug, his arms tight around my shoulders. "I really am glad you're here," he says, his voice gentle in my ears. It reminds me of so many times before this, and I feel the memories deep in my bones.

I've missed him, and I want him now in whatever capacity I can have him. "I'm glad too."

Together, we make our way down to the water, where Tye and Dean are already waiting. When we come into view, their conversation dies off as I see Dean watching us closely, probably trying to decide what's happening.

"We're fine," I tell him as I unhook my towel from around my body, drop it onto the ground, and head for the water. Remembering that Jack is still dressed, I look back at him. "You coming?"

He shakes his head. "Not tonight. I need to get some rest."

I remember his long night last night, trying not to feel bitter, and nod. "Right."

As he walks back to his cabin, I move farther out into the water. The swimming suit I'm wearing is simple and black, perfect for swimming in muddy water like this. I once made the mistake of swimming in a yellow swimming suit in the murky water, and it never fully recovered.

My toes squish in the mud as I make my way into the pond, with Dean and Tye waiting ahead of me.

"Now it's a party!" Tye cries, throwing his hand in the air.

"Sad that this is considered a party," I point out.

"You calling our party boring?" Dean teases.

I grin, memories flooding me. "Compared to the parties we used to have, yeah."

Dean swims toward me. "I remember a few good ones."

"What about that time Tye broke a window playing pool?" I ask.

"That was not a good time," Tye says, wagging a lazy, drunk finger toward me. "I had to work six weeks to pay your parents back for that."

"Well, I'm still not sure what you were trying to do." Dean laughs. "And I think your parents paid mine back, not you."

"Well, whatever. They made me work some of it off, and it was an accident. The cue slipped!" he shouts, waving his hand in the air.

I get deeper into the water, closer to them, until I'm shoulder-deep and having to swim to stay afloat.

"What about the time you two kissed?" Tye asks, wrinkling his nose.

"What about the time you hooked up with that girl from Wilmington, just for her husband to show up and try to kick your ass?" Dean tosses the embarrassment back at him without missing a beat.

Tye chuckles. "Good times."

"Well, we're all old now," I say eventually. "Thank god."

There's a chorus of laughter, then Tye says, "Old, but not dead. There are definitely some aspects of that life that I miss." He's quiet for a minute. "I say we throw another one. For old time's sake."

"A party? No," Dean says quickly.

"Our parents would kill us. There's too much else going on," I agree. "It wouldn't be right."

Tye's hopeful expression falls. "Oh. Right. Well, we can still have fun, can't we? How about truth or dare, then?"

"Oh my god. We are thirty-year-olds. We're not playing truth or dare." I roll my eyes.

"Why? You scared, infant? It's all in good fun."

"Until you both start picking on me," I say. "I'm not playing truth or dare. It's uneven, and I know you guys well enough to know things will get weird."

"You really think we'd do that?" he teases, swimming close to me. "Pick on you?" His arms encircle my waist, and I push him back with one finger.

"I don't *think*. I *know* you would."

He puckers his lip, releasing me. "Aww, Carmie, you're no fun."

"Fine. Truth or dare, Tye?" Dean asks.

Like a dog, Tye turns to him with wide eyes. "Dare."

"I dare you to go home."

The chuckle that escapes my throat is unpreventable. Tye rolls his eyes and flips us both off, diving into the water.

"Why are you friends with him, again?" I ask.

"Oh, you guys pretend you don't love me." Tye groans when he pops back up.

"No one's that good an actor," I tease.

"You're just *so* funny." Tye goes underwater again and comes back up, blowing air from his mouth. "I'll remember that when either of you need a favor."

"Like what? Not to be expelled?" I tease, feeling the buzz of my drink warming my skin.

He lunges forward, grabbing me and tugging me under with him. Dean moves closer suddenly, too, making sure I come back up.

"Jesus, stop it!" I shout, struggling to get out of his arms, laughing as I resurface. We're all so close I can feel their warmth.

As much as they each annoy me, I feel safe with these men. Even Tye, though I'd never admit it aloud. Being with them is a feeling of peace and nostalgia like I've never known.

"So you said you're single, Carmen?" Tye asks, rubbing his hand across his mouth.

"And not looking."

He laughs. "What do you know, neither am I. But that doesn't mean we can't go out while you're in town. I know you always wanted a piece of me back then."

"In your dreams."

"In quite a few of 'em, actually."

Dean's shoulders tense. "Enough, Tye. You're drunk. Leave her alone."

"We're all drunk," Tye points out. "Maybe Carmen's up for a little fun. Like old times."

His hand slides around my waist in the water, dragging me toward him. Something stirs inside my belly. "Old times?" I'm too distracted to pull away.

"Truth or dare, Carmen?" Tye's blue eyes sear into mine.

"She already said she's not playing your stupid game," Dean says.

"Truth." My word sounds bolder than I feel. If I play along, maybe I can get the answer to what they mean by *old times.*

His brows bounce up, and he cuts a glance toward Dean before returning his attention fully to me, his hand still hooked around my waist. "You ever had a threesome, Carmen?"

The muscles between my legs clench. "No. Definitely not."

"Would you?"

"I..." My throat is dry. Tight. His eyes dip down to my chest, lazy and filled with desire. "I don't know. I guess so, under the right circumstances."

Dean's Adam's apple bobs, and his eyes darken with a look of desire I recognize well. "This isn't happening," he says, though his voice is powerless.

The way both men are looking at me sends sparks down to my toes. I feel insanely powerful. "Is that what you meant by 'like old times'? You guys've done that before?"

Tye and Dean exchange a glance.

"Yeah." Tye's grin turns wicked. "You could say we're old pros. We could show you the ropes if you're into it."

"You're not touching her." Dean's words are cutting, spoken through gritted teeth.

Tension crackles through the air. Tye's grip tightens

on me under the water, and like the spell has been broken by Dean's words, I pull out of his arm.

Despite my actions, I snap at Dean, suddenly angry he still thinks he can tell me what to do. I jab a finger at him. "You're not my boss."

He swats my hand away. "Like hell I'm not."

Frustrated and much too inebriated, I turn toward Tye. His brow quirks with a challenge, and I lean forward. He grabs hold of me, pulling me to him, and kisses me. His kiss is sloppy and underwhelming, both too much and too little at the same time. He moans and lifts me up, wrapping my legs around his waist under the water.

As it happens, I'm internally tamping down my panic.

This is so not like me.

I don't even like Tye. But something inside of me wants to make Dean mad. Wants to prove to him he doesn't control me. Wants to prove to Jack I can move on, too.

When a new hand catches my waist, I pull back, releasing a shaky breath. For half a second, I think this is really going to happen. But instead, he snags me away from Tye and spins me around to face him.

I gasp, breathless. "What are you—"

Dean's mouth catches mine, shutting me up. I go weak as I feel him lifting me out of the water. My heart races in my chest so fast I'm certain I'm going to pass out.

Dean's kiss is different. Familiar. Welcome. It sends a

wave of heat more powerful than the alcohol through me. He crushes his mouth to mine, and the world disappears around us. I wrap my arms around him tighter, never wanting to let him go. Before I'm ready, he pulls back, plopping me down in the water with venom-filled eyes. He directs his gaze to Tye. "Don't ever touch her again."

Tye laughs, but there's nothing funny about the way Dean is staring at him. It's as if something dark and dangerous has taken over his body, as if he's ready to fight his best friend right here and now.

I don't know what came over me. It's the alcohol, the tension of the day, the closeness of us all, and my need to prove to them I'm no longer a kid but one of them. That I can do whatever they do.

Without saying a word, Dean takes my hand. "You're drunk. Party's over. Let's get you home."

"What the—" Tye cries. "Come on. We were just having some fun."

"No. I told you back then, and I'll tell you again now...it's not happening with her."

"We got carried away, dude, chill," Tye says, rubbing his eyes as if he's sleepy, as though we've all been in a trance. It's my turn to feel shame, for my cheeks to heat as I realize what I almost let happen. What I kind of wanted to happen.

Dean doesn't look at either of us. "Come on."

"I'm...I'm fine," I try to pull back out of his grasp.

"She's the one who kissed me, man. She was okay with it," Tye says. "Why are you freaking out?"

Dean's jaw goes tight, and he can't seem to look away from me. It's as if he's angry with me, but he has no right to be. I'm certainly not going to let him make me feel bad for considering doing exactly what they've apparently done. Or for kissing someone who's also single. If his best friend is so bad he doesn't trust me with him, maybe he shouldn't be his best friend.

"It's fine, Dean," I tell him. "He's right. Chill. We're all consenting adults. It was just a kiss. Am I not good enough for you or something? Not good enough for...this?"

His eyes narrow. "This is actually something you're asking to do? To fuck us both?" The word zips through the air, slamming into my chest. The reality of what is on the table.

"M-maybe." A chill runs over me.

"No. We're not doing this," he says. "We just need to go inside and sober the hell up."

"Fuck that." Tye grabs hold of me, pulling me toward him and slamming his mouth to mine. I don't pull away for the first second out of pure shock, but then I shove him back. It doesn't feel right anymore.

"Dean's right. Stop."

Tye drops me. "Fine. Whatever. Just trying to have a little fun like old times." His brows rise as he stares at Dean.

"This isn't like old times." He takes hold of my hand

and pulls me out of the water, marching us up the stairs and toward my cabin.

Once inside, he shuts the door. The air between us is practically sparking with anger and tension. He turns to me, and I back into the wall.

"You kissed my best friend."

"Apparently you don't mind when other girls do that."

A muscle in his jaw twitches. "I mind when you do."

His body presses against mine, his fingers tracing lines up my sides. *What are we doing? What is happening?* "Why?"

He swallows, his eyes trailing down my body, then coming back up to meet mine ever so slowly. "You're not his to kiss."

"And whose am I to kiss, Dean?" Shivers line my skin, and I'm so desperate to touch him, but I don't. I keep my hands plastered to the wall behind me as he traces lines over my shoulders, arms, sides, and hips with the most gentle touch.

"You tell me."

"Whoever the hell I want—"

"Wrong." The word leaves his mouth before I've finished my sentence.

"I can sleep with whoever I want, too."

"*Fuck*," he corrects, and the word sends a zap of lightning to my core. "You were going to fuck him, that's it. Make no mistake, he would've used you, Carmen."

"Is that what you did to those girls?"

His nose brushes mine. "I don't want to think about those girls right now." His hand finally comes to rest on my shoulder, nudging the strap of my bikini top down just an inch. With a questioning look in his eyes, almost as if he's already regretting this, he lowers his mouth to my skin.

I release a guttural moan, unable to contain myself. Just the slightest touch from him sends my body into a frenzy. "Dean..."

"Say it again."

My voice catches in my throat. "I—"

"My name. Say it agai—"

A sharp knock sounds at the door, and we both jump apart. The heat evaporates from my skin in an instant as I realize what nearly just happened.

Oh my god.

Oh my god.

Oh my god.

Another knock, this time quicker. Dean pulls the door open, and we find Tye standing there, displaying a bloody palm and holding something with the other hand.

He's hopping up and down. "Shit! Something cut my foot. Do you have a first-aid kit?"

"Yeah," Dean growls, turning away and heading for the kitchen.

"What did you step on? What's that?" I ask, insanely aware of the fact that the goose bumps on my skin from Dean's touch are still disappearing.

"I don't know." He shoves the item toward me, and I stare down at the muddy fabric. "It was lodged down in the pond. I stepped on it when I was getting out." I brush a bit of mud off, not caring that it lands on the floor as my knees go weak.

It's a purse that I'm holding. A yellow, oversized nylon satchel. The zipper is rusting and sharp at this point—and probably easily sliced his foot open—but it's the fabric that catches my eye. The bag is one I'd know anywhere.

CHAPTER SIXTEEN

BEFORE — AGE 17

I walk into the Hunters' cabin without knocking, then cross through the kitchen and into the living room.

"Hey, Carmen!" Jill calls from where she sits on the floor working on a puzzle.

"'Bout damn time someone with some taste came around," Sam says, appearing in the room from the hall. "Carmen, tell her my dip tasted better when we added those extra cans of Ro-Tel."

Jill looks up at me skeptically. "You don't have to agree with him."

"Oh my god, you guys. Don't pull her into this debate. Just make it both ways. It's not like it won't get eaten." Jack's argument comes from down the hall, and it's not until he's done talking that I finally see him. He beams at me. "Hey."

I bounce up on my toes at the sight of him. "Hey."

"Come on." He waves me back toward his room.

"Door open," Sam and Jill warn us at the same time, like we don't already know the rules.

"Yeah, yeah," Jack says, holding my hand as we make our way down the hall.

When we get inside, he turns around, pulling me to him. "Hi," he says again.

"Hi." My cheeks burn from smiling so hard.

His lips press against mine, and we're both smiling so our teeth scrape, causing us to laugh. He quickly kisses me again, twice, then drops my hand. "Want to play?" He gestures toward his Xbox and sits down on the floor against the side of his bed.

"Yeah, sure." I sit down next to him, and he hands me a controller. "So what's the Great Dip Debate of 2010 about?"

He laughs and scratches his forehead. His dark hair is getting long, and it's constantly hanging in his eyes. He flips his head, brushing the hair to the side. "Oh, um, Dean's coming home for winter break, so they've planned this whole welcome-home party for him."

A spark ignites in my stomach. Since he left last May, talk of Dean has been limited. Mom and I visited my grandparents last Christmas when he came home, and he stayed in Nashville over the summer to work. I haven't heard from him a single time, and the only updates I've gotten have been from eavesdropping on my mom and Jill's conversations. As much as I've wanted to, it doesn't feel right to ask Jack about his brother, and as many times as I've pulled up his number in my phone to send him a text, I can't bring myself to do it.

No doubt he's off having a great time at college and doesn't want to be bothered by me.

"Really?"

My response must come off as too shocked, because Jack looks at me with a weird expression.

"Well, you didn't expect him to stay in Nashville for Christmas, did you? He came home last year."

"No, I guess not. I just hadn't really thought about it. You must be excited to have him back."

"Yeah, sure." He shrugs one shoulder.

"Do you get to talk to him much?"

"Nah." He's turned his attention back to the screen, setting up the game for us to play. "You ready to play?"

"Mm-hmm." I'm actually not, and it's painfully obvious because I die within seconds on the screen, leading Jack to laugh and check on me. "You okay?"

"I'm fine."

"I got your Christmas present yesterday, by the way." He grins at me. "You're going to like it."

I've been meaning to shop for Jack, but I haven't yet. Mom says she'll take me into the city next weekend to do it, but I still have no idea what I'm going to get him, which only makes me feel guiltier.

"You did?"

He nods.

"Hmm...what'd you get me?" I giggle, leaning into his side.

"You know I can't tell you. You'll find out on Christmas."

"Mine will be better," I promise—and hope.

"Just seeing you will be present enough." He kisses the side of my head, and butterflies swarm my stomach. "You know, I've never spent Christmas with anyone but my family. I can't believe you guys are staying here this year."

"Me either," I admit. "But the nursing home where my grandparents live had an outbreak of the flu, and they've asked everyone not to visit until things have calmed down. So we can't travel to see them."

"Well, I'm happy to have our first real Christmas together on the actual holiday." He pauses the game and slips his hand into mine, kissing me again. "It's just the first of many."

Two days later, after spending the morning with Shelby on the lake, we've just said goodbye, and I'm watching her head for her car next to the cabin when Dean's dark sedan pulls down the road.

He's home.

He doesn't seem to notice me as he steps out of his car, one bag in hand. He looks older somehow, though I know it's not really possible. He's got stubble—dark facial hair he's always kept shaved before this. I jog toward the Hunters' cabin, coming inside just behind him. Jack is in the kitchen helping Sam and Jill with the food when we walk through the door, Dean with his bag in hand.

"There he is," Jill calls, crossing the room with both arms outstretched. "My big ole college baby." She hugs him quickly, kissing his head several times as he winces. Her fingers trace over his facial hair. "What is this?"

"Hi, Mom." One corner of his mouth tugs upward with a loving smile. He eases her off of him. "Something new I'm trying."

"I don't like it. You look too grown up." She studies him, her lips pursed.

"Leave the kid alone. How was the drive home?" Sam asks, crossing the room to hug his son as Jill backs away with a playful grimace.

"Fine. No trouble."

"Good."

"Were you two together?" Jack asks, pointing between us.

Dean's eyes find mine then...and practically rebound off of me to find literally anything else. He shakes his head.

"No. Shelby just left, and I saw him coming, so I followed him to say hey. Welcome home, Dean," I say, my voice shaking. I have no idea why I'm as nervous as I am.

"Hey." He sucks in a breath as he says it, hoisting the

black duffel bag up over his shoulder. He looks at his mom. "I'm going to unpack and take a shower."

"Okay, baby." She squeezes his hand. "I hope you haven't eaten. We made plenty of food, and Jack invited some of your friends over."

Dean winces. "I'm kind of just in the mood for a low-key night, if that's okay?"

Jill's shoulders drop. "Oh. Well, sure—"

"Never mind. It's fine. I'll just take a quick nap."

"No, honey. We should've checked with you first—"

"Honestly, Mom, it'll be good to see everyone. I'm just tired from the road." He pats her arm. "A party sounds perfect. Seriously, just let me shower, and I'll be fine." His eyes flick to mine, just once, and then he's out of the room and down the hall.

By the time the party rolls around that evening, Sam and Jill have landed on making four different kinds of dips, Little Smokies, a cheese and cracker plate, sausage balls, sliders, and six desserts. There's enough food to feed several families.

My mom arrived with a fruit and veggie tray half an hour ago, and Tye and Daniel wait to show up until it's time to eat.

Tye chose to go to school nearby in Durham, and Daniel isn't in college. He's working at a local restaurant, last I heard. Dean greets them both warmly, but I can see that he's tired. Still, we all gather in the kitchen as Dean fills us in on life in Nashville and how busy his schedule is. He works at a local soda shop that's apparently some kind of Nashville staple. I didn't even know soda shops were still a thing, and I'm picturing people in retro white hats and old-fashioned waitress uniforms, moving around on roller skates, though I have no idea if that's accurate. He tells us how he has a packed schedule with classes but has managed to make a few friends.

"Are you seeing anyone?" Jill asks the million dollar question, and I want to both tell her to shut up and thank her for asking all at once.

He scrunches his nose. "Ma..."

"I'm just asking. I'd like to know you're not alone up there. If you're seeing a nice girl. Or boy." Her hands go up. "You know we don't judge."

"I've gone on a few dates, but nothing serious. I'm trying to focus on school."

"Playing the field...my boy!" Sam pops a sausage ball in his mouth with a wry smirk just before Jill swats him in the stomach. "Oof." He winces.

As the night wears on, my mom heads back home with a kiss to Dean's cheek and a 'welcome home.' Tye and Daniel eventually leave, too, then Jill and Sam head to bed, reminding Jack to walk me home before two, which is my curfew on weekends and over the break.

I don't need anyone to walk me the twenty feet to our cabin, but it's become our ritual, and I don't mind it so much.

When it's just the three of us, the awkwardness of it all sets in. Dean sits on the couch, and Jack takes a seat in the recliner, calling me over to sit on his lap. I'm not sure why, because he's never done it before, but it feels strange to be acting so cozy in front of Dean.

Jack doesn't seem to notice the awkwardness, though, as he slides a hand around my waist, rubbing his palm across my stomach.

"All your classes pretty easy?" he asks Dean, filling the silence.

"Not too bad." Dean doesn't look our way as he cracks open the soda in his hand.

Jack yawns, resting his head against my shoulder. "I could fall asleep."

"Maybe you should walk your girlfriend home and do that, then."

"It's not even midnight yet, and I'm not tired," I argue.

Both boys look at me.

"You heard the woman," Jack says with another yawn. He's always preferred to go to bed earlier than I do. "Let's watch a movie or something."

Dean grabs the remote and scrolls through the channels until he lands on *Four Christmases*—one of my favorites. With the movie on, the room falls quiet, and after several minutes, the awkwardness fades away.

When I feel Jack's lips on my ear, I turn to look at him, and he kisses me firmly. Sloppily. Like he's drunk, but he hasn't had a single drink. I pull away, keeping my voice to a whisper. "*Jack...*"

"It's okay," he whispers back, his hand massaging my hip. "Shh..."

I don't understand what's happening or why he's acting this way, but I'm not okay with it. When I open my eyes, Dean is watching us out of the corner of his eye. I pull back and stand from the recliner. "I need to use the bathroom."

I disappear down the hall, trying to collect myself, and when I return, I sit in the chair next to the couch. Jack pats his leg, calling me like a dog, but I shake my head. "I'm okay here."

He looks ready to argue, but he doesn't.

When the movie is nearly over, I look across the room to realize Jack has fallen asleep.

Dean's eyes are drilling into the television screen like it holds the answers to a pop quiz he's about to take.

"So, you really like Nashville?" I ask, interrupting one of my favorite scenes. I just need to talk to him. I can't explain it. After all this time, he still fascinates me.

He looks over briefly. "Yeah, it's not bad."

"Do you...think you'll stay there?"

He blinks. "Yeah. Maybe."

"Oh."

"What about you two? Are you staying around here after college?"

"Me and Jack?" Jack and I have talked about our future

a lot, but very vaguely and only in theory. Sort of like him mentioning the fact that we have many Christmases in our future, but never making any plans or deciding what that will look like. I guess I've never really thought about what it will actually mean for us to be together long-term. *Forever.* That word feels big and weighty. I have no idea if I want to stay living at The Hollow or even in Cody, nor do I know what Jack's plans are. Should we have discussed that by now? "I don't know."

"But you want to do something with your art, right? You'll need to go to some sort of art school."

"Maybe. Plenty of people don't go to college at all. Maybe I won't. Last Jack mentioned, he still wants to go to film school."

He nods. "Don't let him make that decision for you."

"I'm not saying I would. Whether or not I go to college, and where, it'll be my decision."

"Good."

"Great."

We turn our attention back to the television just in time for Reese Witherspoon and Vince Vaughn to kiss. My cheeks flame.

"You two seemed cozy."

We aren't looking at each other now. "I don't know why he did that."

"Don't you?"

I swallow. "We aren't usually...like that."

"Your business, not mine."

"I...got my license, by the way. Last year, obviously. I didn't know if anyone told you."

It's an abrupt change of subject, but he rolls with it. "Kill anyone yet?"

"No." I scowl, finally turning to look at him. "I'm a just-fine driver, thank you."

"You do know I've ridden in the car with you, right? Remember when you almost killed me after you got your permit?"

My jaw drops, and I adjust in my chair to sit on my legs. "There was not a scratch on you or your car."

He laughs. "Thanks to a miracle."

"Whatever. You're just jealous because I'm clearly the best driver you've ever seen."

"At Mario Kart, maybe."

"So you admit I'm better at that, too?" My eyes widen.

"Than Mom and Jack, sure."

"And you."

He chuckles. "Keep telling yourself that, Carmie." That name on his lips sends a ripple of warmth through me. Once, I hated it, but until this moment, I hadn't realized how much I missed it.

"I've missed you, you know," I say before I can chicken out.

"You don't have to say that."

"It's true."

His jaw is slack as he turns to look at the television. "Well, that's news to me. You never texted."

"I didn't want to bother you."

There's no response for a long time. So long, I think he may have fallen asleep, too. "You're never a bother, Carmen. You know that."

"I'm sure you're off in Nashville with all the cool college girls. You don't want to hear from me." I hate the self-deprecating, pathetic tone to my voice.

"There are no other girls, Carmen. No girls," he corrects himself, removing the *other*. Because there's not me either. The change sends me spiraling. *What does that mean? Why did he say it like that at first? On instinct...*

"I can see the gears turning," he says plainly. "Just stop. I only meant that I'm not seeing anyone. You can text me anytime you want. If I'm not busy kicking someone's ass at Mario Kart, I'll text back."

I glance down at my lap, smiling to myself. "Okay."

When the movie ends, he turns off the television, bathing us in darkness. "You should wake your boyfriend up, let him walk you home."

"Can't you just take me?"

In the pitch-black room, I hear rather than see him sigh. "Is that what you want?"

"He's asleep."

"That's not what I asked. Who do you want to take you, Carmen?"

Take me. Like sex. I don't know if he said the words like that, with that implication, on purpose. "You. Please."

I hear the couch groan as he stands up, and seconds later, I feel his hand slip down the arm of the chair, find my hand, and take it. "Let's go, then."

If it's weird that he's taking my hand and leading me out of the room, he doesn't mention it. I find my shoes next to the door in the dark, my heart pounding in my ears and chest at a rapid speed. He pulls open the door softly, clearly trying to keep quiet, and a smile plays on my lips. He doesn't want Jack to wake up either.

Once we're outside, he drops my hand, and we make our way down the steps. "He's going to be mad you didn't wake him."

"He was tired. I'm only being polite."

He turns around to look at me, and I can see the expression on his face in the moonlight. There, his face is all shadows and dark angles, but still I can read the skepticism. "You weren't."

"Oh, I wasn't, hmm? And you know me so well?"

He nods. "Yeah. I do."

"Then why?"

One corner of his mouth upturns, and he shakes his head. "Nah, I'm not doing that."

"Doing what?"

"Having that conversation. Saying what you won't say out loud."

"What are you talking about?"

"Maybe we'll talk about it someday, Carmen. And maybe we won't. But it won't be up to me. You're the one with a boyfriend. You're the one dating my brother."

"You're the one who said you didn't want me." I can't believe the words, even as they leave my mouth. They're the words that have stung me somewhere deep for the past three years.

He stops in his tracks, turning back to me so swiftly he nearly smacks into me. "When did I ever say that?"

"After you kissed me."

His eyes flick up to the sky, then back down to drill into mine. "You remembered that?"

"It was my first kiss. Of course I remembered—"

"You remembered what I said after? A throwaway comment about not wanting you."

"That's not how it felt to me."

"Well, that's what it was. Let me be clear, Carmen. Regardless of what I want, regardless of the way you've driven me mad from the moment your pale, little legs walked toward me, you are his." He juts his finger toward his cabin. "You were my brother's from the moment you got here. And you were a kid." His eyes trail the length of my body. "You still are a kid."

"I'm seventeen."

"And you're his." He swallows. "Until you make it clear you aren't." His eyes dance between mine, our faces just inches apart. I can feel his breath on my lips, his heat against my skin, and all it would take is a tilt of my chin to feel his kiss again.

Is that what I want?

Honestly, my head is such a mess right now, I'm not sure of anything at all.

"I was not his from the moment I got here. I liked him, yes—"

"You more than liked him. You were crazy about him. Always giggling and blushing. And you said you wanted him that night at the dance. Before anything had ever happened between you two."

"Are you saying...you liked me?"

He scowls. "Don't act like you didn't know I felt something for you. I know you could tell. You felt whatever it was between us, even then. And you chose him."

"You'd said you didn't want me! I didn't know you were an option!"

He moves another step forward—though I don't know how it's possible—until his legs are interwoven with my thighs and his forehead and nose are pressed against mine. "And if I told you that was a lie, if I told you I wanted you right now, would it change anything?"

"I..." My chest hurts, and I try to focus on anything but his face so close to mine. I feel ready to combust. His hands climb my sides.

"Tell me the truth. When he touches you, when he kisses you, do you think of me?"

"Dean..."

His lips brush mine when he responds, just a touch and not nearly enough. "Don't say my name like that unless you're ready for me." Then he pulls away. "You have to make up your mind."

"Are you saying that's what you want? That you want...me?"

His forehead rests against mine, his eyes closed. "I'm saying it's a risk you have to take either way." All at once, he steps back, and I miss the heat of him, but there's no room for discussion as he takes me to the stairs and lets me go. "Good night, Carmen. Sweet dreams."

"Good night."

Sweet dreams. I'm not sure that isn't all this has been.

CHAPTER SEVENTEEN

PRESENT DAY

We're all still damp, though we've thrown clothes over our bathing suits, when the police arrive. It's Tye who hands over the purse to Sheriff Dunlap, explaining to him how he found it.

The sheriff puts the muddy purse inside of a paper bag.

"Will you be able to find any DNA on it?" I ask him. "Will the water have messed that up?"

"Hard to say," he admits. "Most likely, yes. Water usually washes any DNA away in a few days, but there could be something else in the bag that will help us."

"It's hers," I tell him. "I'm positive. Her aunt got it for her for her sixteenth birthday, and she never went anywhere without it."

"It could be anyone's." He dismisses me quickly. "We won't know until we get it down to the station and examine it. The bag's material has held up well, but that doesn't mean anything inside of it is still intact."

"I'm telling you, it was Shelby's. It's too big of a coincidence if not."

He gives me an exasperated nod. "Y'all sure do like to keep me busy, don't you?"

"Will you let us know as soon as you know anything?" Jill asks. "Tracy will want to know. If we found something of Shelby's..."

"You know I'll keep you posted. And, of course, we'll be reaching out to the Brewers to see if they can ID it as Shelby's. Their confirmation will save us a lot of time."

"And if it's hers?" Dean asks. "Will that reopen the investigation?"

"Officially, it's never been closed." The sheriff scratches his temple. "But yes, it would give us more reason to look into it. Her purse ending up in the water while her body is in the woods doesn't make a lick of sense to me." He clicks his tongue. "But we'll have to see. And..." He looks like he doesn't want to say the next part. "If we can connect it to Shelby, we may have to dredge the pond here." He points to it just behind us. "In case there's anything *else* to be found."

"Of course." Sam puts a hand on Jill's shoulder while my mother covers her mouth.

When he leaves, Tye follows close behind him.

"I just can't believe this..." my mom says, shuddering. "After all these years, it was in there the whole time?"

"They don't know anything yet," Sam says, trying to calm us all down. "It could be nothing."

"I know her bag," I tell him. "I promise you, it was hers."

"She could've dropped it," Jack says softly. "I mean, even if it was hers, that doesn't mean..." He can't seem to bring himself to finish his sentence. "It doesn't mean someone definitely hurt her. She could've dropped it at any point."

"It's late," Jill says with a deep breath. "We should all get to bed. It's chilly, and poor Carmen is shivering." She's right, though I hadn't noticed I was so cold until now. "We'll deal with this tomorrow." She looks on the verge of breaking down as they all disappear down the drive and out through the gate.

"She's right. Come on. Let's get you inside." Dean puts a hand behind my back and leads me toward the stairs.

"I've got her," Jack says, trying to swap his arm for Dean's.

"Seems like you've got your hands full," Dean says, pointing toward Jack's phone, which is lighting up in his hand. From here, I can see the name Alissa on his screen. Jack ignores the call, and together, they lead me up the stairs.

Inside, I leave the boys in the living room and change out of my wet swimming suit into something warm. It's only when I'm changed and dried off that I realize the shaking isn't coming from my coldness, but rather something else entirely. Adrenaline and fear over this discovery are doing a number on my body, making me feel nauseous. It's all too real. Though this is what I wanted, to finally know the truth, the possibility of it is terrifying.

I walk out of my bedroom and into the hall in time to hear a whispered conversation between the men.

"It's just like back then, Jack."

"You have no idea what you're talking about."

"Don't I?"

"She's—"

"Right here," I interrupt. "And not in need of anyone arguing tonight. I'm fine, and I'm ready for bed." I'm on edge, my body physically shaking from adrenaline. What I want more than anything else is to go to my mom, to have her hold me and tell me everything is going to be okay. That I'm safe when I feel anything but. It's selfish to ask that of her when I know she's trying to help April's mother, and that is more important than my own silly fears.

"Do you want us to stay with you?" Jack offers.

"No," I say firmly. The last thing I want is to fall apart in front of Jack and Dean. If I can't have my mom right now, I just want to be alone. "I'm okay. You guys should go home and get some rest. I'll see you in the morning." I can barely hold it together as I say the words. I'm seconds from cracking open, splitting at the rib cage and letting all of my ugly fears and anxieties come spilling out.

They exchange a worried look, and for a brief

moment, I worry they'll argue with me. I won't survive it if they do. Everything from that night is ricocheting through my mind.

Every bloody memory.

Every second of the heartbreak.

I'm reliving the nightmare in my head, trying to hold it together long enough to spare myself the embarrassment of them seeing me lose it, like I did so often after I left before.

To my great relief, they eventually accept my answer and make their way toward the door. Maybe they can see that I'm mere seconds from breaking down and are leaving to spare my pride. Either way, I'm thankful.

My heart stalls and tears prick my eyes, threatening to fall at any second when Dean stops and hangs back, waiting for Jack to step outside before he turns to me.

"About tonight—" he says, but I hold up a hand to stop him.

"I really can't talk about it. We'd all had too much to drink, and we got carried away. We're lucky we didn't cross a line we'd regret in the morning." My voice is breathless, panicked. I know he has to hear it, but I silently beg him not to acknowledge it.

"Are you going to be okay?"

"Yes." It comes out as a squeak.

He clearly wants to say something else, but eventually, he nods. "Lock the door, okay?"

"I will," I promise.

"Call if you need anything. I'll be up. You won't be bothering me."

"I'm fine. Just tired."

"I can be back over here in a second."

"Good night, Dean."

With that, I shut them outside of the cabin and turn the dead bolt. Then I collapse on the ground and allow myself to split open, everything from that night replaying in my mind with sudden urgency. Every shattered piece of my heart, every ounce of the terror and devastation, begs to be remembered, demands to be felt.

For once, I don't have the strength to fight it.

The pain overwhelms me, pouring out of my eyes in the form of tears, painting my cheeks with the harrowing memories of the night I've tried so desperately to forget.

CHAPTER EIGHTEEN

BEFORE — AGE 17

I'm lying on Jack's bed with my head hanging over the side while he plays a video game when a text comes through. I'm expecting it to be from Shelby, so I'm shocked to see Dean's name on the screen.

> Quick—I need the name of a Taylor Swift song.

> The Story of Us

I've had that one on repeat lately.

"What's Shelby up to?" Jack asks, clearly assuming that's who I'm talking to.

"I haven't heard from her yet today. She's supposed to be coming over later once she's awake."

I think back to our conversation last night, when I finally told her about what happened with Dean over Christmas break, and she gave me the most Shelby-advice there is. *There are only two things you can do, sister: forget about everyone else and do what makes you happy,* or *put them in an arena and watch them fight to the death. Honestly, I'll support it either way.*

Dean's response comes in quickly.

> Thanks.

> Always happy to be of assistance during Taylor Swift related emergencies

I can practically see him smiling and quickly send another message.

> Can I ask why you needed to know, or is it a top secret spy sort of thing?

I don't notice the music on the television has stopped until I look down and realize Jack is staring at me. "What are you smiling about, then?" He gazes down at my phone.

"Oh. Your brother." I drop the phone casually.

"You're texting my brother?" His brows draw down.

"Sort of. He asked me about a song."

He nods slowly. "Oh. Okay."

"Is that weird for you?" I don't ask if he's okay with it because I'm not sure it's a behavior I'm willing to change if he's not. Dean and I haven't spoken a single time about what happened that night. We went through the rest of his visit like nothing happened at all—and I guess if I think about it, nothing really did. But I make a point to text him a few times a month now, and he does the same.

We don't talk about Jack either, but for the record, there's nothing flirty happening. Dean is a world away, and Jack is here. I can't make decisions based on one night and a whirlwind of confusing emotions. Jack is whom I've wanted since I moved here. He's kind to me. Funny. Gentle. We're the same age, and things with us are just...easy. He's my best friend.

Still, when the next text comes in from Dean, I have to fight against checking it while waiting for Jack to answer.

"No, it's not weird. It's just Dean." He shrugs. "The two of you seem like you can't stand each other most of the time. Weird he'd be texting you, I guess."

"We're friends," I say defensively. "And he texts me sometimes." I'm not sure why his lack of concern bothers me so much, but it does. Shouldn't he be at least a little bit jealous?

"Okay." He shrugs one shoulder and turns back to the TV. I check my phone.

Trivia night.

It's noon

Well trivia day doesn't have the same ring to it

> Lol, and it was easier to text me than just look it up?

> Looking it up would be cheating.

> And texting me isn't?

> Depends on who you ask, I guess.

I swallow, feeling the weight of his answer. I don't think it's what he meant, but still...the question lingers in my mind. Am I cheating on Jack? Not physically, at least. And we haven't crossed any sort of line in our messages either. They're all completely innocent, even though nothing feels innocent with Dean anymore.

But I still don't know that I want to leave Jack. I care about him, and Dean is...a mess. He's a serial dater who never stays with anyone long. I'm not foolish enough to think it would be any different with me.

Jack is looking at me again with a strange expression.

"Don't be jealous," I tease, tossing my phone down.

"I'm not," he says, and there's truly not a hint of jealousy in his voice. "I mean, it's Dean. It's not like he'd be interested in you."

My body goes cold, and I sit up on the bed. "Excuse me?"

"I don't mean it like that." He pauses his game, turning his attention to me. "It's just...well, you've seen the girls that Dean dates. He has a type. He's not into you."

"You're saying, what? I'm not...pretty enough for him?"

"No." He jumps up on the bed with me, rushing to put a balm on the wound he's made. "You're beautiful, Carmen. You know that. It's just you're way too good for him. Too smart and funny. He tends to pick women for their...you know, the way they look and not their personality."

"Still waiting for the part where you aren't calling me too ugly to date your brother." The sting of his words burns my skin, and I'm shaking as I stare at him.

"I'm not calling you ugly." He leans in to kiss me, but I pull away. "You're stunning. Dean just isn't good enough for you. That's all I'm saying. You two would never work."

"I'm not sure you hear yourself right now."

He scoffs. "Why? Do you *want* to date Dean or something?"

"Of course not. I—"

"Then why are we even having this argument? It doesn't matter." He turns the TV off. "I'm bored. Do you want to go down to the lake?"

I don't feel like doing anything except processing what just happened, honestly, but I also don't want to talk about it, so I slip my shoes on and follow him out of the house and down toward the water.

When we're there, I turn to him. "Where are we going, Jack?"

"Right here," he says simply, gesturing toward the

water. "Unless you want to rent a boat or something. We could go to the office and—"

"I mean *us*. You and me. Are we...I mean, is this serious for you?"

He cocks his head to the side. "We've been dating for two years. How can you even ask me that?"

"Because...I mean, it's the summer before our senior year. We have to start thinking about the future, right? Not marriage or anything, but colleges. Mom and I have already been looking at applications and picking between schools. We haven't even talked about where we want to go or if we want to try to apply at the same schools. We've...we've been together for over two years, yes, but some days—*most* days, if I'm honest—it feels like we're still exactly who we were when we were friends. We kiss or whatever, but nothing else has changed between us."

"And that's a bad thing?"

"No, not bad. I guess I just...I want to know where you think this is going. If I go away to school, are you going to come with me? Should we be trying to find schools that offer both our majors?"

He twists his lips. "You've never mentioned leaving before."

I suck in a deep breath. The hurt on his face is evident, and it kills me. This could wait a few days, a few weeks maybe, but the conversation has to happen, and if he won't initiate it, I will. "I'm mentioning it now."

"I never planned to leave Cody, no. I doubt I will go

to college, but maybe I'll go to a trade school or something."

"I thought you wanted to be a director."

He shakes his head. "That's kid stuff. I like movies, but I'd never make it as a director, and I have zero desire to move to LA. Now that I'm older, I've realized I'll probably just stay around here and take over The Hollow for my parents."

"Oh. I wish you'd told me. That feels like a big decision you made without me."

"Is it a problem? I didn't realize we were talking about going anywhere. I wasn't changing anything. Seems like you're the one making big decisions without telling me."

"Of course it's not a problem," I say quickly. "You know I don't care what you do. I don't mean that you have to go to college or anything like that. I just...I guess I need to know if...for the four years I'll need to go, would you come with me?"

"Come where? Why would you need to leave? There are plenty of schools around here."

"I've..." I look down at my feet, the image of the application currently on my computer screen flashing through my mind. "I've been thinking of applying to Nashville. To Vanderbilt like Dean."

"You mean *with* Dean?" His face contorts with its first signs of anger.

"I mean *with* you, if you'll come."

"Why there? Because of him?"

"No," I insist. "But he seems to like it there, which helps, yes. He could show us around. It would be nice to know someone there—"

"We know people *here*. We wouldn't need to be shown around—"

"It's not just that. Mrs. Whitley went there. We were talking about it the other day in art. She mentioned how good the programs are."

"Yeah, but she's an art *teacher*. Not an artist. It's not the same as what you want to do."

"I haven't made up my mind—"

"Really? Because it sort of sounds like you have."

"I don't even know if I'll get in. I'm just applying—"

"So you *are* applying? Oh, great. Because two seconds ago, you were just thinking of applying." He runs a hand over his forehead, stepping back. "Are you doing this to get back at me because I said Dean would never want you?"

"What?" I can't believe he just said that.

"Well? Are you?"

"Of course not! I would never decide my future because I'm angry with you."

"Well, the timing just seems awfully convenient, if I'm being honest."

I scoff. "I don't understand what the problem is, Jack. I'm asking you to go with me. I'm not trying to get back at you."

"And I'm saying no." He shakes his head. "I'm saying no, Carmen. There are plenty of schools here. Stay here."

"So if I decide to go, that's just it?" Tears prick my eyes suddenly. "Are we breaking up? Is that what this is?"

His voice is softer this time when he speaks. "Is that what you want?"

"Of course not." I'm not sure what my life looks like without Jack. Despite whatever is going on with Dean and me, I don't want to find out.

"We could do long-distance," he offers. "It's just four years, and you could come home for breaks."

"Okay." I sniffle, trying not to break down. I can't help noticing he didn't offer to visit me.

"We still have a year," he says. "And you might not even get in."

I nod, but I no longer feel like being here. I wish I'd never brought any of this up. "I...um, I think I'm going to go. Shelby should be here soon." I desperately need to talk to my friend. It's painful to realize that phrase used to mean Jack.

"Don't do that." He holds out a hand to stop me, but I shake my head. "I don't want to fight with you. You just caught me off guard."

"I'm okay. We're okay. I just need a minute." I disappear back to my cabin, my head swimming with emotions.

CHAPTER NINETEEN

PRESENT DAY

When I wake up the next morning, my chest hurts from crying, and my eyes are dry and red. My body is sore from the sobs that kept me up so late, but I know most of the pain is emotional, not physical. I can't believe everything that happened. Not only with the missing girl and the purse and all the things that point to there being a connection between the past and present, but also the heaviness of what nearly happened with Dean.

Thinking back over it, it all feels like a dream. One I'm still not ready to face, though if there's one thing I've learned, it's that I can't put off facing reality any longer, or I will literally overflow. I can't deal with another night like last night.

Time to be a grown-up.

So, I make a cup of coffee while I get ready, and when I'm done, I cross over the grass between our cabins, hoping I'll catch the men still home.

Dean answers the door relatively quickly, dressed for the day, but not yet gone.

"Is Jack here?"

His eyes widen, then narrow. "Uh, yeah. Yeah, he's here."

"I need to talk to you both."

"Okay." He leans toward the hall. "Jack! Get out here." There's a look of confusion and worry on his face as he steps back and allows me into the house. "Is everything okay?"

"I don't know," I admit. "I want to know why you guys were arguing last night."

Jack walks into the room, also dressed for work, a bowl of cereal in his hands, one cheek full.

Dean squares his stance. "We shouldn't have been arguing. It was just a stressful night."

"You said it was *just like back then*." I press my lips together, studying him. "What did you mean by that?"

"We don't have to get into this," Dean says on a breath.

"No, Dean, go ahead. Enlighten us." Jack pins him with a hard glare, and it's only then that I realize they both look exhausted. Is it possible they were up arguing over this after they went home?

"What did you mean?" I ask him. "Please."

He sighs, looking at Jack, then back at me. "I just don't think Jack appreciates you. The fact that he lied to you about Alissa pisses me off. The fact that, even last night, he was trying to act like a hero—telling me to go home, that he had it from there—and the fact that you were buying it."

"Buying it?" I demand. "I hardly spoke to Jack!"

He sucks his lips into his mouth, weighing his words. When he speaks again, it's with precision. "I just think that there were plenty of people back then who would've been grateful to be with you, and he took it for granted. Just like he's doing now. Holding you on a line while you wait for him to make up his mind. I can't watch it happen again."

"Plenty of people..." Jack scoffs, looking away. "And by that, who do you mean, exactly, Dean? *You?*"

Dean's eyes narrow. "Come on, man. Don't make me say it. It's not about me. It's about treating her like she deserves."

Jack's got a cocky look to him now; he sets his feet wider apart, his tongue presses against his jaw. "No, I want to hear you say it. I want to hear you tell me you would have treated her better."

Dean waves a hand in the air. "A fucking paper bag would've treated her better."

"Guys, stop!" I shout, cutting off the argument before it can really begin. "I just want to say..." I put a hand on my chest, catching my breath. "I'm an adult now. And despite the fact that this arguing, everything with Shelby and the missing girl...despite the fact that it makes me want to run away, I'm not going to. I have to be stronger than that this time. I don't need you—either of you—protecting me or fighting over me or trying to tell me how I feel or what I need. Nothing is like it was before, okay? Because I'm not who I was. I'm not waiting for you, Jack. Okay? I'm not. I'm happy to be your friend, but I didn't come back for you." I look at Dean, who's clearly waiting and terrified over what I'm going to say. "And I didn't come back for you either. I'm here for me. For my mom. And everything that's happened has just muddled it. But right now we need to focus on finding out the truth about that night. Finding out what happened to Shelby and what happened to April."

"Agreed," Dean mumbles.

"Yeah." Jack scratches the back of his neck. "Okay."

With that, I turn and march out of the cabin.

CHAPTER TWENTY

BEFORE — AGE 18

After the graduation ceremony ends, I bustle through the crowd of students dressed identical to me. Shelby finds me and wraps her arms around my waist, picking me up.

She giggles loudly. "We did it! We did it! We're officially adults! Can you believe it?"

"It still doesn't feel real," I admit.

"Got your bags packed yet? Have you changed your mind?" She beams. Shelby has been trying to convince me to travel around the country with her for the next year visiting all of the national parks.

"Sorry, the answer's still no. But when you come through Nashville, let me know. You can stay with me."

She sighs. "Alright, I guess that'll be okay."

My chest tightens at the thought of not seeing her again. "I'm going to miss you. I can't believe I might not see you again. Are you coming to the party tonight?"

Her jaw drops. "Duh. Like I would be anywhere else."

"Good. I'll see you tonight, okay? We'll save all the sappy goodbyes for then, deal? Make sure you find me."

"Well, of course." She hugs me again, and when we pull away, both of us have tear-filled eyes. "And just so you know, I'm going to send you, like, so many pictures you'll have no choice but to block my number or drop out of college and come join me. We're not going to fade apart. I won't let it happen."

"I hope not." I hug her a final time and wave goodbye, feeling as if I'm saying goodbye to a piece of myself. It catches me by surprise that I'm finding it harder to leave her than it was to leave my friends in Atlanta. Maybe because I'm not just saying goodbye to one person, but a whole chapter of my life.

Jack's hands slip around my waist from behind, and I spin around. "Hey, graduate."

"Hey, graduate," I repeat, playing with his tassel. "Can you believe it?"

"I can't believe they let me on the stage, to be honest. I think Mr. Jones passed me so he wouldn't have to deal with my inability to remember dates ever again."

I laugh. "Have you seen our parents?"

"They were around here somewhere, yeah. I saw Mom earlier talking to Mrs. Kirkland. Let's go find them." He takes my hand and leads me through the crowd carefully, stopping every so often to let another group of people pass until we see our window to dart forward.

When we finally find our parents, there's not a dry eye in the house.

"I thought it was supposed to get easier with the second kid," Jill whispers, wiping her eyes as she hugs Jack. "That's what they told us, isn't it?" She swats Sam, who nods stoically.

"Proud of you, kids. Both of you."

Mom hugs Jack first, then me, swaying us side to side. "*Te quiero mucho, mi niñita. Tu papá te está mirando desde el cielo y está muy orgulloso.*"

"I love you too, Mama."

She pulls back, cupping my cheeks. "He would be *so* proud." Her dark eyes line with fat tears, and her chin quivers. "Just like I am."

I laugh through tears of my own. "Okay, well, it's not a Nobel Prize. It's just a high school graduation."

She tuts, putting a finger to my lips. "It's enough. It's everything, *mija*."

In her eyes, I see what she means. Not so long ago, it felt like our life was falling apart, yet here, this moment, proves it didn't. Though we're on a new path, some destinations stay the same. Some of this was always meant to be, and in some strange way, it grounds us to a reality where Dad once existed. In another life, he would be with us now. Hugging me, teasing me, cheering me on.

She pats my chest. "He's right here. Always. *Always.*"

I don't know how she manages to do that—read my mind.

I hug her again to hide my tears. Tomorrow, I'll leave her. As of tomorrow, I won't live under the same roof as my mother for the first time in my eighteen years of life. After tomorrow, *she'll* be alone for the first time in even longer. Looking at Jill, Sam, and Jack, I've never been so grateful for them. Without them, I'm not sure I'd feel safe moving away. I wouldn't shake the guilt of leaving her. At least this way, she's among friends.

Eventually, Jack and I make our way around the gymnasium, saying congratulations to our friends and classmates and reminiscing and giving well wishes to the ones who won't make it to the party tonight. When we're both exhausted and ready to leave, we find our families again, who are intermingled with other parents, laughing through their own sets of teary eyes.

"We're heading home," Jack says as we make our way out the door.

When we get into his car, he starts it up and looks over at me. "Last time we ever have to walk in or out of those doors."

I throw my hands into the air. "Freedom!"

He laughs and pulls us out of the parking lot. I know we're both trying not to think about the fact that we're officially in countdown mode to goodbye. The guilt of that knowledge, and knowing that it's entirely my fault and I could change it in a second, is heavy.

Jack has been gracious with me since the fight. He

celebrated with our families when I was accepted into Vanderbilt and went with my mom and me when we shopped for things to fill my new apartment.

He hasn't tried to make me feel guilty—though it wouldn't be hard to do—even during our most emotional moments. In fact, nothing at all has changed between us. Even with the impending goodbye, he's still my closest friend.

When we get home, Jack and I make our way to our respective houses to change into more comfortable clothes for the party. I choose a simple dress and flats, touch up my makeup, and then leave the house for Jack's.

The air is still warm, but the sun has tucked itself behind a few clouds, making the day look gloomier than it should. It reflects the bittersweet feeling of graduation, in a way.

Jack's just leaving his house, too, and I wait for him at the bottom of the stairs. He holds out his hand, taking mine and kissing my knuckles. "You ready?"

"As ever," I say, though in truth, I'm not and never will be.

We walk slowly toward cabin ten. It'll be at least an hour before anyone arrives, so we're in no hurry at all. The walk is heavy with the weight of knowing it will be our last for a while.

Like the last day of school, suddenly everything that I once easily overlooked or even annoyed me is something interesting, something I'll miss. Like the way the dirt from the road clings to my shoes. Once, I hated it. Now, it's strange the way it makes me feel at home.

The walk once made my legs tired. It's easily a mile and a half from our cabins to the campground, and cabin ten is in the back, almost directly across from the gate that leads to cabins fifteen and sixteen, where Jack and I like to hang out when no one is staying there.

By the time we reach the cabin, I realize we've walked entirely in silence, clearly both lost in thought. There's a thin sheen of sweat across my forehead, and I'm sure my makeup is beginning to smear.

Strangely, I don't care.

Everything feels okay right now. Maybe it's the promise of tomorrow or the strong desire not to mess things up today, this one last perfect day before everything changes, but I can't bring myself to get upset over anything right now.

Our parents spent the day getting the cabin ready for our party, so the food and drinks are already here and just have to be pulled out of the refrigerator and heated up. There were several jokes made about getting a two-for-one deal thanks to both of us graduating the same year, so there's a larger guest list and amount of food than at Dean's.

Also, the parents decided as a group that since their 'babies are all grown up,' they deserved a night out on the town. I can't decide if it's because they want the freedom to be sad without making us feel bad, or if they're genuinely relieved to finally be done with the whole parenting thing.

I think, if I ever have kids, the day they graduate will feel like an accomplishment for me as much as it does them. It'll mean I did something right, I hope.

As Jack and I pull the food out of the fridge and place it on the table, heating up the random platters and bowls of food in the microwave, I can't help thinking of Dean's party. It feels weird with him not being here. He texted me this morning to say congratulations, but that he had finals this week and couldn't make it back.

I understood, of course, and Sam and Jill had already let us know that was the case, but still. As of the last few years, Dean has been present for all the big moments. Not having him here for this one feels...empty, I guess. Like my dad. There's a them-shaped hole in this day, and it makes me sad that—at least in regard to my dad—it will always be that way.

I try not to think about it as I set the platter of meats and cheeses out, and Jack empties the first few boxes of drinks into a cooler, which he takes into the living room.

A few of his friends are bringing alcohol, but we want to wait until our parents are definitely gone for the night for that. Honestly, I'm not sure they'll care, but it's better to be safe than sorry.

He grabs a Cheerwine and hands me a Sprite. "Last big party?"

"Well, hopefully not the last."

He smiles with one corner of his mouth. "Here's to tonight. And to never forgetting how this moment feels."

I tap my can to his. We're on the cusp of everything. Somehow, I hope he's right. I never want to forget a second of it.

———

By nine, the party is going strong. Most of our class is here, including Shelby, who is currently riding on Colton's back as he darts through the living room with his tie tied around his head.

Alissa and her friends are here, too, which surprised me at first until I realized ours turned out to be the biggest graduation party in town.

Jack reappears to find me on the couch, his cheeks flushed because of the alcohol. He plops down next to me, grinning from ear to ear.

"What are you up to?"

He chuckles. "Nothing. I'm just happy to see you."

"You've seen me all day."

He taps my nose. "Not enough."

"Well, I'm happy to see you too, weirdo."

"Prove it." He winks.

"How would you like me to prove it?" I stare at him skeptically.

"Kiss me." He puckers his lips, and I lean forward and kiss them.

"Happy now?"

Instead of answering, he sighs and rests his head against the back of the couch.

"What's the matter?"

He sighs again, and this time when he speaks, his voice is soft. Sad. "I'm just really going to miss you."

I put a hand on his arm. "I'm going to miss you, too." Tears burn my eyes with the truth and sadness of it all. This is our last night together until winter break. I have no idea what will happen to us. For now, we plan to try to make the long-distance thing work, but it's clear we both have our doubts. Maybe this is a huge mistake. Maybe I shouldn't ruin a good thing. I could stay here, and nothing would have to change.

He swallows and looks up at me with glassy eyes. "Come with me."

"Okay." I don't question it for a second. He barely has to ask. I follow his lead as he stands and takes my hand, leading me down the hallway and toward a bedroom. Once we're inside, he shuts the door, bathing us in darkness.

"What are you do—"

His lips crash into mine, interrupting my sentence. I return his kiss with equal fervor. My hands lift, slipping around his neck and holding the back of his head. His palms slide down my sides and he picks me up with ease. He leans his body against mine, pressing me against the wall. My mind is dizzy with this moment, and the alcohol, and the surge of desire pulsing through me.

His hands grip me tightly, like if he just holds me

here, I might never leave. The next second, I'm on the ground, and he's pulling me farther into the room. We stop when I hear him bump into what must be the bed, and then he's kissing me again, spinning us around. When he lies down, his kisses slow, becoming softer and more meaningful.

My heart pounds in my chest over how much I love him and will miss him. I want this moment, these kisses, to tell him everything I can't put into words.

He curls his body into me, and I feel the hardness of him everywhere. This isn't the closest Jack and I have come to having sex, but it's happening more frequently now. To be fair, for most of our relationship, it was rare we had a moment alone. Conveniently, one of our parents always seemed to be walking into the room or house unannounced to check this or grab that. And with them all working where we lived, the opportunity had never presented itself.

We'd gone on dates, sure, but I wasn't interested in losing my virginity in the back seat of his car or outside in the woods, and neither was he. We wanted it to be special. Right. We said when the time came, we'd have a conversation about it. Prepare precautions.

As his hand slips under my dress, his kisses grow faster, and he trails them down my neck. As he does, I wonder if he's forgotten that plan.

His hand slides up my inner thigh, tracing the outline of my panties, and I freeze. I pull back. "Jack, wait."

He leans in, trying and failing to land another kiss. "I don't want to wait anymore," he says. "Come on. We have the whole night to ourselves."

Suddenly, he doesn't sound so drunk.

"No," I tell him firmly. "Not like this. You don't have protection. We haven't—"

"I do," he corrects me, shoving his hand into his pocket. I hear the crinkle of the foil package.

"We didn't talk about this." I prop myself up on my elbows.

"I know. I just thought...it's your last night. It's now or never."

His words are like a hit to the funny bone. I sit up straighter. "No. This...it feels too much like you're saying goodbye. Like you're doing it to...I don't know, to claim me or something. Now or never?" I groan, covering my face with my hands.

He speaks faster. "I just meant that this is the last time I'll be alone with you for a while. We've waited all this time for it to be special. What could be more special than this? Graduation night."

"Oh, yeah. With all our friends just outside the door." I stand, adjusting my dress. "No, Jack." I'm crying now, and I don't fully understand why. "This feels like an ending, and it shouldn't be like this. Come see me in Nashville, prove to me this can still work, and then... maybe. But not now."

"I didn't realize you had such a plan laid out."

"Clearly, you're the one with the plan I wasn't made aware of."

"It was our first night alone. Our parents took off. What else did you think was going to happen?"

I set my jaw. "You did not just say that."

He grabs my arm. "Wait, it came out wrong!"

"I'm not doing this tonight, Jack. I'm not sleeping with you because you think you're losing me."

"Well, am I right in thinking that?" he shouts after me.

I want to tell him no, to say it's ridiculous, but I'm angry. I'm so angry I could combust. "We'll talk about this tomorrow."

And then, without another word, I walk out of the room, past all of my friends, and go home. All alone.

CHAPTER TWENTY-ONE

PRESENT DAY

I spend most of my morning in the office with Mom and Jill. Though they adamantly refuse to let me help with any actual work, I get away with hanging out in the office, listening to their gossip, and filling them in on life in the city.

We're trying aimlessly to fill the void that exists because April is still missing, and we have yet to get another update from the police, when we hear the little chime over the door, letting us know someone has come into the office.

"Be right with you!" Jill calls, standing up from her desk.

"It's me, Jill." I'd recognize Sheriff Dunlap's dry voice anywhere.

"Robbie?"

Now we're all on our feet, making our way out into the hallway. When I see him, I know something terrible

212

has happened. "Good and bad news," he says. "Daniel's talking to Ms. Moore now, but I wanted to give you a heads up that we found her daughter. April."

"Is she...please tell me she's not..." Jill whispers, clearly afraid to put our greatest fear into words.

"No." He shakes his head. "She's alive and okay. She was in the woods walking toward town. Alexander Allen happened to catch her on his trail cam and called it in. She was mostly clean and appeared unharmed, but she's at the hospital now getting checked out just to be safe. Understandably, she had a few abrasions on her arms and legs, likely from the woods, but we want to be sure."

"Of course." She nods, clutching her chest. "I'm so glad you found her."

Mom whispers a prayer under her breath, something I recognize after years of hearing it.

"There's bad news, too," the sheriff reminds us.

"And that is?"

He folds his hands together in front of his round belly, squaring his shoulders. "The bag the kids found in the water last night has been confirmed to have belonged to Shelby Brewer. At this point, I'm going to have to get the state police involved again. There's a chance we'll be dredging the pond. You may have to shut down Hunter's Hollow for a day or two if it comes to that."

She puffs out a breath. "Well, we'll do whatever we have to do. Just like before. Do you really think there could be something found? Poor Tracy. She never got answers for what happened. This will just devastate her all over again."

He shuffles his feet. "There's nothing any of us want more than to get Tracy Brewer some answers about her daughter, but I don't think the state boys will want to do anything if I'm being totally honest. It's a decade-old case with very little to go on, and even with the purse being found, any DNA or evidence is long gone. Nearly everything in the bag had completely disintegrated. But they'll have to be notified since the investigation was handed over to them, and it'll be up to them where we go from here."

After the sheriff leaves, Mom and Jill call Sam to come to the office so they can tell him what we've learned. Taking it as my cue, I slip out and head back toward my cabin. My heart is so light knowing that at least April has been found.

Whatever was happening, it wasn't related to Shelby, and that makes me happier than I've been in what feels like ages.

When I see Jack walking up ahead, I put my head down, pretending to be studying the plants along the path in a way that would make you think I had a degree in botany. No one has ever looked at plants harder than I currently am, but it does no good.

Jack makes a beeline for me. "Carmen, can we talk?"

I pretend I hadn't seen him and look up as if I'm shocked. "Did you hear they found April?"

"Yeah, I was over there while Daniel was telling her

mom. They just left for the hospital to go and see her. I'm glad she's okay."

I nod, staring at him as I wait for him to say more.

"Can we talk?" he asks again.

"We are talking."

"I mean in private." He waves me over toward the woods behind the cabins, and I follow.

"Okay. What's up?"

When we're far enough away from the main path that we won't be easily overheard, he turns to me. "What Dean said last night—and this morning—it got me thinking."

"Okay..."

"I didn't deserve you back then. I tried to. I really did. I cared about you, but I was also scared, and I let my fear control me. I..." He bounces his hand in the air, palm side up, staring down at it. "I don't want to do that anymore. I want to be honest with you."

"About what?"

"I told Alissa I don't want to get back together."

My chest chills. "Oh?"

"Because...because I'm in love with you, Carmen. I was back then, and I still am. I never fell out of love with you."

I bite down on my inner lip. For years, I've waited to hear these words from him, but now they just feel empty. "You broke my heart, Jack."

"I know."

"No, you don't know. You don't know all of it. You

didn't see who I was when I moved to Atlanta. You don't know how badly you screwed me up and for how long. I'm finally in a good place again. Finally. I had to fight for that."

"I'm sorry. I was so messed up and confused back then. I was hurt, too, but it's no excuse."

"I thought I wanted to come back here and drag all of this up and demand answers for things that don't truly matter anymore, but I just...don't. I'm tired of this, Jack. Of letting you toy with my emotions and of letting myself feel this way. I deserve better."

"I know you do. I want to be better for you. I do."

"You made me feel like I wasn't good enough." To my surprise, I'm not crying as I say the words, painful as they are. I've done all my crying over him, and now I'm just firm in where we stand. "Like I was never good enough. And for all I know, you're only saying this now because you think Dean wants me, too."

"That's not it at all. You were good enough. You *are*. You're everything. I don't care about Dean. This is about us."

"For now, maybe. But I'm sorry...I just can't. I don't want to." I step forward and kiss his cheek.

"I love you."

"I wish that were enough, but Jack, it just isn't. I'm sorry." And then I walk away without a single regret. I feel clean for the first time in so long, like I've finally broken his grasp on me.

CHAPTER TWENTY-TWO

BEFORE — AGE 18

Jack doesn't come with us to drop me off at my new apartment. I don't ask him, and he doesn't reach out, so when my mom asks where he is that morning before we leave, I tell her I don't think he's feeling well.

I think she assumes he's hungover after our party last night, but she's too polite to ask. The drive to Nashville is about eight hours long and completely scenic, with picturesque mountains and winding roads. It's like something you'd see in a movie, the mountains all covered in fog, sun shining brightly, reflecting off yet another body of water as we pass over it.

Mom's oddly calm this morning. No tears yet. She packed my favorite candy like when I was a kid and would go on a road trip with both of my parents. It was a rule that we'd stop at the first gas station we saw, and I could get as much as I could carry in my arms. I always tried to test my limits, carrying a little bit more than I should've until something inevitably dropped from my hands, and Dad scooped it up and claimed it was just what he wanted. Then, in the car, he magically changed his mind and asked if I wanted it instead.

While there's no gas station stop this time, Mom has a bag full of all my favorites—sour gummy worms, chocolate-covered raisins, Swedish Fish, and hot buffalo wing pretzel pieces. As we drive, I tear into each of the packages like little scraps of my childhood. Next to me, Mom has a bag of dark chocolate pretzels that she's grazing on.

When a song comes on that I like, I turn it up, and the two of us sing it at the top of our lungs. It's been so long since we were like this, and it makes me sad to think we should've been all along. I hate the child I was who was angry with my mom for moving us to Hunter's Hollow. In hindsight, I know she was doing her best.

My world was so small then. I had no concept of life outside of my home and my city, no idea how life would or could go on without my dad or my friends. I get it now.

"Mom?" I say after the song ends, and I've turned the radio back to a normal volume.

"Yeah?" She looks over at me briefly.

"I'm really glad we moved to Hunter's Hollow. I know I was a brat about it in the beginning, but...I just wanted you to know I stopped being mad about the move a long time ago."

Her chin draws up, pushing her lips into a sad smile.

"I'm glad we did, too. And you weren't a brat. You were hurting. We both were."

"Are you...I mean, are you happy now? Are things okay for you?"

She reaches across the console and squeezes my hand just once. "Yes, *mija*. I'm happy. Hunter's Hollow has been good to me too, you know. Jill and Sam have given me a support system when I needed it, but also the freedom to feel like we're on our own when I didn't. Jack and Dean became your friends. You built a life there. We built a home. It's everything I could've asked for when we moved there, everything I hoped would happen."

"Me too." It's all I can manage to say. I never imagined what the move to Hunter's Hollow would mean for my life, but it's been the best thing to ever happen to me. Of that much, I'm sure.

When we get to Nashville, we follow the GPS toward the part of the city called West End and navigate our way to my new apartment building. When it comes into view, it's taller than I expected, towering over the city in a way that feels intimidating. My room is on the sixth floor, so Mom and I load up the few boxes I have onto a rolling cart we brought and head for the door to meet my leasing consultant.

With just a few more trips, the entirety of my belongings and furniture sits on the floor of my new apartment. The place is small, but it feels positively cavernous as it sits empty. It's a one-bedroom, as Mom and I both agreed we'd feel better about me not having a roommate. We're using some of Dad's life insurance mixed with savings from the sale of the house that Mom had put back to help me until I can get a job here.

We walk through the apartment, musing about what can go where and imagining what my life will look like in this tiny space.

"Is it going to be alright?" Mom asks, and though I'm not sure if she means this place or life in general, I nod.

"It's going to be perfect." I fake the confidence I certainly don't feel as she hugs me, tears finally gleaming in her eyes.

"Do you need me to stay with you?" she offers, drying her cheeks. "I could stay the first night."

"You need to get back, Mom." We both know the longer she stays, the harder it will be to say goodbye. And while I could let her stay—we could camp out on the living room floor and pretend none of this is happening —it is happening, and I need her to be gone so I can accept it and move forward.

Her face wrinkles with sadness, and I notice the lines around her eyes for what feels like the first time. In my mind, my mom will always be as young as she ever was, but every once in a while, I'm hit with a stark reminder that time is passing whether we like it or not. A reminder that someday I'm going to lose her, too.

She gives me a hug, holding on for so long it feels like we may never let go, and when she pulls back, she touches my cheek and whispers, "Go change the world, *mija*."

"I love you, Mama." Both of our voices are choked with tears as she kisses my cheek.

"I'm just a phone call away. You call me, anytime. At least once a week. And don't worry about money, at least not right now. I'm here to help. I'll help you get a car as soon as you find a job, but it has to be a good job. No shaking your tatas around for the boys, you hear me?"

I chuckle. "Yes."

"Make us proud. Both of us." She kisses her fingers and points toward the sky, then touches her chest.

"I'll do my best."

With that, we walk toward the door and say our final goodbyes. It feels like I'll never see her again, and my chest aches with sadness like I've never felt. The moment the door closes, it's as if I've been marooned on an island, left completely and utterly alone.

I walk to the window with my vision blurred from tears and watch for her to exit the building. She does eventually, walking too slowly. When she reaches her car, she looks back up at the building, shielding her eyes from the sun. I press my hands on the glass of the window, feeling like a child who's been left at daycare watching her mom—the one piece of safety she's known her entire life—walk away. She can't see me through the reflective glass, but somehow, it's like she knows I'm there. Watching.

She presses her hand to her lips, then pushes the kiss

toward me, just like she's done so many times. And then...she's gone.

I watch her drive away as I'm openly sobbing. When she's so far out of sight I can no longer see her, I sink down against the wall and cry. All my life, it's been the two of us against the world, and now she'll be eight hours away. A whole day.

What was I thinking coming here?

Angrily, I search through my bags until I find my comforter and wrap up in it, crying on the floor until I fall asleep.

Knock, knock.

I wake to the sound of someone knocking on the door. *My* door. It only occurs to me then that I'll be the one who has to answer it from now on. I'm the adult now. But who could be knocking in the first place?

My mind flicks to Dean, who knows I'm arriving today, but I still haven't given him the address, so it can't be him. I don't know anyone else here. My heart flutters in my chest as I stand and rub my eyes.

I cross the empty room slowly, each footstep seeming to echo like a cathedral. When I reach the door, I move the peephole cover aside and stare out.

His face is a welcome surprise.

I pull the door open and stare at him, hardly believing it. "Dean?"

He smirks, lifting the beer and pizza in his hands. "Hey, I heard there was an old lady living here who might need some company."

"If I'm old, you're ancient." I step back, allowing him to come into the apartment. It feels like a dream, and I'm still not sure it isn't one. "H-how did you...I mean, I didn't tell you I was here. I didn't tell you where *here* was."

He sets the pizza and beer on the countertop in the kitchen and turns back toward me, giving me a look that says the answer should be obvious. "Your mom called. Asked me to check in on you."

"Oh." Of course she did. Even as I tried to tell her I'd be okay, she knew I needed someone. Knew I needed him.

"First night's the hardest." He opens the box of pizza and nudges it toward me.

I step forward, taking a beer instead. "Was it this hard for you?"

He cracks open a beer of his own and takes a sip. "Anyone who says it isn't would be a liar. Everything you've ever known has changed overnight. It's normal for that to feel weird. Sad, even. You just have to make it through."

"I really didn't think it would be this hard." My voice cracks, and I wipe my eyes with the back of my arm. "I thought I'd be fine."

"And you will be. In a day or two, this will all start to feel normal again." He stares around the room. "But we should get things set up and feeling like home." Without asking permission, he places his beer down, grabs the bed frame resting against my wall, and heads for the bedroom.

"What are you doing?" I follow him.

"I'm helping. What does it look like? Do you have tools?"

I grab the small tool bag Mom gave me for my eighteenth birthday and carry it into the bedroom, and he sets to work. Meanwhile, I grab my clothes and begin hanging them in the closet. It feels good to stay busy. To keep my mind occupied.

"So, how was graduation?" he calls. When I look through the closet doorway, he's lying on the floor under the bed, one arm working to screw the bed frame together while the other holds the pieces in place. His shirt has ridden up, and there's a sliver of stomach visible —a trail of dark hair that makes me blush.

I look away. "It was fine."

"Just fine?"

"Sad, I guess. Happy, but sad. And then we had the party—" My mind flashes to Jack. "Which was...sad too, really."

He chuckles. "I think you're doing graduation wrong, Carmie."

"How were you so happy back then? Did you not think you'd miss home?"

"I miss...parts of home, sure. But Nashville has been fun. It was good to get away."

"Will you go back?"

There's a long pause. "Will you?"

"Jack wants me to, yeah."

"That's not really an answer." When I look back into the room again, he's sitting up, his arms resting on his knees.

"I like the city." My voice is small. It feels like a betrayal to say it. "It will always feel like home."

"Atlanta?"

I nod, fighting to get my shirt on a hanger. "Yeah. Maybe Nashville, I don't know. Don't get me wrong. I love Cody, and I love The Hollow. And some days it feels like home, but it's not home, you know? But...for Jack, it is. He's...he's mad that I'm here. That I dared to leave at all." My words are soaked in bitterness like a brine. "He hasn't said it, but I know he is."

When I spin around to grab another shirt from the pile, he's standing there, one arm resting on the door-frame. "That doesn't surprise me."

"He didn't want me to come."

"You're your own person, Carmen. You made a decision."

"I know."

"Do you regret it?"

I suck in a breath, trying to find the answer inside myself. "Ask me again in a few days."

A small smile plays on his lips. "You're going to be just fine."

He goes back to work, leaving me alone with my

thoughts. A few hours later, we've gotten the bed together, my clothes put away, some of the kitchen unpacked, the small couch against the wall, and my television hooked up and resting on top of a mostly empty bookshelf.

Exhausted, I grab a piece of cold pizza from the box, another beer, and collapse on the couch. Dean stands in the kitchen, looking around the place with his hands on his hips. "Not bad for a day's work."

"Not at all." I pat the seat beside me. "Come. Sit. Enjoy the fruits of your labor."

He shakes his head with a chuckle and comes to sit down. I check my phone, disappointed that I still haven't heard from Jack.

"Want to watch a movie?" I grab the remote and turn it on. "*Horrible Bosses* is still in the DVD player."

He lets out a breath. "Like I'd turn down watching my celebrity crush."

"You have a thing for Jennifer Aniston?" I smirk. "I don't think I knew that."

"Please. Clearly, I'm talking about Charlie Day." He sits back, getting comfortable, but eyes me. "Did you tell Jack I'm here?"

I stare at him, my head resting against the back of the couch. "Why?"

"Just wondering."

"Actually, Jack and I haven't spoken today."

His brows dart up.

"We kind of had a fight last night, and he decided not to come with me today."

"He's that mad that you're here?"

"At first, it seemed like it, but then he sort of warmed up to the idea."

"When I spoke to him last, he didn't want to talk about it."

"Yeah, I mean, obviously, it wasn't his favorite idea, but he seemed like he'd accepted it."

"Jack will get over it." He adjusts, turning to face me with his arm up over the back of the couch. "You guys are good together. He'll figure his shit out, and you'll be okay."

"Thanks." I sigh. "He's worried we won't be able to make the long-distance thing work, but I think it's more than that. Some of it feels like spite."

He nods. "Jack has always liked things done his way."

Guilt sinks in my chest. "We shouldn't be talking about this. I'm sorry. I don't want to talk badly about him. I really do..." I can't say the words, not to Dean. Not when I already know how he feels about me—or how he once felt about me, at least. "I really do," I say finally.

"I know you do. Truth be told, the reason I asked if he knew I was here was because he doesn't like us being alone together. I've tried to respect that, but when your mom asked if I'd come by, I couldn't say no."

"I'm not going to lie to him," I say firmly. "If that's what you're asking."

"I wouldn't want you to. I just thought I should prepare you for the fact that he probably won't like it."

"It's not like you're ever not going to be in my life. We're friends." I nudge him, then sigh. "I don't think he ever got over the fact that you were my first kiss. It's like there's this rift between us over that. He brings it up whenever he can, I swear. Every single time we argue about anything. It still really seems to bother him."

He leans his head back on the couch, staring at the ceiling. "Yeah, but...who cares? That was it. Your first kiss, and for a game. He was your first everything else. He has nothing to be jealous of."

Warmth blooms in my stomach as I realize what he's just implied.

"Sorry," he says quickly. "I didn't mean...that's none of my business."

Clearly, though, he's thought about it. "It's okay." I bite my bottom lip, turning on the TV, and we go silent as we watch the movie.

As the night drags on, I begin to doze off on the couch, and I feel Dean nudge me. "You should go to bed. I'll head out."

"Stay," I tell him, grabbing his arm. "Please. I don't want to be alone tonight."

He studies me.

"We'll make a bed on the floor with blankets." Sleeping in my bed feels like crossing a line, but this way feels childish and innocent. "Like New Year's Eve parties when we were kids."

I can tell he's thinking it over, weighing the pros and cons, but eventually, he nods. "Okay."

We lay out the blankets carefully, putting our pillows far apart. Once we've lain down, close to falling asleep, I feel a truth bubbling in my chest. "Dean?"

It takes him a long time to answer. "Yeah?"

"He wasn't." My voice is so soft I'm not sure if he's heard me.

"Hmm?"

"You said earlier Jack was my first everything, but...he wasn't. I...I mean, my first love, yes. But if you meant..."

"Sex." The word sends chills over me, tracing a line of goose bumps across my skin as real as if I were being touched by his hand instead. "Yes, that's what I meant."

"Jack and I...we haven't slept together." I pull the covers closer around me.

He's silent for several seconds. "Oh."

"That's what the fight last night was about. He wanted to, and I...I mean, I *do* want to. But last night felt like he was saying goodbye." I wince. "Do you promise you won't tell him I told you this? I just have no one else to talk to."

He rolls over on the floor, then takes his pinkie and wraps it around mine. "Cross my heart."

"It felt wrong. Like it was his last chance, and he had to go for it. I didn't want to...I didn't want it to be like that."

He studies me, waiting for me to say more. "I think that's very smart of you."

229

I smile.

"Now go to sleep." He dusts a bit of hair from my eyes before closing his, and almost on command, I feel myself drifting off.

I wake up in the middle of the night to the sound of my phone buzzing, and when I pick it up, Jack's name is on my screen. I scramble to answer it and get out of the room, keeping my voice low.

"Hello?"

"I didn't know if you'd be up." His voice is dry. Lifeless.

I rub my eyes, trying to clear my blurry vision. "I was asleep, but the phone woke me up."

"I'm sorry I didn't come with you today."

"It's okay," I tell him. "Are you...mad at me?"

"I'm not mad, no. But...listen, Carmen, I've been thinking a lot about this. I think we should break up."

"What?" My world shatters into a million pieces.

"I'm sorry. I just...I can't do this. You were right. Last night would've been a mistake because in my head, it was goodbye. You didn't deserve that."

"I don't understand." I'm crying now, and I hate that he can hear it, hate that he seems unaffected by the sound.

"I just can't be with someone who lives a world away.

I still want to be friends, and after you graduate, who knows? But right now, my life is here. And you aren't."

"Jack, please. Can't we just talk about this? I mean—"

"I'm sorry. I have to go." He ends the call, and I'm plunged into silence. I drop onto my bed, sobs shaking my body as I try to keep quiet. I shove my face into my pillow, crying so hard it physically hurts.

When I feel the bed dip down at the foot, I know he's there, but I can't bring myself to look at him. He climbs up beside me and wraps his arms around me, pulling me into his chest.

He doesn't say anything, doesn't ask any questions. Somehow, he seems to understand. My tears soak his shirt as I sob, crying for all that I lost and knowing it's all my fault.

What did I do?

What did I do?

All through the night, Dean holds me. His warm arms keep me grounded when nothing else could. When I wake myself up crying in my sleep multiple times, he's still there, his hands on my back, his body against mine.

There's nothing sexual or inappropriate about this moment between us. He's simply here for me in a way no one else could be. And I've never been more grateful for him.

CHAPTER TWENTY-THREE

PRESENT DAY

That evening, Dean finds me on the porch working on one of my illustrations. The slow, methodical art of drawing always seems to calm me down, and with the news that we could be one step closer to learning the truth about what happened to Shelby, my nerves are frazzled.

I turn my head to look at him, setting my Apple Pencil down. "Hey."

"Hey." He scrapes a hand over his dark beard. "Can we talk?"

I lock the screen on my iPad, closing it and turning toward him in my seat. "Sure. That seems to be the theme of the day. What's up?"

"About last night...I'm sorry if I overstepped. I didn't mean to. I know you can take care of yourself and stand up for yourself. It's just...when it comes to you...I can't help myself. But it's not an excuse. It won't happen again." He leans against the railing, studying me. "It's not my place to tell you who's good enough for you."

I fold my hands into my lap. "No. It's not."

"And I'm really sorry I—"

"But you were right."

His eyes widen. "What?"

"You were right for what you said. I'd already told Jack as much, but for what it's worth, I appreciate you for...so many things. Last night included."

He fights against a small smile. "And listen, I'm glad you came back for your mom. Hell, I'm glad you came back for *my* mom. But if I'm ever too much, friendship or otherwise, just tell me, okay? I don't want either of us to scare you off again. I don't think I could handle it."

"You never scared me off." I'm on my feet. "You know that's not why I left. You...you hurt me, yes, but—"

"I never meant to hurt you, Carmen. I thought I was doing the right thing. You clearly still had feelings for Jack, and—"

"That's not why I left either. Not really. I left because it felt like I needed to. For me. After her funeral—after everything that happened—I couldn't stay here anymore."

"I know." Again, his hand finds his chin, and he scrubs his palm across it. "I'm just so terrified you're going to let him in again, and he's going to destroy you. That night he broke up with you, the night I held you...it nearly killed me to just lie there. To watch you cry over someone who was never good enough for you."

"Jack and I are friends," I say firmly. "We talked, and he told me how he feels—"

"How does he feel?" His head cocks to the side.

"You'd have to ask him that."

He gives me a knowing look. "I don't think I have to at all. What did you tell him?"

"I told him I care about him as a friend. But he has a lot of things to figure out, and I don't feel the same way about him anymore. When I came here, I thought maybe I could again. My head was so messed up, and I thought things might be different now that so much time has passed. But I'm here, and...and all I really know is that I don't want to lose either of you."

His jaw twitches. "Sometimes it's worth the risk."

"You both really hurt me back then, Dean. I don't want...I don't want to punish anyone for mistakes or choices that were made years ago. We have to be better than that. We have to move forward."

He leans back. "We are not the same, and you know it. I was there for you when he wasn't. I protected you over and over again." He stops, taking a moment to cool down. "I'm not going to beg you to want me. And I'm damn sure not going to be his replacement. Or your backup option. A second choice because you can't have who you really want. Not then, not now. So just be honest with me. Tell me the truth like you did him."

Before I can respond, movement catches my eye.

Somewhere over by the playground, I saw something—some*one*—moving through the trees. I take a step forward on the deck, looking closer.

"Look, I'm sorry if I—"

"Shh!" I warn him, a finger to my lips. "I saw someone over there."

"Someone? Who? Jack?"

"No." I shake my head, rushing for the stairs. "Someone else." The gate swings open with a groan, cutting me off before I can cross the street, and Tye's familiar red truck pulls inside.

I try to hide my frustration.

He looks surprised to see me here. "Deanie-weenie and the infant," he cries, waving at us. "What's up, my dudes?"

I scramble behind him in a hurry to follow the trail, though there's a good chance whoever was lurking in the woods is already long gone.

I dart past the playground and into the treeline, and then, up ahead, I see her. She checks over her shoulder, picking up her pace as she tries to get away from me.

Her red hair blows in the breeze as she moves.

"Hey! You! Wait up." I jog to catch her, and soon, Tye and Dean are on my heels.

"Who the hell is that?" Tye calls after me.

"Stop, or I'm calling the police. You're not allowed to be back here!" I shout, a final attempt as the girl slips farther away. To my surprise, her pace slows until she eventually halts.

With her head hung down, she spins back to face us. She's a teenager from the looks of it—young enough to still be in high school, perhaps. "Please don't tell my mom." She covers her face. "I was just going for a walk."

"How did you even get in here without a code?"

"There's a place where the fence is falling down in the woods. I just climbed over it." She shrugs, her voice small. "I wasn't going to mess with anything. I just wanted to be alone."

"What's your name?" Dean asks. "Are you staying here?"

"I'm..." I can see her weighing her options as she stares at us. "April."

My heart picks up speed. "*April*. You're the girl who went missing?"

She nods. "Yeah. I just got back from the hospital a few hours ago. I'm fine, by the way. I just got lost out here."

"And you're already running off to do the same thing again?" Tye asks.

Her eyes flick to meet his, then back down. "I wasn't...I'm not going to get lost this time. Last time, it was dark. Late. I lost track of where I was. I'm fine now."

Something about the way she's acting has me suspicious. She's nervous. Something isn't right. I take a step toward her. "I'm Carmen, April. I live here at the campground with my family. I..." I look over my shoulder at the men and lower my voice. "I can get you help if you need it. If someone, maybe someone here, is being mean to you? Maybe you're trying to run away from home?"

Her eyes widen. "What? No! No. Of course not. My mom doesn't hurt me if that's what you mean. I'm fine. I'm not even leaving. It's literally just a walk."

An idea flashes in my head like a light bulb. She'd been roaming through the woods, never straying far from the campsite. Robbie said she was clean and unharmed.

She wasn't alone.

"Are you meeting someone? Another camper?"

Again, her eyes flick up to me, then to the men behind me, and finally back down. "I told you I was just walking."

"But why back here? There are plenty of places you could walk. Safer places. Unless you're trying to meet someone somewhere where your mom won't find out."

"I'm not meeting anyone," she says, but there's a shake to her voice that wasn't there before. "Look, whatever. I'll just go back to my cabin, okay? Forget it." She huffs and storms past me.

"I can help you if you trust me," I call after her.

"I don't need your help, lady. Leave me alone."

With that, she's gone. But there's one thing I'm nearly certain of. She was meeting someone she doesn't want me to know about. Someone who made her sneak through the woods. Someone who might not have thought we'd be here. The only question is...who?

CHAPTER TWENTY-FOUR

BEFORE — AGES 18-19

Knock, knock.

Two knocks. Every time.

I stand from the floor where I've been painting my toenails and waddle across the room. When I open it, Dean is there, his hair still damp from his shower after work. He grins at me broadly, holding up a brown sack of food from his shift.

"Hey, stranger."

Dean has become a regular fixture at my apartment. He's here more than he's home at this point, and I don't mind a bit.

It's been four months since Jack and I broke up, and slowly, I'm healing. His loss still hurts, but with time I find myself thinking about him less and less. Like Dean promised, Nashville is starting to feel more normal by the day. I've been in school for a month now, I'm finally settled in like an adult with a job and a car, and I've even made a few friends. Dean was right. It took time, but it happened.

Once my toenails have dried, we find our usual places on the couch and dig into the bag while deciding what movie to watch tonight. It's Dean's turn to choose.

It comes as no surprise when he chooses yet another rom-com. He says it's for me, but we both know they're his favorites, too.

We settle into our routine: watching the movie, filling each other in on our days, and asking about what tomorrow holds. I tell him I talked to my mom, and he tells me he heard from his dad, and we fill in the blanks about what's going on at home.

We have all the habits of an old married couple, but he hasn't kissed me or even made an attempt. Despite the familiarity we share and the feelings we both know are there between us, neither of us has crossed the line. We haven't spoken about the night Jack broke up with me, haven't mentioned his name more than a few times, and then it was only when relaying a message or update from our parents.

Dean, being Dean, is giving me space and time, and to be honest, it's exactly what I've needed. I could've jumped into something with him, could've let him erase the pain I was feeling over the breakup temporarily, but I know it wouldn't have been a long-term solution and would've left me feeling worse in the end. He deserves more than that from me.

So, we've been friends. Best friends, I think. He's shown

me around Nashville and also around campus once the semester started. He introduced me to some of his friends and helped me decide which restaurants to apply to. Once I accepted a job at a coffee shop, he helped me pick out a car at a local lot, talked to Mom on the phone throughout the whole process, and helped me with the test drive. He was here when my washing machine went out, and we had to take my clothes to the laundromat until it was fixed. He helped me when the icemaker in my fridge quit working and when I needed blackout curtains installed so I could sleep in.

In short, he has been my saving grace since my move to Nashville, and I know if I mess that up somehow, I will always regret it.

He looks over at me as if he can tell I'm thinking of him, and a weird look comes across his face. "You okay?"

"Yep." I pop a fry into my mouth. "How was work?"

"Oh my god." He rolls his eyes. "Let me tell you about this one guy. Okay, so dude comes in, says, 'I only have thirty bucks, so don't let me go over that.' Then he proceeds to order, like, seventy bucks' worth of food. I kept telling him, 'Oh, we're close to thirty. Oh, we're over thirty. We're at forty now. We're at sixty.' Every time, he's like, 'Okay, just a little more.' In the end, when I told him his total, he was like, 'But I told you not to let me go over thirty.' And then..." He pauses for dramatic effect. "He just walked out."

"Oh my god." My eyes widen as I laugh. "Was he high or something? What the heck?"

He shrugs. "I have no idea. It was probably the weirdest thing that's ever happened to me."

"So he just dined and dashed?"

He nods, chewing. "Yeah, I guess so. Pete was furious, and I really thought he might fire me or make me pay for it or something, but he just let it go. We have security footage that we turned over to the police, but it was insane."

"Well, more eventful than my day, for sure."

He clears his throat. "Um, Dad asked me if we're planning to come home for Thanksgiving break."

"Well, yeah. Of course." I pause. "What did you tell him?"

"I wasn't sure. I told him I'd let him know. I didn't know how you were feeling about going home right now. If you were ready..." He trails off, and I realize what he's really asking. *Am I ready to see Jack?*

"Ready or not, I already told Mom I wasn't coming home for my birthday since it's so close to Thanksgiving," I tell him. "She'd be devastated if I missed the holiday, too. My grandparents live too far away for her to visit them except for at Christmas. We've never spent Thanksgiving apart."

He nods. "Okay. Totally cool with me. I just wanted to make sure before I told him yes."

I study him. "You mean you weren't going to go if I didn't?"

He purses his lips, looking at me like I should know

better. "I'm not going to leave you here by yourself for Thanksgiving, Carmie. Clearly."

I don't know what to say to that. The gesture, the thought of us spending Thanksgiving here, together, alone, is enough that my chest is full. "I thought you couldn't usually get Thanksgiving off. You don't usually come home."

He looks away then. "Pete would've always given it to me if I'd asked, but I haven't."

"Why?" But I think I already know the answer. When he turns back to look at me, his eyes say it without having to move his lips. "Because of me?"

He scrubs a hand over his face. "No. Not because of you. Because of me. It was too hard to go back and see you guys together. And I didn't want to make it awkward for anyone. So I visited on Christmas when I knew you'd be in Ohio visiting your grandparents. At least, I assumed you would be, until the year you didn't go, but I didn't know you'd still be home until I got there."

"And the summers, too? You stayed away because..."

He sets his jaw. "I stayed away because I needed to. Not because of you, okay? You did nothing wrong."

"I hurt you," I say softly. Sadly.

"Carmen, I..." His eyes are wide with words he can't seem to find. "Look, growing up, you were always Jack's girl. Mom and Dad talked about it. Joked about it. Jack seemed to understand. You both got along, and you were the same age. It made sense. You were never supposed to be mine, and so I let it go. I teased you because it was the only way I knew I could be near you without driving myself crazy. And then...and then, just once, I let myself do what I'd been wanting to do for years. I let myself kiss you that night at your party. It was just a game, so I thought, what was the harm? But I was wrong because from that moment on, you were all I thought about. It was like, you'd walk into a room, and I could feel you before I'd see you. And then, the feelings were harder to ignore. I thought by taking you to that dance I could make you see how it could be with us, but I wasn't blind. It was obvious I had no chance, so I let you go. All that talk about how love is worth the risk, and I couldn't take a risk on you." He scoffs. "I beat myself up over that for years. And then, finally, that night I came home and walked you back to your cabin, I thought 'it's now or never,' and I risked it in the only way I knew how. And I knew you didn't feel the same. Maybe a little, but not enough. You were in love with my brother, and it was shitty on my part. But after that, even before that really, it was just too hard. I wanted you to be happy, I just...I wanted you to be happy with me." He stares at his hands, unable to meet my eyes, his cheeks burning red.

My heart aches from his words, from the kindness, from the love that's always been there. When I sit down and add it all up, Dean has been there for me in every way that matters. He was a bratty kid once, but as we've grown up, he's shown me the truth in his actions without ever having to put the words out there. And deep down, I think I've always known the feelings were here on my end, too. I was just so scared to mess anything up with Jack. To cause drama and have Jill and Sam ask us to leave. To lose what foothold I had on our home. Our makeshift family. Now I realize he's been the family I needed all this time. Even when it's just the two of us.

Slowly, I lift my hand to his jaw, using my fingers to turn his face toward me. "I think, in some way, I've always felt it between us. But...you were older. You said you didn't like me the night you kissed me. You'd always teased me. I thought I was just some annoying little sister to you. I thought... Even after you hinted that you had feelings for me that night, I knew, but I've seen how you treat women. I thought I'd be someone you'd use and throw away. I thought...I thought there was no way you could want me for long."

His face visibly breaks after my words. "How many girls did I date after I kissed you, Carmen? Can you tell me?"

I think back. "I don't know."

"Let me think. There was..." He pretends to count on his fingers. "Oh, right. None. Zero. Sure, I wasn't a saint. I had my fun, but I never dated anyone else. Not seriously. Because I guess in some weird way, I was always waiting on you."

"Then stop waiting." The words leave my lips on a soft breath.

His brows rise. "Wh—"

"Stop waiting, Dean." I lean into him before he can move, then my lips are on his. It takes him a second to react, but then it's as if he's come to life. Both hands catch my head, pulling me to him. The kiss that night we played spin the bottle is nothing compared to this one.

That night was reservation and nerves and tenderness, and this night is pure flame. Nothing but fire and want and need.

His lips claim mine over and over, his tongue in my mouth, hands in my hair. We gasp for breath between kisses, and a storm rages in my stomach as he pulls me to him until I'm sitting on his lap right there in my living room.

He breaks us apart for one terrible minute, his forehead pressed to mine. "I have wanted this for so long."

I kiss him again, my hands exploring his body as our kisses grow more intense. I feel as if I'm going to explode. This night is like nothing I've ever experienced—the way it feels to kiss him, to finally give in to what I've wanted, deep down on a cellular level, for as long as I can remember.

He kisses me with the expert precision of someone experienced, someone who knows exactly what he wants and how to get it. Eventually, his mouth leaves mine, peppering my jaw and neck with desperate kisses.

My hands slip under his shirt, pulling it up over his head. Once it's off, he looks at me, his eyes hot with desire. He licks his lips, running a hand over his mouth as he visibly tries to calm himself down.

"Carmen...are you sure about this?"

My full name on his lips sends a zap of longing running through me.

I nod. "Yes."

"I don't...we don't have to do anything you don't want to do. I don't want to force you or assume or...we can just do this." He kisses my lips. "Do you have any idea how long I've waited to just do this?" A smile warms his face like a kid on Christmas.

I kiss him back. "I want this, Dean. I want...I want you." Then, forcing more confidence than I feel, I say the words that have been playing in the back of my mind for weeks now. "I want you to be my first everything."

The happiness evaporates from his expression like water on a hot day, replaced with dark determination. He reaches for the bottom of my shirt, pulling it up over my head and returning his lips to mine. We're chest to chest now, him holding me so close to him it's like he's afraid if we separate, I might change my mind.

He pulls my bottom lip between his teeth. "You have no idea how many dreams I've had like this."

The words send a bolt of lightning through me, turning my core molten. I can't breathe, can't think. There is only him and the way he's making me feel.

His arms hook around my back, and I feel his fingers on the clasp of my bra. My breathing hitches, and he pauses, but I kiss him deeper, not wanting him to stop. Not wanting any of this to stop.

With my bra off, he leans back, breathing heavily as he looks over me. It's as if I'm a hen, and he's a fox. His gaze is hungry. Practically ravenous, in fact. He looks up at me, his dark eyes meeting mine, and something softens in him.

"I want to take it slow with you. For you." His hands grip my waist so hard I think he might leave a bruise. "But you have no idea how hard that's going to be."

"I don't need you to take it slow," I tell him, but it's no secret I'm nervous. I don't know if it's going to hurt. I don't know anything at all.

He nods, leaning forward and kissing my collarbone. "I know. I will, though. Just this once."

With that, we're standing, and he leads me into the bedroom. We stop at the bed, and he pushes me backward until my legs hit the edge. Then his hands are on me again, and he's kissing me like I'm the only source of air in the room, and he can hardly breathe.

His body is warm against mine, skin on skin, heartbeat to heartbeat. He eases me down on the bed and lowers his mouth to my breasts. I suck in a breath. Nothing—*nothing*—has ever felt this good. Why didn't anyone tell me it could feel like this? That *I* could feel like this?

He lifts his head and moves to the other breast, his hand coming up to replace the warmth of his mouth on the first. My back arches off of the bed at the feeling, my body screaming *more, more, more!*

The sounds escaping me don't even sound human. I sound like I'm being tortured, rather than made to feel like...whatever this is. He looks up at me with a wicked grin, and the sight is one I will take to my grave.

His hand slips down my stomach slowly, followed by his mouth, and I know what comes next, though only in theory. He lowers my pants and places kisses in the newly bare places, inch by inch, until he rips them straight off my legs.

With his eyes locked on mine, he pulls his own pants off next, and I see the hard outline of him in his boxers, trying to spring free. He lowers himself at the edge of the bed and, when I sit up, he pushes me down, keeping his palm on my stomach to hold me in place. "Stay."

Like a dog.

One corner of his mouth upturns deviously when I stop fighting him. "Good girl."

Why the hell does that turn me on so much?

I don't dare try to move as he removes my underwear, and I feel his warm breath between my legs. My heart races, and I close my eyes just seconds before his mouth is there.

Is this really happening?

Is this a dream?

Expertly, his mouth works over the most sensitive parts of my body, his noises echoing mine. I'm a mess of desire and longing and confusion and fear. I want to do this right, to be whatever Dean wants, but as his tongue laps over me, his thumb moving in circles just above his mouth, I can't think about any of that.

I can only think of...this.

I never ever want this to end.

My body is numb, loose like spaghetti, under his hands, against his mouth. He hooks my legs over his shoulders to get a better angle, and then I'm crying out.

"Dean! Oh my god!" My body goes lightning hot, a current of lava coursing through me like I've only been able to do to myself up until this point. Somehow, with him it's even better.

I can feel his grin between my legs as he waits for the final aftershocks to pass through my body, and when they have, he lifts up, wiping his face with his hand.

He crosses the room to his pants, and I watch as he pulls a condom from his wallet.

"You were prepared?" I ask breathlessly.

"I've always had hope." As he makes his way back to me, I take in the sight of him. He's lean and muscled as he's always been, with ropy arms and the hint of muscles underneath the skin of his stomach, mostly covered by hair.

I've seen him shirtless before, obviously, though not when I was free to look at him. Still, it's only the part of him that is usually *underneath* his swimming suit I haven't seen at all before this. I'm shameless in my staring, though he seems to appreciate it. I watch as he rolls the condom over his length and steps toward me.

He slides me back farther on the bed and climbs on top of me, pressing kisses to my lips. His tongue invades my mouth, and I tilt my head up, welcoming him. He lowers down slowly.

"Tell me if I hurt you," he whispers.

I nod and brace myself.

He slides between my legs, using one hand to guide himself. I feel the pressure of him at my entrance. He takes a deep breath, meeting my eyes. There's something so pure and overwhelming about them. I can't bring myself to look away.

Then, there's the sudden feeling of fullness in a place that's always been empty. It doesn't hurt necessarily, just feels...sore. Like muscles after a long workout.

"You good?" His forehead is pressed to mine, hand on the bed next to my face. I can feel his arm shaking.

"I'm great," I say with a laugh.

He runs his teeth over his bottom lip, and then we're moving together. My body knows what to do even if I don't. We're both slick with sweat, skin clinging together as he moves within me, slow at first but gaining speed.

The fullness is exciting and overwhelming and intoxicating. My body melds to his, making perfect space for him like we're meant to be together. Like he was made for me.

He sits up, spreading my legs and staring down at the place where the two of us join with newfound passion in his eyes. Seeing him like this, I feel like I could explode. The two of us together—I never thought this would happen.

I never dreamed—

His thumb returns to the sensitive place where it was earlier, and my legs begin to quake. I have no idea how he already knows my body so well, but soon, his eyes meet mine again.

"Let go, baby," he whispers. "For me."

And so I do. We go over the edge of the cliff together, and I close my eyes, never wanting to wake up from this dream.

When Thanksgiving comes around, Dean and I have been dating—*god, it feels so weird to say that*—for just over two months. We still haven't told our families, and we're probably not going to while we're on this trip. We both feel like Jack deserves to have his feelings considered for a while longer.

The last thing I want is for him to think I only moved to Nashville to get with Dean, or that this was somehow my plan all along. I don't want him to think he was so easy to move on from or that I'm not still healing from our breakup.

I know Jack, and despite how much he hurt me, I know he did it because he was hurting, too. I don't want to add to that.

On the way home, Dean and I take turns picking albums to listen to and sing along to the songs we know. We stop for snacks and meals along the way, and by the time we reach Hunter's Hollow, we're both exhausted and ready to find our beds and crash.

Except, for the last few months, Dean has been

sleeping over more often than not, which means I'll be missing him a little extra for the next few nights.

"It's going to be torture not to kiss you for the next... one hundred and twenty hours." He peers over at me, smiling sadly.

"Tell me about it."

"Are you sure you don't want to just tell them?"

"We'll tell them over the summer," I say, squeezing his hand. "I want to tell them now just as much as you do, but we owe it to Jack to be gentle with this."

I know Dean doesn't completely agree. It's not that he doesn't care about hurting Jack, it's just that he's—*we're*—insanely happy, and he wants to share it. But I can't shake the feeling we've done something wrong somehow, and I don't want to hurt Jack.

He pulls to the end of the road leading to Hunter's Hollow and stops the car.

"What are you—"

He puts it in park and leans across the console. I'm laughing as he pulls my face toward his, kissing my lips firmly. The feeling never fails to send my heart soaring, stomach fluttering. I kiss him back with just as much passion, vaguely considering a game plan to sneak into his room each night.

"Now that I've had you, I can't get enough of this," he murmurs, pulling away just to say that before his lips return to mine.

He kisses me twice more quickly and sinks back down into his seat.

"I know the feeling," I admit.

"What do you say we just hit the road and go back home? Tell them we had car trouble and couldn't make it?"

I raise a brow. "*Both* of our cars had trouble?"

"Isn't that a funny coincidence?" He grins devilishly.

I shake my head and swat his chest. "You're impossible. We can't do that. Come on."

He sighs and takes my hand. "Oh, fine."

The rest of the drive down the long dirt road, past the office, and to our families' cabins is done in silence. I'm an odd mixture of sad and worried, not to mention uncomfortable, over seeing Jack again.

When Dean pulls the car to a stop, we make our way to the trunk and unload our bags. I see Mom first. She comes out of the cabin almost at once and rushes down the stairs, wrapping me in a hug.

"There she is! My big old nineteen-year-old. When did you get so old?" She sways us back and forth, only releasing me when I'm nearly dizzy. Then she reaches for Dean, who hugs her back just as tightly and only lets go when she does. Somehow, it warms my heart. The smallest things he does send me spiraling.

Now I'm rethinking the idea of telling our families. I'm finding it hard to resist the urge to kiss him right now.

"How was the drive?" Mom asks. "No trouble? Did Carmen provide you with a free concert the whole way?"

"Oh, a hundred percent," he says with a grin. He winks at me. "But I didn't mind."

I feel heat rush to my cheeks and realize we have a secret now. Maybe this won't be so bad after all—stolen moments, hushed conversations, and secret kisses. It could be kind of hot if we play our cards right.

When I look at Mom, she's staring at me oddly, and I realize we may have already blown our cover.

"I'm, uh"—Dean clears his throat, and I think he's realized it, too—"going to go take my bags inside and see Mom and Dad. I'll see you later, Carmen? Ms. M?"

"O-okay," I choke out.

"Mm-hmm." Mom's lips are pursed, and her eyes are drilling into me. *We are so busted.*

With Dean gone, Mom loops her arm through mine, a sly look on her face. "What?" I ask, feigning both innocence and ignorance, though not well.

"What was that about?" she asks, swaying her hips like someone who knows a secret.

"What was *what* about?"

"That look he just gave you. Those cheeks." She brushes a finger over my cheek and clicks her tongue. "And since when has that boy ever called you Carmen?"

I shake my head. "He was just being nice. I hate Carmie."

She pouts. "I think Carmie's cute."

"I don't want to be cute," I admit. "I'm grown up, Mama. You just said so yourself."

She blows a raspberry. "No, you're not. If you're grown, I'm old, and I'm not okay with that."

When we enter the house, I set my bag down on the floor and kiss her cheek. "You could never be old."

She crosses her arms. "You sure that's all that was?"

I roll my eyes. "Positive."

I'm still not sure she believes me, but she lets the subject drop for the moment. In the kitchen, I pour myself a glass of water and lean against the countertop. "So...what's on the agenda?"

"A whole lot of nothing." She chuckles. "I thought we could catch up on the new season of *Hart of Dixie*. I've got them all recorded."

"Oh! You haven't watched them without me?"

"Well, no. Of course not. What kind of monster do you think I am?"

"Good." I take a sip of my water. "Have you been painting?"

She nods. "Do you want to see? I just bought a little schoolhouse."

She takes me toward the corner of the living room where she has a little table set up with the most perfect ceramic village. Dad has been buying her a new addition for her birthday every year for as long as I can remember and, at this point, her collection has outgrown its place at least three times.

I bend down, examining the village closely, along with its newest addition—a one-room schoolhouse that she's painted bright red with cute little bushes all around it.

"It's beautiful, Mama."

She beams. "Thanks, *Carmen*." She imitates Dean's dreamy voice, and I can't help but laugh.

"Oh, hush," I tease.

She winks at me dramatically, imitating him again, and I fall into a fit of giggles. She walks away, clearly proud of herself. "You just better hope Jack doesn't find out. Those boys'll be fighting in the potatoes at Thanksgiving."

Like usual, Mom falls asleep twenty minutes into the second episode, leaving me alone on the couch with my thoughts. Somehow, I've managed to avoid Jack all day.

I guess a part of me thought he might try to come see me, but he hasn't.

I pull out my phone and open my text thread with Dean, sending him a quick message.

> How'd today go?

> Fine. Better if you were here.

> I'm just feet away

> Don't tease.

> I think Mom knows

What? How?

> That little wink you did was less than subtle

I can't help it if I think you're cute ;)

I try and fail to suppress the smile that spreads across my lips.

> How'd it go with Jack?

Haven't seen him.

> What? Seriously?

He's out with friends, apparently.

I don't know what to make of that, except that he must be staying away to avoid me.

> Can't wait to see you tomorrow

His response is quick.

That's too long to wait.

> Oh yeah?

Yeah. Can you sneak out?

Like we're twelve?

Twelve-year-olds have no business doing what I have planned.

You forgot the wink

Brat.

You know just how to turn me on

Come let me prove it.

I sigh, looking out the window. It's nearly dark, and this is a terrible idea, but...I miss him.

Meet you outside in ten seconds

Make it eight.

I stand up and drape a blanket from the back of the couch across Mom's body, then jot down a note to let her know I went for a walk and will be back, just in case she wakes up.

With that taken care of, I slip on my shoes and am out the door quickly. Dean's already there waiting for me. He pulls me into the shadows against the house, kissing my lips.

"We're going to get caught!" I warn him, kissing him back.

"Worth the risk," he reminds me, and at least for the moment, I can't help thinking he's right.

He takes my hand and leads me to the car, and I follow his lead, trying to understand the plan. We get into the front seats, and he starts it up.

"Where are we going?" I ask, breathless as my heart races.

He buckles in. "You'll see." We back out of the driveway and down the road toward the campground, stopping next to cabin fourteen, just beside the gate that leads to the private cabins: fifteen and sixteen.

"What are we doing?" I ask again.

"Shhh!" he teases, opening his door and stepping out. He takes my hand and pulls me past the gate, along the fence, and toward the woods.

"Will you just tell me where we're going?"

He laughs. "Will you just be patient?"

"I'm not a patient person. You should know this about me."

"Oh, I do." He chuckles.

When we reach a small dip in the fence, he stops. "I might've asked Mom and Dad if anyone was staying in cabin fifteen or sixteen when I got home, and they might've told me yes, which meant we couldn't go through the gates if we wanted to be alone. So..." He gestures toward the iron fence where it's bent—a small dip that means it's around a foot shorter in this spot than anywhere else.

"What? We climb?"

He nods, stepping on the bottom rung. "Unless you're a 'fraidy cat." He hoists himself over the fence and waits on the other side.

I practically leap over the fence, nearly falling head-first in my effort to prove I'm not afraid. Also to get my hands on him again. And then we're running and kissing and making fools of ourselves as we hurry on our way farther out into the woods.

When we reach the old cabin, my heart sputters. I look around, realizing how far we've come.

"Devil's cabin? Really?" I stare at him. "After what you and Jack told me about this place?"

He cups my cheeks, kissing my lips. "Don't worry about that. This place has been empty for years. No...*religious experiences* to speak of. At least none that have involved me." He chuckles under his breath, and I poke him in the side as he pulls me toward the door. "I deserved that, but this is the only place I can have you alone to do...devilish things."

I roll my eyes but follow along, too drunk on him to care about the cabin's history of him with other people. There is only us now. It's like the entire universe has shrunk down to the size of just two people. He's all I see, all I think about. I've never felt like this. Not with anyone.

He pulls open the door of the cabin, his eyes on me.

And then someone starts to scream.

Soon, we're all screaming, four voices filling the

night. It takes me all of ten seconds for my eyes to adjust and my head to wrap itself around what I'm seeing.

Inside, Jack is there with a girl, sans clothing.

When I look closer, I realize I know her.

Her eyes widen as she uses Jack to shield her body from sight, and he looks at me as if he's seen a ghost.

I stare at her in disbelief. Last I heard, she was supposed to be somewhere near Vegas. Yet here she is, decidedly not. *"Shelby?"*

CHAPTER TWENTY-FIVE

PRESENT DAY

From the porch of my house, I watch as the girl reappears at the edge of the woods. It's been less than two hours since she went back to her cabin, and it turns out my gut instinct was right—she wasn't done trying to meet whoever she's planning to find in the woods. Dean and Tye gave up within an hour, Tye going home and Dean returning to his cabin.

But I was right.

I watch her shadow move through the trees. She's keeping close to the treeline because she's unfamiliar with the woods, clearly. It would be all too easy to get lost here, which seems to be what happened when she ended up on the wrong property and on camera.

I'm hidden in the shadows of the house right now, and she's completely oblivious that she's being watched. I remember that time so well, so in love—or lust, though probably both—that you can't see anything else around you.

I make my way down the stairs quietly. With Tye's truck out of the driveway, it's easy enough to move along the wall of the cabin and stay tucked in the shadows with a clear view of her. She thinks she's being sneaky, hiding behind trees for a few seconds before she runs again.

Maybe I should just call the police or alert the girl's mother and let them handle this, but it doesn't feel like there's enough time. If we want to find out who she's meeting and why she's being so secretive, it's now or never.

Maybe it's harmless, a simple meeting of two love-struck teens, but I don't think that's it either. Her mother was convinced she hadn't met anyone since she came here and that her ex-boyfriend wouldn't have followed her—and even if he had, why would they be sneaking around? It has to be something else. No matter how badly I want to believe it's not related to Shelby's death, I just can't.

I lose sight of her as she goes deeper in the woods, and my stomach plummets. I have to chance it. I squeeze my hands into fists, steel myself, and make a run for the woods. It's darker there—so dark I can hardly see a thing. The sky is masked by trees, blocking the light from the moon, and I have to be careful about where I step so I don't trip and fall.

I listen for the sounds of her footsteps, identifying them up ahead, and move toward the sound. I walk slowly, trying to keep my own footsteps in sync with hers so they'll be concealed.

When I run smack into someone I don't see until it's too late, I let out a yelp. A hand clasps over my mouth, and I recognize the scent in an instant, though his face is cloaked in shadows.

"Dean?"

His hand releases me. "Shhh..." he warns.

"What are you doing here?" My heart sinks. *No. No. No.* "Are you...are you meeting her? The girl? April?" I'm going to be sick.

"*What?*" Though I can hardly see him, I can so clearly imagine the scowl on his face. "No. Of course not. I was following her. I thought she might try to sneak out again. What are you doing here?"

"Same thing."

"Stay close. Before we lose her." He takes my hand, leading me forward and through the woods.

CHAPTER TWENTY-SIX

BEFORE — AGE 19

When Thanksgiving Day rolls around, things are no less awkward between Jack and Dean. Mom says Jack has had a new girl here each week since the summer, but Shelby seems to be a bit more permanent since she's going to be joining us for the holiday.

Inside the Hunters' cabin, Jill has a full spread waiting for us. Dean and I sit next to each other, with Jack and Shelby across from us.

The meal is mostly eaten in silence, though I try to make small talk for Jill's sake. She asks Dean and me about school and work, and Shelby about how she's feeling since being home again.

We all answer, but there's clearly something awkward going on between us.

When there's literally nothing else to talk about, Jill tells us about her run-in with the school principal at the grocery store and how one of the guests' dogs stole a birthday cake from a party down by the playground last week.

Soon, the meal ends, and since Mom and Jill cooked, it's the boys' and my job to clean up. I zip around Jack, putting food into Tupperware and handing him things without making eye contact. When we're nearly done, Shelby reappears from whatever she's been doing, her yellow purse tucked over her shoulder.

"Could I talk to you, Carmen?" she asks softly, almost like she's afraid I'll yell at her.

"When I'm finished," I tell her, putting the lid on the mashed potatoes and passing them to Sam, who's standing in front of the refrigerator. He stares at me, then her, and gets a knowing look on his face.

"Go on." He nudges the bowl of potatoes in her direction, the command directed at me. "We've got this."

"But—"

"No buts," he says. "Go."

I turn and follow Shelby outside and to the porch. She stops in her tracks, spinning to face me, and all in one breath, she says, "I'm sorry."

"Sorry?"

"Are you mad at me?" Her doe eyes grow larger, and she digs in her purse and produces a cigarette. "I'm so sorry. I didn't—I mean, obviously I didn't plan for you to find out like that. But I wanted to tell you. Jack said you broke up with him when you went off to Nashville, and I came back last month to save up some more money —what do you know, traveling's expensive. Anyway, Jack came into Tucker's—out by the school, you know? That's where I'm working now. Anyway, he came in, and we started talking, and well, it just sort of...happened." She covers her face, wincing. "That is the worst explanation out there, and I won't blame you if you totally hate me. *I* would hate me. Girl code. I should've asked you first. But, well, I didn't think it was anything serious, just a hookup, and then it turned into three, and...anyway, I'm leaving town again next month, so you don't have to worry about me. Not that you have to worry about me, but—"

"Shelby," I interrupt her, mostly because I'm afraid she's going to pass out from lack of oxygen soon.

Her eyes find mine as she stops digging in her purse, finally having found her lighter. "Yeah?"

"I'm not mad at you, okay? Jack's version of our breakup is a little...questionable, but what matters is that we're not together anymore. I'm not mad at you." I repeat the words slowly, watching them wash over her. "I was shocked to see you guys together, obviously, and that was not a mental image I wanted." I chuckle. "But...seriously, it's cool. Awkward, maybe, but cool."

"Okay, thank god. I mean, I've always liked him, but Alissa told me you guys hooked up after your birthday party that year, and I didn't want to overstep, so I immediately backed off and have been—"

"Wait, what?" White-hot rage coils through me.
"What?"

"She told you Jack and I hooked up after a party?"

She lights her cigarette, inhaling deeply. The scent fills the air. "Yeah. Your birthday party. She told me you guys hooked up, and I put him on my 'do not touch' list right then."

"Why would she tell you that?"

"Oh. Was it a secret or something? I'm sorry. You know I won't say anything. I just thought—"

"It's a lie," I say angrily. "Jack and I never..." I lower my voice, pushing her farther away from the door. "We never hooked up. Not once."

"Oh." Her face falls.

"Why would he tell her that?"

Something about her expression changes. Something I really, really don't like.

"What is it?" I demand. "What was that look?"

"Nothing. I don't know. I have no idea why he'd tell her that. Maybe he was just being a guy." Her laugh is forced and uncomfortable.

"Shelby..." I warn her.

She sighs. "I don't know this for a fact, but Alissa has this...rule. She won't sleep with virgins."

I swallow, her words buzzing in my ears like bees.

"So...maybe Jack told her he slept with someone— you—so they could hook up."

"But they didn't..." My voice is powerless.

Her eyes widen, and she looks away. "Maybe I should go."

"They slept together?"

"Back in high school. Before you guys dated. He didn't cheat on you." She rushes to add that last part.

Jack told me he was a virgin. All this time...he lied to me. He lied to me about everything. He didn't cheat, but the lie feels worse. He promised me something he could never give me. We were meant to be each other's firsts, and while that possibility is long gone now, it stings to know I would've spent my life believing something that wasn't true.

Why would he lie about sleeping with her?

Why would he lie to her about me?

I'm practically seeing red when Jack comes outside, holding two beers. "You guys okay out here?" He hands one beer to Shelby, who takes it and blows a puff of smoke in the other direction.

I could say something. I could confront him and demand to know the truth about everything, but what good will it do? Jack was never the man I thought he was. He lied to me about so much. And now he's lying to her about who broke up with whom in our relationship and god knows what else. Just like he lied to Alissa. Why didn't I see it?

"Fine." I spit the word out. "Just heading back inside, actually. You guys have fun."

"Where are you going?" Shelby calls.

I'm not mad at her. Really, I'm not. But I also can't be around her right now. "Inside."

"We're going to party with some friends out by the dock. Do you want to come?" she asks. I know she's really asking me if we're still friends. If we're okay. And the truth is, I don't know anymore. What I know is that I want to get far away from this place. I want to find Dean and get out of Hunter's Hollow for good. "Please."

"Sorry, no. I'm tired."

With that, I slam the door in their faces and disappear inside.

I find our parents and Dean in the living room and sink down on the couch next to him.

"Where's Jack?" Jill asks.

"They were meeting some friends, I think." I can't bear to look at her. I know somehow I've managed to ruin all of this. I know this wasn't the Thanksgiving she planned, and that guilt eats at me.

It's our family tradition to watch our first Christmas movie of the year on Thanksgiving, so Sam picks one, and we all settle in to watch it.

I'm grateful for the silence, but in truth, I don't hear a word of the movie.

Dean spends most of the night texting me. He knows something's wrong, but I can't tell him what. The next day, I avoid him, though he doesn't deserve it.

It's not his fault, and I have no one to truly be angry at except for Jack. And even he isn't worth my anger.

I spend the day doing a puzzle with Mom, finishing the last few episodes of *Hart of Dixie*, and frying sopapillas. It's a day I desperately need, and though she's kind enough not to ask, I know she understands that I'm hurting.

When night comes, there's a knock at the door. Two knocks, actually.

I know who it is in an instant.

I pull open the door to find him standing there. "Hey." He appears to be surprised that I opened the door.

"Hey."

Mom looks up from the couch. "Hey, Dean."

"Ms. M." His eyes trace the lines of my face. "Can we talk, Car?"

A new nickname. Despite my strange emotional state, it seems to awaken something in my core. "Do you want to come inside?"

"I was hoping you'd go for a walk with me."

I glance over my shoulder at Mom, who waves me away. "Go on. I need a shower anyway."

I slip on my shoes and head outside with him, and the second I do, my walls break. He holds me, not understanding why I'm crying in his arms, but he's there for me, nonetheless.

"It's okay," he says, his voice firm. "It's okay."

It's not, though, and I can't tell him why. I just can't tell him. As bad as it may make Jack look, it makes me look stupid, too. Naïve. Trusting. I want him to think I'm smart.

"We should talk," he says. When I look up at him, it's

like he's actively processing what's happened aloud. Something has changed in the way he's looking at me. "Can we go somewhere? Alone?"

"Where?"

He shakes his head. His eyes are strangely empty. "Just come with me. Please."

"Take me somewhere," I beg. "Literally anywhere where I don't have to see anyone."

Without another word, he takes my hand, and we set off. When we reach the cabin, I'm in a sort of daze.

He turns to face me, drawing in a long inhale. "Carmen, we should break up."

"What?" My chest collapses. I can't process this much pain at once.

"This was fun, but it's...we both knew it wasn't going to be permanent, okay? Clearly. I just think we should cut our losses before anyone gets too attached."

"What? What are you saying?"

His words make no sense. I can't understand what he's saying. Two days ago, we were fine. Happy. In love. Now, we're breaking up. *What did I do?*

"I just think it's for the best," he says blankly.

I should've known this would happen. I know Dean. I know how he is. How he dates. I know the timelines of his relationships, and ours has run its course. But...I thought this was different. I thought *we* were different. *How have I been so stupid? So blind with both of them?*

"Please just talk to me," I beg him, no longer caring if I look naïve. I just want to understand. I grab hold of the door to the cabin, trying to bring us somewhere private and quiet, where the wind howling through the trees won't fill my ears so loudly I can't focus.

I pull open the door and shriek.

This time, there are no naked bodies. There's something worse. It's Shelby, but it's not. Half of her is gone, and what remains is a shredded, bloody mess. Less human, more tissue.

She's dead.

Destroyed.

Someone—something—*destroyed her.*

It takes me several seconds to realize the scream I'm hearing is coming from my chest.

CHAPTER TWENTY-SEVEN

PRESENT DAY

When the girl reaches the cabin, approaching it slowly, my gaze lands on the door just as something clicks in my mind.

"Dean." I grab his arm from where we're hidden behind a tree. "The maintenance shed isn't locked."

Dean looks at me as if I've had a stroke.

"The maintenance shed isn't locked. The day April went missing, your mom and I went by there and got light bulbs. But it wasn't locked."

In the clearing, a bit of extra moonlight peeks through the trees, so I can see the exact moment where he decides I've lost it. He looks toward the cabin, then back at me, trying to understand where it all connects.

"Okay. What does that mean?"

"Jack told me your dad sent him to get the key for the maintenance building's padlock, but it doesn't have a lock. The only building I've seen with a padlock is..." I look up ahead again and, sure enough, there's a silver metal padlock hanging on the door of the cabin. Jack had mentioned it when I first saw him that day in the woods.

"It's Jack." A screwdriver wedges in between my ribs, the pain of my realization astonishing. "Jack is who she's meeting." I grab Dean's arm to hold him back from coming out of hiding as the girl approaches the door. Before she can knock, the door swings open, and we stare at the person who walks out.

Only...it's not Jack.

CHAPTER TWENTY-EIGHT

PRESENT DAY

"Dad?" With my entire body numb, I can't stop Dean as he walks out from behind the trees then, directly in front of Sam.

Sam stares at us in horror. "Dean? Carmen? What are you doing here?"

"We could ask you the same thing."

"I'm..." His eyes fall to the girl. "I was checking the cabin. Who are you?"

"It was you." It clicks for me then as I remember again what Jack said that day. He was getting the key for Sam, not for himself. If it was for himself, why would he have told me? Jack doesn't handle maintenance, so he wouldn't have thought about the fact that there is no padlock on the door. "You were getting the key to give to April. So she could meet you here."

He presses his lips together. "April? Who's April? What are you talking about?" He laughs under his breath. "I think she's losing it, Dean. Has she been getting enough sleep?"

"Do you know he's married?" I ask April.

She shakes her head, looking every bit the very *young* adult she is. "He told me—"

"Okay, chill out, guys," Sam says, hands out in the air. "We're jumping to a lot of conclusions here. At least let me explain."

"Go on, then. Explain," I beg.

"I..." He sighs, rubbing a hand across his forehead. He averts his attention from me and toward Dean. "Look, son, your mother and I...we've had our share of problems. It sounds awful, I know, but you have to know how much I love her. We're a unit. I love her, and she loves me, but..." He looks down. "But I make mistakes, just like the rest of you. I never wanted you to see me like this. To see that your father is human."

Dean groans. "Please don't do that. Don't play the pity card right now. What you mean to say is that my father is a cheater."

"Human," Sam corrects. "Yes, I was meeting April. You're no saint, are you? Can you really judge me?"

Dean's arms go out to his sides. "I've never cheated! Never. I wouldn't do that to the person I loved. Mom doesn't deserve this. You were...you were meeting her before, too? When she went missing?"

"Yes. We'd just met when they checked in." He looks sheepish, and I don't understand how I've spent so long looking up to this man. Considering him a father figure.

"She was supposed to meet me here, and I was going to unlock the cabin so we'd have somewhere to be, but she never showed up. She got lost in the dark."

"And what about Shelby?" I ask, the thing I have to know. "Were you meeting her, too?"

Sam's face falls, wrinkles with sadness, and he covers his eyes. "Both girls were over eighteen. I asked." He points at April, like it's any consolation. "Didn't I ask?"

She nods, wringing her hands together in front of her.

"I haven't done anything to hurt anyone except your mother, and she's...she's too important to me to lose."

"Did you kill her?" I demand, the weight of the words filling the quiet of the forest around us. The wind falls silent, like the trees want to hear the answer, too.

"*What?* Shelby?" He drops his jaw open like it's a ridiculous theory.

"Was she going to tell, so you took care of her?" Hot, bitter tears fill my eyes. All this time, we haven't known. She was just another dead girl without answers. Just one of many.

"I..." He drops his shoulders, looking at April. "Can you go home? I'm sorry about all of this."

Obviously relieved, she darts away, not looking back.

"Answer the question, Dad," Dean barks, moving closer to me.

"No," Sam says, bouncing his hands in the air to calm us down. "I think you know me better than that. I wouldn't hurt anyone. Not on purpose." He pinches the bridge of his nose, clearly exasperated. "Look, it was an accident. We'd seen each other a few times at the restaurant where she worked, and I'd invited her to come over one day when your mom and Jill were out shopping. I didn't expect Jack to be home, but he was, and they... well, you know. Hit it off. Once I saw that Jack liked her, I ended it."

He pauses, squeezing his eyes shut and shaking his head. "Until she called me the night she died. She was crying and drunk. Jack had gotten mad at her. Left her. They'd had some fight over..." He gestures to me. "You, Carmen. I think. She was hard to understand. Anyway, she asked me to come pick her up by cabin fifteen. I drove back there, and..." Suddenly, he's sobbing. "It was an accident, I swear to you. I didn't see her. She was lying in the road, passed out drunk, and I hit her. I didn't know. I tried to help her, to save her, but it was too late. She was already gone. I took her out to the cabin to hide her body until I could decide what to do and threw her purse in the lake. None of it was malicious. I acted out of fear, not violence or rage. She was already gone. There was no saving her. No one was supposed to find her. I thought I could get rid of the body, make it look like she'd run off again. Her parents would never know. But then... the animals got to her, even inside the cabin. And you guys found her body before I could do anything." He waves a hand at us.

"If she called you that night, there would've been a

record. The police would've questioned you," I point out.

"They did," Sam insists. "Robbie asked me as soon as they got her phone records. Jack had an alibi because he and his friends went out after his fight with Shelby, so it didn't look good for me. I told him the truth—came clean about the affair—but I swore to him she'd called, and I told her she needed to call her parents. That I never went to see her." He drops his head. "It's what I should've done. What I would give anything to have done. I swear to you I wasn't going to sleep with her again. I just wanted to get her home. I thought I was doing the right thing." Tears line his cheeks, glistening in the moonlight.

"The right thing would've been to leave the eighteen-year-old girl alone in the first place," I say bitterly. "Clearly, you haven't learned that lesson."

"I know." His face is crumpled with disgust. "I don't know why. It was only then. I swear it was." He gestures toward me. "I never touched you. I was the father you didn't have—"

"Don't talk about my dad," I snap, venom pouring from my words like an open wound. "Don't you dare."

"You need to tell Mom," Dean says, taking my hand.

"No." Sam shakes his head. "This will kill her. I'm not asking you to keep this a secret for myself, son. I swear I'm not. It's your mother I'm trying to protect. She won't survive this."

"She's strong," I say firmly. "Jill is everything you're

not. She's been through so much, and she's still here. Still kind. Still loving. She let us stay here. She helped us. She made this feel like home."

"And I didn't? I love her. I love you all. I just messed up. I'm human." His words are stony. "If I tell her the truth, we'll never be the same. None of us. There's no coming back from that. Right now, we can walk away, and this can be our secret. Ours. No one else has to get hurt."

"If you don't tell her," Dean says, "we will."

Sam looks at us as if we're the monsters. "I'm your father. Doesn't that mean anything to you?"

"She's my mother."

"And you'd really hurt her like that?"

"He hasn't hurt anyone. You're the one who's done this," I shout, my voice echoing through the silent, dark woods.

"Fine. I'll tell your mother, sure. Then what?" He looks like he's testing us, trying to prove a point.

"Then the police." Dean's voice is empty. I squeeze his hand, trying to assure him I'm here in whatever way I can.

Sam's face goes sallow, horror-stricken. "No. Not the police. Not Robbie. He'll arrest me. I'm not a killer, son. It was an accident, I swear it was. I don't deserve to go to jail. I don't deserve to have my life ruined for trying to do a good thing." He looks at Dean, then back at me. "Tell him, Carmen. You believe me, don't you? Wasn't I good to you? I know I didn't replace your father, but I tried. I tried to be the father you didn't have."

His words are a gut punch. "I had a father. A great one. One who would never do what you did. One who would never hurt my mom like this."

"You don't know that. No one's perfect. You think you know what people are capable of...what you're capable of, even, but you don't. You're not perfect either."

"My dad loved my mom. So much. You have an amazing wife. Jill is a great person, and you hurt her. And you killed my friend. And even after all that, you were looking to do it again. Even after the worst thing that could have happened, happened, you went back for more."

"Years later." He speaks through gritted teeth, begging us to understand the impossible. "Years and years later. Infidelity isn't a crime here. How can you sentence me to jail, punish me for an accident?"

"No one is sentencing you, Dad," Dean says, his voice cracking. "But you have to tell Mom. And then let her decide what to do."

"But—" I try to argue.

"Mom will do the right thing," he says, "even if I can't. But the decision has to be hers." He's not looking at me as he says it.

Eventually, I nod in agreement. "Fine. But we have to tell her everything. All of it."

Sam just looks at us both, his eyes swollen with tears,

face gray in the moonlight. He won't hurt us. I know that much. He watches us walk away, and a small part of me wants to save him. But that part is easily squashed when I picture Jill working as hard as she has to save this place while the blood of Shelby's body was on his hands all along. He could've told the truth and then explained what happened. But he lied. Tried to save himself and cover it up. Because of him, every time I close my eyes, I see my friend's dead body.

Because of him, I've spent years running, searching for a home I left behind. Because of him, so much of my life has been messed up. And he had the audacity to sit across the dinner table—across from all of us—and smile.

I hate that doing this, getting justice for Shelby, will mean hurting Jill, but I have to believe she would want to know. She's strong, smart. She'll be okay. Just like Mom, she'll make it through.

She doesn't deserve this. Her only mistake was marrying such an ass. And...like the ass said, no one's perfect.

CHAPTER TWENTY-NINE

PRESENT DAY

Telling Jill and Mom what we've learned is the hardest thing I've ever had to do. There are a lot of tears and a lot of questions, and it breaks my heart that we don't have answers for all of them.

Sam stands in the corner of the living room like a child ready to accept his punishment. He begs Jill not to go to the police, to let them deal with it behind closed doors.

I can't tell what she's thinking, honestly. Which way she's leaning.

By the end of the evening, once all the secrets are spilled, she looks up at Sam, the man she's loved for so long, the man she met at this very campground.

"Is that where the money was going?" Her face is stoic, despite the tears falling down her porcelain cheeks.

"What money?"

"Right before Shelby died, there were a few transactions on our account that didn't make sense. But then we got caught up in the murder investigation, and I forgot about it. There've been a few other times here or there, where a little bit was missing. Not enough to raise red flags, but enough that I asked you what it was. You always said you'd look into it, then explained it away with a gift you'd bought me or something." She pauses, staring down into her lap. "On the day Carmen arrived, I noticed a charge to our account. Seventy bucks or so, not a lot, but I assumed Jack had used the wrong card." She sniffles, dusting a finger under her nose. "Were you buying these girls things?"

Sam presses his lips together. "Small things, yes. Nothing that mattered. Dinner. Jewelry."

"What did you buy her?"

"A pair of jeans she said she'd been wanting but couldn't afford." His words are dry, lifeless. "I didn't see the harm. I'm sorry, Jill. I took the money out with no idea you'd think anything of it."

She lets out a breath. "*That's* what you're sorry for?"

"I'm sorry for all of it, obviously. I screwed up, okay? I screwed up. But that's all this is. We can fix it. Go to counseling, start doing dates again. Like when we were kids."

"I'm not eighteen years old anymore, Sam. Is that going to be a problem for you?" Her brows rise.

He runs a hand over his hair. "It's just a stupid fantasy. I'm human. I'm sorry I can't be perfect."

She stands. "Kids, can you give us a minute, please? Elena, go back to your house and call Robbie."

Mom stands in a heartbeat. "I'm not leaving you alone with him."

Jill scowls. "He won't hurt me. I'll be fine."

"Elena, please don't do this," Sam calls after her, watching as she walks past him without looking his way. "Please. She's just mad. She doesn't know what she's saying."

"I'm not mad, Sam."

Dean pulls me down the hall, giving them the privacy she's requested.

"I'm not mad. I hate that you've put me in this position, a position that I desperately don't want to be in because I don't want to tell Robbie—"

"Then don't!"

"What if it were our kid? What if someone knew the truth about what happened to our child, and they—"

Dean closes the door to his old bedroom, resting against the wall with his head in his hands. Even after all this time, the room smells of him. On the dresser next to his bed, I notice the framed photographs of us at the winter formal all those years ago. I had no idea he'd kept them, not to mention framed them. Somehow, I'd always pictured the photos shoved into one of Jill's junk drawers, if they hadn't been thrown away.

The simple smiles on our faces break my heart. Life felt so hard back then, but we had no idea what was coming.

"Are you okay?" I ask.

"No." His answer is simple, but so complicated. "I hate this, Carmen. He's my dad. He's...I can't just hate him. I don't understand how he could do this. I don't know how..."

I hug him, holding him as tightly as he's held me in my darkest moments. "I know." It's all I can say because the truth is that it's not so easy. I love Sam, too. Now that my adrenaline is waning and my anger is starting to fade, it's made way for heartbreak of a new kind. None of this is easy. None of this makes any sense. All I can do is hold him.

And so, I do.

CHAPTER THIRTY

ONE WEEK LATER

Nothing will ever be the same.

With Sam gone, the house is quieter than ever. My mom has been here with Jill every day. Mostly, they sit in silence. Though it's not the same, I know Mom is the best person to help her through this. Their losses are different, but the same.

Dean and I bring them food and water, covering them with blankets when they fall asleep on the couch, and in general making sure they're...still breathing, I guess. It feels wrong to say we're making sure they're okay.

None of us will ever be okay again.

I remember this part. The early stages of grief when everything feels like you're being buried with sadness. Like you may never get up again. Like no one has ever felt the way you do—they couldn't have, because how could they ever function again if they had?

Jack comes and goes, too, but mostly he stays away. I think he's angry with his mom for the decision she made, but she's too broken to notice.

After a week, Jill takes a shower for the first time. She looks better, but not good. Not whole. A piece of her is missing in the same way a piece of me is missing. A piece of Mom.

What Sam did doesn't erase what he was to her. Or to us.

I won't lie and say there haven't been moments of regret sprinkled in throughout the week. Moments of wondering if we made a mistake or how we could be heartless enough to do this. Moments where I contemplate whether Sam would've done the same thing to me.

I think the answer is no, if I'm being honest, and I'm not sure if that makes me love or hate him more.

"Can we talk?" Dean's voice startles me as he appears at the door, walking out toward me on the porch.

I stand. "Of course."

He runs a hand over his face. He's exhausted, despite all of the sleep. I remember that, too. Grief is no different than a car accident, in my experience, with the way it affects your body. The soreness, the pain, the exhaustion.

And when you're in the thick of it, no matter how many people are around, you're always completely alone.

"This is the worst timing," he says slowly. "But...I need to say this. If this week has taught me anything, it's that nothing is guaranteed. Not even the constant you've had your whole life." Tears blur his eyes.

"What are you saying—"

"I'm saying I love you, Carmen." He looks up at me then, his face serious. "I love you in a way that makes my whole body feel like the sun when you're around. In a way that makes me crazy. That makes me act like I've never met a girl before in my life. I get jealous and speechless and...I love you in a way that hurts, but in the best way possible. You are everything to me. You have been from the moment I saw you get out of that car all those years ago, and nothing has changed."

He looks away, tears on his cheeks. "I broke up with you back then because I thought you wanted to be with Jack. You'd gone outside with him and then came back in a weird place. The next day you avoided me, and I knew. I knew what was going on. You'd come back home and realized you missed him. I thought I was saving myself the heartache of you being the one to end it. I thought I was helping you out so you didn't have to do it yourself. Instead of fighting for you, telling you all the reasons you should pick me instead of him, I gave up. And I've never forgiven myself. You left back then because you were scared and upset. Because he'd hurt you. And I'd hurt you. And"—he rolls his eyes—"my dad had hurt you, apparently. I still don't fully understand what happened back then, but I don't care. Because I love you. And I want our shot to be together again. For real this time. No secrets. No hiding. Just...us" —he takes my hand—"against the world. Love is worth the risk, so I want to risk it with you. And if you don't feel the same, just say so. But I can't wait one more day not knowing."

"Dean..." Tears cascade down my own cheeks, and I brush them away. "I never wanted Jack back. The reason I was avoiding you that day was because I realized he'd lied to me. About major, major stuff. And I was hurt, but I felt like it wasn't fair to talk to you about it."

He takes a step backward as if he's been shot. "You weren't going to break up with me?"

"No." I shake my head fiercely. "I loved you so much. I still love you. But I thought you'd realized it was a mistake. That we were a mistake."

"We were never a mistake." He rushes toward me, cupping my face. "You are the best thing that has ever happened to me. And you are mine. I've just been waiting for you to figure that out."

"Despite the fact that our world is literally imploding, or maybe because of it, this feels like the perfect time. I love you, too, Dean. You have been there for me in every way that ever mattered. Even when we were never meant to be together, it's been you. It will always be you."

When I think about Jack and Dean, they remind me of the two homes I've known in my life. Jack is the home in Atlanta. The home I was supposed to have, even when it no longer fit. The nostalgic home. The one that felt warm and cozy and normal.

Dean is Hunter's Hollow. Wild and unpredictable. He's the home I rebelled against. The home I fought with every fiber of my being, even when it welcomed me with open arms...eventually, anyway. I had a picture of my life growing up, and Dean didn't fit it.

But life has a way of sneaking up on you, for better and for worse. Despite not wanting to love The Hollow, I've found a family here. A home.

Because sometimes, I'm realizing, home isn't a place at all. It's a person. It's a feeling. It's the place where you're always welcome no matter what is happening outside or what choices you make. For me, home isn't where I am, but where I belong. With my mom. With Jill. And here with Dean.

His dark eyes dance between mine, still brimming with tears, and then he pulls me into a kiss, crushing his lips to mine, and the rest of the world disappears. There is only him and me. No madness, no sadness, just that warm feeling that I can only describe as home.

My heart beats rapidly in my chest, warmth spreading throughout me like a flower taking root, staking its claim, and reminding me of how this is supposed to feel. When we pull back, he smiles at me with that crooked grin, and his eyes radiate love like I've been waiting for. Love that he's always had ready for me. In that moment, I know with everything in me, the boy who took my first kiss in a silly game will be the man who gets my last.

WOULD YOU RECOMMEND THE HOLLOW?

If you enjoyed this story, please consider leaving me a quick review. It doesn't have to be long—just a few words will do. Who knows? Your review might be the thing that encourages a future reader to take a chance on my work!
To leave a review, please visit:
http://kierstenmodglinauthor.com/thehollow

Let everyone know how much you loved
The Hollow on Goodreads:
https://bit.ly/thehollowkm

STAY UP TO DATE ON EVERYTHING KMOD!

Thank you so much for reading this story. I'd love to invite you to sign up for my mailing list and text alerts so we can be sure you don't miss my next release.
Sign up for my mailing list here:
kierstenmodglinauthor.com/nlsignup

Sign up for my text alerts here:
kierstenmodglinauthor.com/textalerts

ACKNOWLEDGMENTS

As I wrote this story, I spent a lot of time thinking about home, and about what that word means to me. Like Carmen, my life was split between two homes. For most of my childhood, I grew up in Western Kentucky, though I later relocated and eventually graduated from a school in Southern Illinois. So when people ask where I'm from, I often hesitate. Both homes feel like parts of me in strange ways, but it also makes me feel like I can't call either of them home, especially when you add in the fact that I later moved again and now live in Tennessee. Like Carmen, it often makes me feel like I don't actually belong anywhere. I'm working on that.

Also like Carmen, and as some of you may know, I lost my father in 2021. In most of my books since his loss, the main character has also lost at least one parent. In ways, I'm trying to work through my own feelings about grief and loss by losing myself in stories and characters like I always have, but I also realized recently I've been creating a world where losing a parent isn't so uncommon so those of us who have experienced it will feel less alone. Carmen's loss—her grief, her anger, her confusion, the way she lived and dealt with her grief—

was so raw, realistic, and refreshing for me. Some of the lines I wrote for her will stick with me for a long time.

As I wrote this book, those two ideas were always top of mind: grief and the true meaning of home. For those of us who have lost someone, it's often hard to have a grasp on home when the person who once made your home so special is gone. So while Carmen searched for her true home, I wanted to make the story and the emotions within (including alllllllllll the teenage angst and bad decisions) as honest and unflinching as I could for anyone who can relate to her. I hope I did that well.

While the themes in this book were heavy, the story was also filled with hope. As I've mentioned before in these author notes (honestly, should we just start to call them journal entries, because goodness, I'm really just pulling back the curtain at this point), I write to entertain and to let the stories in my head loose, but also to show that even in the darkest story, on our worst day, there is hope. And love. Family. Kindness. Grace.

Because just like Carmen found out, home isn't always a place. Or even a few different places. Sometimes it's just a person. A feeling. Sometimes, it's just you, and the peace and gentleness you show yourself over bad decisions, mistakes, hard times, and regrets. We're all just trying our best.

So to the people who make me feel at home, no matter where I am:

To the world's best husband and sweetest little girl— thank you for making our home a place filled with love and laughter. Of early-morning sing-alongs, quiet afternoons with books and music, evenings filled with games, and roadtrips with all the snacks. I love you guys more than I could ever put into words.

To my incredible editor, Sarah West—thank you for loving this story and helping it to shine! I'm so glad my books have found a home with you.

To the awesome proofreading team at My Brother's Editor—thank you for all you do for my books! I'm so grateful to have you as my last set of eyes.

To my loyal readers (AKA the #KMod Squad)—thank you, thank you, thank you! Oh my gosh, you guys mean the absolute world to me. Have I mentioned that? Above, I talked a lot about not ever feeling like I had a home, but when I really think about it, stories were always my home. When I had a bad day, a fight with friends, when my heart was broken, when I didn't understand something, when I had a good day, when I was in love, when I felt on top of the world—the one constant was storytelling. I can't tell you the number of days—summers, evenings, late nights, weekends—that I spent bent over a notebook or (eventually) my computer, writing away on my latest story. And all the while, I dreamed of a future where people would read my books. Where they might hold a paperback with my name on it. Where they would recommend my books to their friends. Where they would want my autograph in their books. Where they might travel to meet me at signings. I dreamed and wished and hoped, but in truth, I never could've dreamed up what you guys have done for me. You've changed my life in every way imaginable. You've given me everything I've ever hoped for and more, shown my daughter that dreams can come true, and taught me to trust myself even when the world doubts my goals and abilities. Because you don't. You have shown up for me when so many people said 'no' or 'not for me.' I could never tell you what that has meant to me, but I will spend my life trying. Thank you for being everything I wished for.

To my book club/gang/besties—Sara, both Erins, June, Heather, and Dee—thank you for being the best friends a girl could ask for. For the pizza and laughter, the daily check-ins, the movies and books, the trips, the inside jokes that I always manage to throw into stories, and the truest, most beautiful friendship I've ever known. I love you, ladies.

To my bestie, Emerald O'Brien—thank you for being my sounding board and cheerleader. I'm so grateful for your advice, wisdom, and trust. I love you, friend.

To Becca and Lexy—thank you for being in my corner. I'm so thankful for you both!

To my agent, Carly, and my audiobook publishing team at Dreamscape—thank you for putting your trust in me, for being a true team, and for helping to get these books into the most hands possible.

To Dewi Hargreaves—thank you for the beautiful map of Hunter's Hollow Campground, for seeing my vision and making it happen (and not laughing too hard at my drawing).

To Natasha Gonzalez—thank you for helping to bring Elena's Spanish to life and keep her character authentic. I could never have done it without you and I appreciate you so much. You're the absolute best!

Last but certainly not least, to you, dear reader— thank you for taking a chance on this story. I know there are SO many books out there that you could've been reading, so the fact that you took the time to read THIS ONE?! Seriously, I don't take that for granted. Thank you for spending this time with me in this wild and twisted world I created. Thank you for seeing this book cover or reading the blurb, for listening to someone's recommendation, or seeing my name, for remembering that post you saw on social media, or seeing this book out in the wild and deciding to take a chance on it. Your trust and belief in me is something I will never stop saying thank you for (seriously, I might get annoying with it). When I write these stories, I spend so much time thinking of you. I wonder which parts will resonate with you, which ones might bring you to tears, which moments will make your jaw drop, which twists will shock you the most, and whether you'll love (or hate) the characters as much as I do. I truly hope you enjoyed Carmen's story. And, as always, whether this is your first Kiersten Modglin novel or your 44th, my greatest wish is that it was everything you hoped for and nothing like you expected.

ABOUT THE AUTHOR

KIERSTEN MODGLIN is a Top 10 bestselling author of psychological thrillers. Her books have sold over a million copies and been translated into multiple languages. Kiersten is a member of International Thriller Writers, Novelists, Inc., and the Alliance of Independent Authors. She is a KDP Select All-Star and a recipient of *ThrillerFix's* Best Psychological Thriller Award, *Suspense Magazine's* Best Book of 2021 Award, a 2022 Silver Falchion for Best Suspense, and a 2022 Silver Falchion for Best Overall Book of 2021. Kiersten grew up in rural western Kentucky and later relocated to Nashville, Tennessee, where she now lives with her family. Kiersten's readers across the world lovingly refer to her as "KMod." A binge-watching expert, psychology fanatic, and *indoor* enthusiast, Kiersten enjoys rainy days spent with her favorite people and evenings with her nose in a book.

Sign up for Kiersten's newsletter here:
kierstenmodglinauthor.com/nlsignup

Sign up for text alerts from Kiersten here:
kierstenmodglinauthor.com/textalerts

kierstenmodglinauthor.com
www.facebook.com/kierstenmodglinauthor
www.facebook.com/groups/kmodsquad
www.threads.net/kierstenmodglinauthor
www.instagram.com/kierstenmodglinauthor
www.tiktok.com/@kierstenmodglinauthor
www.goodreads.com/kierstenmodglinauthor
www.bookbub.com/authors/kiersten-modglin

ALSO BY KIERSTEN MODGLIN

<u>STANDALONE NOVELS</u>

Widow Falls

Missing Daughter

The Reunion

Tell Me the Truth

The Dinner Guests

If You're Reading This...

A Quiet Retreat

The Family Secret

Don't Go Down There

Wait for Dark

You Can Trust Me

Hemlock

Do Not Open

You'll Never Know I'm Here

The Stranger

The Hollow

ARRANGEMENT TRILOGY

The Arrangement (Book 1)

The Amendment (Book 2)

The Atonement (Book 3)

THE MESSES SERIES

The Cleaner (Book 1)

The Healer (Book 2)

The Liar (Book 3)

The Prisoner (Book 4)

<u>NOVELLAS</u>

The Long Route: A Lover's Landing Novella

The Stranger in the Woods: A Crimson Falls Novella